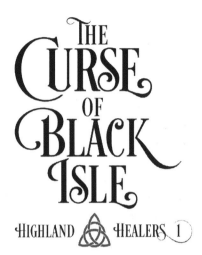

THE CURSE OF BLACK ISLE

HIGHLAND HEALERS 1

KEIRA MONTCLAIR

CHAPTER ONE

———◆———

Spring 1292, The Highlands of Scotland

THIS ONE STEP, this one act he was about to commit, would change his life—irrevocably.

Marcas Matheson prepared to climb over the curtain wall. To do so was to breach the gates of Clan Ramsay, a move that would make him hunted and condemned by every Highland warrior until he was caught, but he didn't care.

He had to save the person most important to him, but he knew that doing so would also save himself. Saving her would give his life the twist he'd always wanted, the one thing he'd long hoped to achieve but didn't know how.

One step at a time. What followed would come. He climbed the wall and hesitated at the top, taking in the great fortress's landscape, confirming he was alone and would not be caught.

If he was, he knew the reputation of the Ramsays guaranteed he would not be returning to Black Isle. Instead, his head would be displayed on a pike at the front gates. His body shivered at the thought, but he couldn't allow it to slow him.

For now, his breach of the strong keep's cold stone walls would allow him to locate and steal away the best healer in all the Highlands, whom he prayed could save his daughter Kara's life. At the tender age of three winters, seeing Kara suffer was more than he could bear.

He'd failed at saving everyone else of importance. Now he turned to save the life of an innocent, one of two people he adored more than life itself, repercussions be damned. He'd say the same about his son, Tiernay, nearly a year now, but Tiernay was presently safely ensconced in his keep. Kara was there as well, but far from hale.

Kara needed a healer, desperately.

Since he'd already failed his clan by inadvertently sending away the one healer they'd had before the curse, the others had little faith in him. But he would reclaim his honor. This act was the only way he could think of to do so. He had vowed to improve things in his clan, and he needed a powerful healer to do it.

He prayed for success for himself and his two brothers, then swiftly cursed. Why should he pray to a God that had no concern for him? The Almighty had placed a curse on his homeland, which had nearly been destroyed. And now the lairdship was his if he wanted it.

He wasn't sure if he could step into that role.

Marcas was known as one of the stealthiest of all hunters, able to move without being seen or heard, which would help him get inside the walls of the Ramsay keep before returning to Black Isle.

The Black Isle of Death.

He scanned the area again from the top of the curtain wall, then jumped down, silently landing on the walkway behind a Ramsay guard. He grabbed his stunted club, a weapon he'd had made special, and crept up behind the warrior, swinging his club in a practiced arc that knocked the man out with one blow.

How he loved this weapon. Upon seeing him fashion it, others had sneered and called him a weakling. But Marcas preferred to injure, not kill.

Once he found the back staircase to the keep's third floor, he stepped inside and gave his eyes a few moments to adjust to the darkness, his weapon still in hand. His source had told him where the healer slept, so he made his way up the staircase and down the passageway, awakening no one in the dark of night.

To guarantee the success of this mission, his source had offered him the most valuable information of all: the best healers in the land were Brenna Ramsay and Jennie Cameron.

He wanted both. He was here to find Brenna; his brothers were out to grab Jennie from Cameron land about two hours away. They would use the same method: sneak in, sneak out, hope the king would never identify the guilty parties. A sound of giggling caught him, and he froze, leaning over the balcony to listen to where it rose from the floor where the great hall sat beneath him.

His source had told him Brenna and Jennie both had large healing chambers off the great hall inside the main keep, unlike most clans, who kept their healers in the village. Sisters living in different keeps, Brenna and Jennie did nearly everything the same. Because of their talent and its value, everyone in the land would hear about their captures, especially since the two were married to chiefs or prior chieftains of their clans. But it was their brother who guaranteed it would not go unnoticed. Both Jennie and Brenna were younger sisters of the great Alexander Grant of Clan Grant, which was home to over a thousand warriors. His only concern was making sure he had the right woman, something that could prove difficult in the dark of night.

The Grants wouldn't begin to follow the captors for a day, but Logan Ramsay, known for his tracking skills, would start the chase as soon as he learned Brenna was missing. And the Camerons? Of their tracking ability, Marcas had no idea. He guessed Cameron would send word to Clan Ramsay and Clan Grant for help. The disappearance of the two healers would not go unnoticed. He guessed he would need an hour ahead of the Ramsay trackers to be safe. They did have a reputation, but his was better.

He'd not be caught. Too much depended on his success.

He hurried down the staircase and moved to the doorway, listening to a conversation between two females, their voices indicating a respect and a camaraderie many never know. One spoke of a bairn just delivered in the village. He guessed this was Brenna Ramsay's voice. Marcas opened the door a crack and quickly assessed that there were only two women inside, both refilling supplies in a large sack, tying up cloths and filling vials as they spoke. Both women were brown-haired, one a bit lighter in coloring than the other, and clearly different heights. All he needed to do was determine which one was the healer. He hadn't expected to find two. He hoped his brothers were not faced with the same quandary. While both women could be healers, only one could be the renowned healer. Other than that she had brown hair, he knew nothing about the woman he meant to capture. Now, searching for clues, he guessed she might be tall, as she was sister to Alex Grant.

Brown hair was what he was told, yet one was nearly blonde, the other had shades of red in her hair. But they would still be called brown haired.

Suddenly, he had an odd thought. Was it possible these could be the two sisters? As quickly as the idea popped into his mind, he shook it off. His source had just left Cameron land and said Jennie was at home. He'd have to make a choice, but what if he was wrong?

Both froze when he entered.

"Are you ill?" the taller one asked.

"Nay." He grabbed the lass and held his knife at her throat while he spoke to the shorter of the two. "I'm in need of a healer, so I'm taking her with me. Close that sack. We're taking your healer's tools with us. Not a sound," he said to both of them. "Or I'll slit her throat."

The shorter woman said, "We're both healers. Take me along, too."

"Suits me. You'll both come." He pointed to the shorter one, "Grab your mantles and the sack."

"But—"

"No more buts," Marcas hissed. "Cease your prattle, both of you. You'll find out why you're needed later."

The two lasses glanced at each other, silently, and fortunately for them.

He shoved them out the door and whispered, "Lead through the back way, Lady Ramsay."

And they were gone.

———— ◆ ————

Brigid Ramsay silently cursed the moment she made her mistake. Why had she told him they were both healers? She should have tried to convince him to take her and leave Jennet behind. But she'd blurted out the truth without thinking. How could she have made such a foolish mistake?

But she knew why, and she was quite sure Jennet knew too. Brigid didn't consider herself a healer without Jennet by her side. She'd had a quick fear that the man would only take her and leave Jennet behind, and she'd be found out. Instead, she'd dragged Jennet into her bad fortune.

Jennet would never forgive her.

Frozen by the surprise of the attack, Jennet blindly did as she was told. Of course, the dagger at her throat might have had something to do with her compliance. Brigid half expected Jennet to refuse to go along, but in another total surprise, she followed along willingly.

Would she ever understand her cousin?

Best of friends since as far back as Brigid could remember, she and Jennet had gone along on many of Aunt Brenna's healing ventures, which they both found to be quite interesting. But Jennet, with her clever mind, was far more skilled than Brigid. Brigid believed her cousin was of a mind stronger than any man they knew, even her father, though she had wavered on that thought over the years. Right now, Brigid was convinced Jennet was smarter than anyone in the clan.

If anyone, Brigid thought, could out-smart Jennet, it would be her mother Brenna, but in time, she believed, even Brenna's intelligence would pale before her daughter's.

Once they left through the gate's back entrance, the man tossed Jennet up onto a horse, taking the reins in his own hands, then put Brigid on another and climbed up behind her. He spurred the beasts on, and they headed away from Ramsay land, from the home Brigid had rarely left, from her truest family.

There was no sign anyone had discovered their absence. Brigid said a silent prayer that her sire would be advised of her absence, or that someone at the gates would soon hear of the breach.

How had this man eluded the guards of Ramsay Castle? It was known for having the best group of trained guards besides the Grants farther north. But in the southern part of the Highlands, no one could contest their excellence.

Yet Brigid and her cousin had been stolen in the middle of the night, just as her mother had many years ago.

Brigid glanced over at Jennet, who stared straight ahead. Her beloved cousin would think of something, surely she would. But then Brigid reminded herself that both her father and mother would be out after the two of them, as soon as they realized the girls' disappearance. Or the other possibility was Brigid's older sister and her husband who worked for the Crown. They would surely be able to find her if her sire failed.

The night was quiet, yet beautiful, the only sound the horses' breath, their hooves thumping the soil soft from recent rain, and the occasional hoot of an owl. There was no wind or rain, and clouds rippled across the moon, allowing enough light to see. Brigid guessed her captor had planned the event for a night when the moon was full. It allowed just enough light to ease his travel.

They moved at an unrelenting pace for about three hours. Then, he slowed his horse, looked for a break in the trees, then followed one he found into a small clearing. Dismounting, he set his hands on Brigid's waist and lowered her to the ground, pointing to the surrounding trees. "Take care of your needs. You'll go first, before your friend. We will wait here until two more horses join us. This will be your only chance for the rest of the night, so make good use of it."

Brigid moved into the brush and briefly thought about running, but dismissed the thought. She had no horse and no idea where she was. Nor could she leave Jennet behind after foolishly guaranteeing their dual bad fate.

When she finished, she stepped back into the

clearing. Their captor said to Jennet, with a shove at the small of her back, "You go next."

Jennet silently headed into the brush from which Brigid had just emerged.

"Do you have a name? I'd like to know who kidnapped me," Brigid crossed her arms and stared up at the man. He was good-looking, something to which she rarely paid attention, since her sire would kill any man who dared look at her. She'd never find a husband the way her sisters had.

Her captor didn't speak, finding an oatcake in his saddlebag and eating it rudely in front of her. "Why does my name matter?"

Jennet joined them from the brush and said, "So we know what name to put on your grave marker after our sires skin you alive then leave you for the buzzards to peck your eyes out."

Brigid nearly smiled at her cousin's crude remarks, but she recalled a previous time the two of them had been taken captive when they were much younger. Jennet had shown no fear, and instead used her quick wits to upset her captors. Because of her mother's work, Jennet had known one of the bastards who'd stolen them away had a strong fear of blood, so powerful that he often fainted from the sight of red liquid streaming down pale skin.

So Jennet used that fear against him toward their escape, something Brigid would've never thought to do. It had been a brilliant act, one applauded and repeated many times. Jennet claimed to be a witch with the ability to make someone fall asleep with just a look. Then, she intentionally cut herself, showing the fool her blood, and he'd crumpled to the ground in a second.

Could Jennet think of something now that would work against this captor?

The man shot Jennet an amused look. "Fair enough. If I'm caught, I'd prefer death, and I would want my brothers to know 'tis me beneath the pecked-out, empty eye sockets. Marcas is my name. I'm not known in these parts, so you'll never guess my clan." He took a bite of his oatcake, then smiled.

"Why do we wait, *Marcas*?" Brigid asked, drawing his name out. "Who's coming with the two horses?"

"My brothers."

He said nothing else, so Jennet walked around the periphery of the clearing, looking at the leaves of the surrounding plants, pulling up the roots of a couple to inspect.

"What the bloody hell are you doing?" Marcas asked, throwing an annoyed glance at both of them.

"Looking for something to use when I cast a spell on you," Jennet smirked, continuing her pursuit of the plants, ignoring his foul mood.

Marcas nearly spit his food out with a chortle. "You think I'm afraid of witchery? I'm not, so don't waste your time."

Jennet glared at him and rolled her eyes. "No sense, then."

Brigid almost laughed but contained her mirth. Marcas had outsmarted Jennet, guessing exactly what she was looking for and why. Few she knew had ever outsmarted her cousin. But Brigid still believed in her. She was aware of exactly how fast Jennet's mind worked, how quickly she was likely to come up with a solution to get them free. For now, if she knew Jennet well enough, she was biding her time as she considered the purpose of this abduction. They'd been stolen in the middle of the night, and up to this point, Marcas had gotten away with it.

Jennet would get as much information as possible.

But they weren't given the opportunity to wonder much more as the sound of horses' hooves appeared, silencing all three. Marcas's horse gave a small blow, its breath coming out in a huff, a greeting toward a familiar horse, and Marcas smiled, patting its withers in appreciation or so she assumed. "Aye, I know who's coming, also, but I thank you for the update."

Two horses broke through the trees, a man on each, one with woman in front.

It was their cousin—Tara Cameron.

CHAPTER TWO

———◆———

MARCAS STARED AT his two brothers and the lass riding with them. She was indeed a beauty, freckles sprinkled about her pert nose, but she didn't look old enough to be a healer. She had nearly the same hair color as the women with him, telling him they were related, but this new lass had brown eyes that looked different, like there was gold inside. He glanced at the first two he'd taken, thinking they were both brown-eyed.

But were they?

Then he stopped to stare at the one, her eyes now appearing green like the forest. They were indeed a deep green, and he'd hardly noticed. Those eyes called to him, but he chose to ignore the call of the siren.

Instead, he made a point to observe the expressions between the three lasses to see if they knew each other. That would tell him the truth of the matter.

If they were truly sisters, as was said, then they would recognize each other. The one who was said to be Jennie sat in front of his brother Shaw.

Her eyes widened, and she nearly spoke when she saw the one called Brenna and her friend, but she said nothing.

One of the women with him shook her head to silence Jennie, then all three immediately stared at the ground.

They knew each other. That small movement of the head was all the confirmation he needed to know they'd grabbed the right ones. Considering a question to propose, he thought carefully, but Ethan barked, "There are Ramsay patrols not far from here. We need to move."

He saw a smirk cross Brenna's face, but he had to ignore it. He tossed the two women near him up on their horses again and prepared to head toward Black Isle. Time was of the essence. His daughter was already quite sick, though not as sickly as the others had been.

Not as bad as his wife, whom he'd already buried, or his sister's husband. Or his mother and father.

They'd each heaved and deteriorated so quickly he feared his daughter would be dead by the time he returned. He was about to mount his horse when something stopped him. A white rose on a bush at the edge of the clearing caught his eye, glowing through the night air and seeming to call to him. He paced over to it, reached down, and, pleased to see it was not solitary but surrounded by other blooms tucked into the thicket, he plucked two of them off, hurried back, and stuffed them in his saddlebag.

He caught the looks that crossed between the

women, but he ignored them and spoke to the group, "We must hurry. Do not tarry for any reason. We'll settle once we get near our own land. We'll have no trouble losing them then."

The riders kept a brutal pace, flying across the countryside. The punishing route allowed Marcas a chance to take in all the lass in front of him.

He wasn't sure why, but he'd thought Brenna would be an old woman, much older than this lass. It had been a long time since he'd been with his wife, Freda. She'd been a good wife for most of their time together, and a loving mother to their bairns, but they'd never shared the friendship and playfulness of many couples he knew. Others married for love, but theirs had been an arranged marriage to tie their two clans together. He liked Freda well enough, but he'd never known the feelings others spoke of, the kind of undying love and devotion he had once wished for, which had never come to him. Others had said to be patient, but their love had never blossomed. Just respect.

These three lasses were all beautiful, each in their own way, but especially the brunette in front of him. Her hair was unplaited, the long, silky strands falling down her back. He had a vision of burying his face in the thick locks, then tasting her neck and slipping his hand around to the front of her frock, untying the ribbons to free the two mounds they bound, giving them the freedom they deserved.

Embarrassed by his crude yearnings, he reminded himself that he hadn't been with his wife, or any other woman, since she'd delivered their son, Tiernay. A year without release was enough to make him sensitive to a woman so close. Perhaps he'd have her ride with Ethan the rest of the trip so he'd not be confronted with the temptation of a lass so close.

But Ethan didn't like to be touched by strangers.

He forced himself to think of any other thought but the woman in front of him before he did something he would regret, like growing hard enough that she'd notice.

"Marcas, will you not stop, please?" Ethan shouted.

"As you wish," he called back. Half the night had nearly passed. He decided they could each use a break to take care of their needs.

He stopped his horse, waving for his brothers to follow him. He pointed to an area off the main path, and they led their horses in that direction, ducking underneath trees and around a hill to a spot invisible to anyone on the path.

"You foolish arse!" Ethan yelled.

"Shut your mouth, Ethan!" he bellowed back, leaping off his horse and going after his brother. "Or do you wish to explain your problem? You've always got a problem with how I handle things."

"The hell I do, but I do have a problem with your decisions when you're headed in the wrong direction. Maps were never your strong suit, were they?"

Marcas helped the woman he thought was Brenna down, then reached for the taller lass, setting her down. "What the hell are you talking about, Ethan? This is the correct way," he said, starting to wonder if his brother was right. Ethan was usually best at following directions, but Marcas had made this trip before. Had he made a mistake?

Shaw said, "Instead of you two hollering at each other, why don't you kindly tell him your view, Ethan? Making him mad will bring no help at all."

The lasses had all disappeared into the bushes, but Marcas ignored them. The party was too far north now for them to consider running away. "He doesn't listen, Shaw."

Shaw directed his comment to Ethan. "After all the people he's lost to the curse, I think 'tis reasonable for him to have his mind cluttered with other thoughts. Just say what you mean."

Marcas grabbed Shaw's shirt and said, "You'll not be announcing all my troubles to everyone. I've given the women my first name only. The rest is private, and I'll respectfully ask you to keep it that way." Then he gave his attention to Ethan. "Forgive my outburst. Tell me where I went wrong."

Ethan, the middle brother, nodded, accepting Marcas's apology, and said, "That fork in the path, back in the last hour. We should have taken the other trail."

The tall Ramsay lass with the brown eyes came out of the forest and said, "If you're planning to go anywhere near Inverness, you definitely took the wrong path. You're headed to the west coast of Scotland."

"Shite!" Marcas tossed his anger out to the

group, though it had not been aimed at anyone but himself. "Why did you not stop me back then?"

"I tried to, but you ignored me. You were lost thinking about something. What had you so blind to everything?" Ethan looked from his brother to the lasses, which Marcas knew made Ethan uncomfortable. Ethan didn't like strangers, especially women. But Marcas was glad he had brought Ethan along since he was best at directions, as he had just proven.

Marcas couldn't admit the truth of the matter, that the soft, round bottom of the woman in front of him had distracted him. And the scent of her hair. And the curve of her neck.

"You agree, we're headed northwest?" he asked the tall lass, because she seemed to know her directions well enough. Now the sun was up, he noticed her hair was lighter than the others, streaks of gold snaking through it.

"Aye."

"Your name?"

"Jennet."

"Tell Brenna to hurry up."

Jennet choked on the water she was drinking from the skein. "Brenna? Brenna is my mother, and she's not here. Is that who you sought?"

Marcas felt like someone had punched him. Brenna was her mother? It couldn't be true. He had too much at stake here. He couldn't have been wrong! His hands shook at the thought that he hadn't brought healers at all.

His clan would laugh at his mistake. Some would

cry. He couldn't be wrong. He just couldn't. He ran his hand through his hair, tugging on its ends as if straightening the waves would fix the mess in front of him.

Ethan snorted. "Well done, Marcas. You grabbed the wrong person. It's a good thing we grabbed Jennie so we have one healer in the three."

"Jennie?" Tara asked. "Which one do you think is Jennie? She's *my* mother. So is that who you were after at my castle? My mother?"

Ethan stared at the lasses, a shocked expression on his face. Shaw started to laugh, the sound rolling off his tongue and sending squirrels skittering across the branches as it changed into a thunderous roar of frustration. "Didn't we do a hell of a fine job. All three of us!" He pointed to the brunette. "So if you're not Brenna, then who are you?"

"Brigid."

Jennet, the tall one, smirked. "My mother is the famous healer, Brenna, and her sister Jennie is the other renowned one, and her mother." She pointed to her shortest cousin with the freckles across her nose. "Her name is Tara."

Marcas cursed so loudly birds flew from the trees, squawking a curse back at him. "What the hell do we do now? We're too far to take them back." He stared up at the sky, wondering how the gods could go against him so often. But as his gaze returned to the group, the oddest thing happened.

All he saw was *her*.

Something had happened to him while they

rode together, an awakening or awareness, something that made her stand out from the others. Five people stood before him, but his eyes locked on her, the beauty, the one whose aura shone. He had thought her name to be Brenna, but instead it was Brigid. A name that fit her much better—more regal, majestic, noble. The name of someone who could handle whatever life threw at her.

Unlike him. In his moment of failure, he felt desperate for someone like that in his life.

"I'll tell you what to do. You take us along anyway." Brigid's gaze locked on his, her green eyes drawing him in. Where he had expected judgment and hatred, he found the most sincere eyes he'd ever seen. Not just sincere, her eyes were warm, compassionate, the color of the forest foliage with golden flecks inside. Her eyes held promise.

He couldn't help but take a step closer to her. In that quick moment, he knew he'd never leave her behind.

But what she said next sealed their fate. "We're all healers."

———— ◆ ————

Brigid had overheard Marcas's talk with his brothers. "Who did you lose to the curse? And the better question is, who are you afraid to lose to this curse?"

"You don't need to know the answer to either of those questions," he replied as he repacked the few things in his saddlebag. "You need to answer my questions. Give me one good reason to take all three of you along with us. I don't have time to waste on female issues. I can choose which one to take with me and send the other two home."

"Female issues? Why, you arrogant bastard—" Jennet shot at him, her eyes lit with a fury she hadn't felt in a long time.

Brigid set her hand on Jennet's shoulder, stopping her brief tirade. "You take us along, Marcas, because you now have three healers instead of two."

He looked from one lass to the other two, his hands on his hips as he assessed the three women. "How do I know you're telling the truth?"

"You won't, until you see us at our vocation, but Jennet and I have worked with her mother since she was six summers and I was five. We've seen nearly everything. We've both learned how to stitch, and we have the best poultices to fight off fever. Luckily, we were packing our healing bag when you stole us away, so we have a full stock of everything we could need. And Tara is Jennie Cameron's daughter. She's learned from her mother nearly as long as we have. Any Grant healer has abundant poultices, salves, potions, and needles ready at all times—Tara probably brought her own along."

She looked to her cousin, who was smiling and nodding. Tara added, "Healers are happiest when we're healing. If you truly have need of our skills, we'll go along willingly, as long as you promise to take us back when we are no longer needed."

Marcas thought for a moment, then said, "I'll

agree to that."

Ethan said, "So we have the offspring of the two finest healers. Think you we're lucky enough to get a talented one in the group?"

Jennet drawled, "I think 'tis worth taking a chance. You'd have a hard time getting my mother to ride a horse for this long. She's no longer young."

"You can prove your worth when we get there. You've convinced me to keep the three of you together, at least until we ascertain the most skilled." Marcas dropped his gaze and gave the trio his back.

Jennet said, "I'm the most skilled when I have a good assistant, so you'd be foolish to leave any of us behind."

"Fine. Mount up then. We have plenty of patients for you."

They mounted and left, retracing their steps with the hope of getting to Inverness by the next night.

Brigid couldn't help but wonder if she'd made a huge mistake admitting their identities, but Aunt Brenna had always preached honesty. Her father never did, but he wasn't usually in these kinds of predicaments. He was more often a bull who acted without thought, relying on intuition instead. She wished to hone such powers but hadn't any idea how to go about it. He was also lacking in one other aspect that was inherent in her two aunts and her cousins.

Logan Ramsay didn't understand a healer's need to help wherever they could, the way few healers would walk away from a sick person.

She'd overheard Marcas talking about a curse that had killed people in his clan. What clan, and where were they headed? Clan Ross was well known for being around Inverness, but they didn't wear Ross colors, or any colors at all. Instead, they wore dark clothing, probably to help hide their identities.

Brigid had no idea who they could be.

They spent the first night not far off the path but well hidden from any passers-by. The lasses huddled together over the fire while the men hunted. Brigid whispered, "I think I know this spot. I think we've stopped on our way to Grant land here before. Jennet, do you recognize it?"

Jennet slowly nodded, scanning the area as she wrapped her woolen garment around her legs. "I think so. I wish I'd traveled more often, but I only went in the summer for the festivals."

Brigid looked at Tara's garment, noticing some tears on her clothing. "That wasn't ripped before."

Tara's eyes lit up smugly. "Nay, do you not recall your sire is the best tracker of all? I've left him hints wherever we've stopped and sometimes when we are riding. When I relieve myself, I cut a piece of material with my dagger and toss it down as we go."

Jennet's eyes widened, but she covered her surprise quickly in case the men returned. "I have an idea. Recall you when we traveled with Bearchun, Brigid?"

"Aye, what of it?" Brigid responded. She thought back on that horrid time when they'd been kidnapped at such a young age. She and Jennet had been taken by a crazed group of men in retaliation against their clan. A sudden memory popped into her mind—Jennet scratching messages in tree bark. She gasped and quickly covered her mouth with her hand. "The tree bark!"

"Aye," Jennet said. "Every time we stop, you need to cover me so I can scratch messages in the bark."

"And you should put the same message each time."

Jennet nodded. "Inverness."

They repositioned themselves so the group of three was a bit away from the fire. Jennet sat at the base of a tree. She pulled out her small dagger used mostly to cut bandages and began to scratch into the bark. "Tara," she said. "You need to drop a piece of your fabric when we leave. Not before."

Tara nodded, cutting a few more pieces in a hidden spot so as not to be discovered. She shoved them into an inside pocket.

The voices of the men came quickly, shouting, "Horses. Get on the horses!"

Jennet jumped up and leaped on a horse while Tara ran to hers, though Brigid had no idea why. Brigid wasn't ready to move until she learned what was making the men yell so.

She didn't have to wait long. Moments later, a large boar came barreling straight at her, his mouth frothing with spittle as it charged. She screamed, running toward the horse. She should have listened to the warning and not questioned the men. Too late now. Once she noticed there was no mount for her, she changed her tactics and ran toward a tree she thought she could climb quickly.

She leaped at the strong oak, hoping she could make it to the first branch and swing herself up and over like she did for archery posts, but the beast attempted to gore her, just missing her with his tusk and getting it stuck in the tree momentarily. The wild pig bleated and struggled in a fury to get free, but so strong he shook the tree tugging his tusk loose, and Brigid lost her balance, falling to the ground. Flat on her back, the only thing she saw was a wide speckled face with flaring nostrils too close.

Way too close.

Bolting to her feet, she took off back toward a different tree, but she was too late. The beast charged her and caught her from the side, sending her airborne, and she landed with a loud thud.

Pushing herself to her feet as fast as she could, she was barely beyond its reach when Marcas leaped on the boar from behind, plunging his dagger into his throat, sending its blood spurting everywhere. His brothers followed, Shaw striking his sword deep into the animal's belly.

Brigid fell back on her bottom as the pain in her side finally registered. Collapsing onto soft moss, she did her best to catch her breath, her own body heaving from fright. Once her panting slowed, she shoved herself to sitting, her eyes darting the area to ensure there were no more beasts headed in their direction. Wild boar rarely traveled alone.

She searched her skin for blood but didn't see any. Her ankle had turned when she fell, and it was swelling already, but she found no sign of a major wound there either.

Ethan and Shaw dragged the dead beast away while Marcas knelt down next to her, brushing errant hairs back from her face. "You are hurt? What happened?"

"My ankle. I turned it." She wished to cry and have her auntie tend her, but that wasn't likely to happen.

"I thought he gored your side," Marcas stated, his concern evident.

Brigid tossed her mantle back off her shoulders, letting it drop on the ground. "I don't see any blood so he didn't break my skin, but 'tis a wee bit sore." She touched her side again and peeked at it, but still no blood.

Jennet hopped down and looked at Brigid's foot, her twisted boot. "I'll take your boot off, see how it looks. I don't see any blood near your ankle. Do you?"

Brigid shook her head, the pain in her ankle now throbbing. "Cold water. I'm going to walk to the burn and put it under the cold water to numb the pain. Wash the beast off my leg."

"Nay, you'll not walk anywhere." Marcas scooped her up and began to carry her away. Jennet followed, but he barked at her, "Stay with the others. I'll care for her. I don't need you running away while I'm focused on her."

"I'll be fine, Jennet. I'll check it myself."

Marcas found a boulder to set her on, rinsed his hands in the water, then helped her roll her woolen hose down. "I'll not ask because we cannot waste any more time. I'm sorry if you feel I'm violating your dignity, but this is necessary. Please do not be offended."

Brigid found herself saying words she hadn't expected. "I trust you, Marcas." Why, she wasn't sure, but she felt after voicing it that she did.

Marcas arched a brow at her, his gray eyes catching hers. His gaze was a steel gray, with a strength behind it that told her she'd never need to worry with him around, that he'd protect her. His long lashes fluttered as he focused on her hose again, and she studied his face. Prominent cheekbones gave a striking look to his appearance, and his mouth was, well, kissable. Marcas was a handsome man, she found herself thinking, his brown locks falling in messy waves that suited him just fine.

Resting her eyes on his lips made her wonder how it would feel to be kissed by this man. She envisioned him trailing kisses down her neck and to other places no man had touched. She was close enough to him that she pictured his long lashes lifting to peer at her, a look of want and need so expressive that had he not had a firm hold on her foot, it would curl her toes. Her imagination ran wild over this man who gently removed her stocking and peered at her foot, carefully turning it.

"Does this hurt?" His voice came out in a husky tone that undid her. She guessed his mind had traveled to thoughts that were nearly as carnal as her own. Since she had little experience with men, she'd had to depend on her imagination. Her father had a way of scaring them all away.

She didn't want him to stop. She shook her head to deny the pain, unable to speak intelligibly at the moment, fearing her voice would betray her innermost thoughts.

Her desire.

Her raw, unbridled desire for this man to want her in the same manner she found she wanted him.

He lifted her to carry her to the water's edge, stopping for a moment as something tangibly passed between them. The flare of need evident on his face, words of her feelings caught on the edge of her tongue, both of them apparently curious if desire would be accepted or rebuffed. His eyes locked on her lips, then her eyes. He opened his mouth to speak, his head dipping closer to hers, so close she wished he would finish it and kiss her, but he didn't.

"Hurry up, Marcas," Shaw called out.

The spell broken, he set her on a soft mossy spot next to the water's edge and said, "Go ahead and dip it in."

She did as he said, pulling back with a gasp quickly as the cold hit her skin, but he cupped her calf and eased it back under the water.

"You'll get used to it." He splashed the water over her leg below the knee, washing off the dirt that had found its way between the weave of the wool.

She craved his touch.

"My apologies to you. I should not have allowed this to happen," he said earnestly.

"You cannot stop a boar from charging."

"But the only reason you are here is because of me. That makes you my responsibility. We should not have tarried. I will make sure you injure your ankle no further."

She looked into his gray eyes, where flecks of dark blue mingled with the gray, and knew he meant what he said. His heartfelt apology was unlike any she'd ever heard. "You're forgiven." This close, she caught something else. "You chew mint leaves."

"I do." His lips moved as if he had more to say, but she'd never know what because they were no longer alone.

Ethan appeared and called, "Is she well enough? Because I don't think we wish to stay here next to the dead animal for long."

"We'll be back in a moment." Whatever had passed between them was gone, his gruff exterior returning as he said, "We better return."

He handed her the hose and allowed her a moment to put it back on, then lifted her and returned to the group. He settled her on a log with instructions. "Put your boot back on and we'll move. I don't wish to wait here where the smell of blood will draw other animals." He turned toward Ethan, "Douse the fire and we move on. Shaw and I will cut a piece of the boar to cook for our dinner. I'll find a stick to carry it on."

Several minutes later, they were off, this time with Ethan in the lead directing them toward Inverness. They stopped an hour later, feasted on boar meat roasted over a fire, and fell asleep. The lasses huddled together in the middle while the men lay outside them in a circle.

Brigid went to sleep with images of strong shoulders and soft lips calling to her. This could be the adventure she'd been looking for.

CHAPTER THREE

———————— ◆ ————————

AFTER A GRUELING day where little was said, the travelers stopped a short distance outside Inverness.

"Where are we headed, Marcas? I know we said toward Inverness, but do you plan to travel through the burgh or head home?" Shaw asked, after relieving himself and returning to the clearing. The six sat around the fire after they had finished eating.

"Can you tell us more about what we're looking for? What kind of sickness has beset your clan?" Brigid asked.

"If I knew that, I wouldn't need you. You'll find out when the time is nigh," Marcas said, answering her out of the corner of his mouth before turning to his brothers. "The reason I'm traveling to Inverness first is to throw off the Ramsay group coming behind us." Then he reached into his saddlebag and tossed down a few pieces of cloth. "I picked these up from one of you," he said, slowly scanning the lasses. "I've heard Logan Ramsay is a hell of a tracker, but I decided there was no reason for you to give him assistance."

Tara stared at the cloth, her gaze narrowing. "You may think you're so wise, but only half of the scraps I left are there. Uncle Logan will find the others."

Then Marcas turned to Shaw. "Do you think either of you might start to trust me? At this point, we're going to need to band together. We left the clan, so others may attempt to take over the castle. We don't know how many of our guards will have survived the curse. If we work together, we'll have a better chance at becoming strong again."

"We might if you would consult us in your decisions before you make them. You just decided to come to Inverness and now you won't explain why," Ethan said. "It's a foolish decision because it makes our journey longer."

Marcas ran his hand down the front of his face to keep himself from cursing at his brothers. As the eldest, he was used to making decisions, but Ethan was extra sensitive and Shaw held a wisdom he depended on. It was time to share his thoughts.

"I decided we'd have a better chance of losing the Ramsays if we travel through one end of Inverness and head out the other. They'll not know which way we left." Then he glared at Tara. "True, I may not have found them all, but I have enough. Even if the great Logan Ramsay manages to track us thus far, he'll not track us from here. We'll sleep here, enter the town on the morrow, purchase some supplies, and leave. I'll not wait long, but I thought it important we try to throw the Ramsay contingent off."

Shaw tipped his head one way, then the other, scratching the rough stubble on his chin. "True that they may easily follow us here. I agree with your reasoning, but why you won't consult with your brothers before you make a decision, I don't know. Can you rethink your strategies next time?"

Marcas couldn't disagree with his brother. In fact, Shaw was correct—he tended to make decisions quickly without considering repercussions. Usually, he was lucky. Would he continue to be? He wasn't sure.

"I'll agree you have a point," he said, sitting on the log. "I'll try to improve."

"How many others are in your family?" Brigid asked. "And what clan are you from?"

Shaw started to speak, but Marcas stopped him. "Shut your mouth, Shaw. They don't need to know."

Shaw said, "Mayhap if they did, they'd understand the dire circumstances we're in and be more willing to help."

Ethan said, "He might be right." He looked at Marcas, awaiting his response. Marcas got up and paced a circle around the group, picking new leaves off the trees and tossing them in the air.

Jennet pursed her lips and crossed her arms. "Why must you ruin new growth on the tree?"

"What?" Marcas stopped his movement to stare at her. "Are you daft or something?"

"Nay, I'm far from daft. More intelligent than you, I'd wager." Jennet's chin shot up a notch, her glare challenging him. "The time is spring, when trees are ready to burst into blossom, the light green vibrant shades showing how young and delicate the foliage you so callously rip and toss to the ground."

"They're *leaves*." Marcas's voice raised as he pointed to the branch of the tree he'd assaulted.

"Back to the topic. I think if you told us what the curse is mayhap we would be more prepared to help you upon arrival." Jennet locked gazes with Marcas for a moment, clearly not intimidated by him.

"I don't see 'tis necessary to tell you anything ahead of time." Marcas's hands planted on his narrow hips as he continued to pace.

Shaw broached the topic again. "I don't see how it could hurt, brother. We need help. You've brought them this far, and we haven't far to go. I doubt they'll be running off anytime soon, as they don't have horses to return upon."

"Marcas," Brigid said, "If you knew anything about healers, you'd know that telling us what you fight is more likely to attract our interest. We are all drawn to help, especially when it comes to nursing sickness and developing remedies. Tara's mother has a beautiful volume showing where blood flows through the body, a virtual image of what our insides look like. We've all studied it."

"She's trying to tell you nicely that if you reveal and share what you know, we're more likely to willingly stay with you," Tara said. "'Tis like a puzzle to us. And having the ability to consult on this puzzle with my two cousins is a kind of treat."

"I agree with her," Shaw said, Ethan nodding next to him. "Tell them. I don't want to die."

Marcas threw his hands up in the air. His brothers now sided with the healers, though since they were all beauties in their own right and showed a courage to rival many men, he understood why his brothers were drawn to them.

Nor could he deny how attracted he was to Brigid. He glanced at her and finally nodded after giving the issue thorough consideration. Shaw was right. What could it hurt to tell them what his clan had endured?

Brigid added, "If we need special herbs, we may only be able to get them in the forest or Inverness."

"Do you not carry special herbs with you at all times? I thought all healers did that." He wouldn't admit how close he'd been to telling them the truth before the Cameron woman had spoken.

"We carry small amounts of everything, but 'tis more likely we'll require large quantities of whatever we need since your entire clan has been affected. Sizable amounts will take longer to harvest. And some herbs are difficult to find in spring."

She'd just given him the strongest argument yet. He sank onto the closest empty spot on a log and folded his hands in front of him, staring into the dying flames of the fire, considering his words carefully. "They have the heaves. All of them. They heave and heave until 'tis naught left inside. Then blood starts to come with it. They spout fluid from every opening they have. 'Tis making it difficult to care for them."

"Ah," Jennet said. "No one likes to be spewed upon, do they?"

"Exactly the problem. So what causes the heaves? And why does everyone have it?"

"Did all start retching at the same time?" Jennet asked.

The three men glanced at each other, thinking about her question before they answered.

"And a few more questions while you think on it," Jennet continued. "Did you have waves of people who came down with it? Like five, then eight more in another day, then ten more the next day? Did the numbers grow like that? Did it affect everyone? Warriors? Bairns? The eldest in your clan? Men and women the same?"

Ethan jumped off his log and stepped back. "Too many. Too many questions. I cannot answer that quickly. One at a time."

Marcas stood and moved next to his brother. "Do not worry, Ethan. Shaw and I can answer most of the questions."

"I wish to answer, but not all at once. 'Tis too much." He wrung his hands in front of his body as he stared up at Marcas.

Marcas patted his brother's shoulder, which often calmed him. Ethan got overwhelmed easily. He was probably the quickest of them all, but he struggled to maintain his composure when he felt threatened. He preferred everything orderly. Not that too many questions were always a threat, but in this moment, to his mind, they were. That much Marcas understood. "You think on one question, and Shaw and I will answer the others."

"My thanks to you," Ethan said, letting out a breath. "Which one is mine to answer?"

"You think on how many came down with the sickness each day and if it came in waves. Can you do that?"

Ethan's eyes lit up and he nodded, sitting down again. Numbers were always a good thing for him. He thrived on them. Ethan counted everything he could.

Marcas sat down next to his brother, facing Brigid. "Here is the situation. We lost both of our parents first, then my wife sickened with our son. Our parents and my wife died within a sennight, but my son of less than a year survived. My daughter of three winters was never sick until just before we left. She is the primary reason we came for you. I couldn't sit by and watch her die. I had to find a healer for her. And I can't lose anyone else. The answer to your question is that this curse doesn't care what age or whether its prey is a lad or lass. It has sickened nearly everyone."

"Bairns? Ones that were still at their mother's breast?" Brigid asked.

Marcas sighed and said, "Aye, our son was only ten moons, and he had naught but his mother's milk. But he healed, and she did not."

"And you three?" Jennet asked.

"I survived along with Shaw. Ethan hasn't had it yet. He didn't catch it."

"Truly? 'Tis most unusual," Brigid said. "We must think on it."

"Then we should all get some rest. Please do think carefully on it." Marcas stirred the fire to keep the flames going, tossing in another two large sticks.

"But what about my answer?" Ethan asked. "Are you no longer interested?"

Tara said, "Aye, we are. Tell us what you know."

"Five the first day after our parents, three men and two women. Day two, ten more were sick, four men, four women, one lass, one laddie. Day three, ten more. Three men, two women, three lasses, two lads. Day four and day five, no new ones. Then it started again on day six. Seven men, four lads…"

Jennet said, "Nicely done, Ethan. You've provided valuable information, but you've given us enough for now. We may ask more on the morrow. Verra helpful."

Ethan smiled, then found a spot on the grass and fell fast asleep.

Marcas said to the ladies, "He's overtired. You sleep there—Shaw will be on one side, I'll be on the other."

What would he find when they returned? Would his lass be alive? His sister? Any of their remaining guards?

Or no one?

CHAPTER FOUR

———◆———

BRIGID FELL FAST asleep but awakened a few hours later. She glanced at her cousins, not surprised to see Jennet was awake and staring at the stars overhead.

"What say you, Jennet?" she said quietly as possible, not wanting to awaken the others.

"'Tis not from the buttery." Jennet chewed on a blade of grass. "Or a bottle of wine."

"It could be one of those sicknesses that moves from person to person. If that were the case, there's little we can do and we must protect ourselves."

Jennet rolled onto a side and leaned up on her elbow. "We'll have to boil all the water. Check their well."

"And speak with their cook. It could be a new cook who leaves goat's milk for too long," Tara said, rubbing her eyes as she sat up. "Mama always insists on throwing away good goat's milk after a short time."

"Something else bothers me. Why not Ethan?" Brigid asked.

"'Tis a good question. We'll have to observe him carefully. He has a different way of looking at things," Jennet said. Her tone dropped to a whisper. "Besides that, I find him quite appealing. He is both clever and shrewd, something I admire. His hair is dark and the gray eyes feel as though they see right through me."

Tara said, "I think Shaw is attractive and amusing. His hair is that dark shade of red I like, and just being around him makes me smile." She giggled. Tara had soft brown eyes that matched her hair color perfectly, but she was a little more rounded than her two trim cousins. "How is your ankle, Brigid? The swelling looks much better. It didn't even appear you were favoring it."

"'Tis much better. The cold water stopped the swelling rather quickly. Riding allowed it to calm down. It only hurts a wee bit, though my side is still sore." Brigid looked at each of the three men, making sure they were all asleep, soft snores still emanating from each. "So are we in agreement we stay to help?"

Jennet said, "Of course. 'Tis our duty to assist. Besides, it pleases me to investigate such a wonderful puzzle."

Tara sighed. "I have no idea how to get home from here. I've never come this far north. Nothing is familiar. We'd have to steal their horses to leave, but I doubt we'd get far."

Brigid lay back down and stared up at the stars. "They'd get horses from Inverness and follow us. Have they said their clan name yet? Did I miss it?"

"Nay, I've not heard yet," Tara said, glancing at Jennet. "You?"

"Nay."

"Then we agree to go willingly, do our best, see if we can stop it?"

"Aye," Jennet said. "But we must be verra careful or we'll get it. I don't wish to lose either of you. Our mamas' rules for everything. Boil all fluids we ingest, don't share with others. Wash our hands. Lots of fluids for the sick. Take the daily herb brew Aunt Jennie uses to protect ourselves. Have you some, Tara? Do you know the recipe well enough?"

"Aye," Tara said, lying back down again. "We'll do fine."

"And make our mamas proud when they get here," Brigid said. "Because you know my mother will be here soon. I don't care what end of Inverness we leave from. Mama and Papa will find us if they have to raze the burgh from one end to the other."

"I can't wait to see the effect your mother has on these three," Jennet said. "Will be worth the wait. They have no idea what Aunt Gwyneth is capable of when she's protecting her bairns."

Brigid laughed. Her cousin was so right.

———— ◆ ————

The party rode their horses through most of Inverness to determine how active the market was and if there were healers selling wares. Marcas noticed two at the end of the busiest area and pointed them out to the lasses. "You should be able to find what you need here." They stopped at the stable at the edge of town, and Marcas helped

Brigid down while the others dismounted. "You can walk on your ankle?"

"Aye, I'm fine."

He led them through the burgh to the nearest inn, then turned to the group. "We'll sleep here this eve. I'll get one large chamber."

Marcas knew it was probably wrong, but he didn't know how else to do it. He couldn't risk the three women banding together and leaving. They entered the inn, surprised to see the dining hall full for the midday meal.

"I'll take your largest chamber with six pallets."

The innkeeper looked the group over and said, "You don't want three large pallets?"

"Nay, my wife prefers to sleep alone, and so do the others."

The innkeeper nodded and said, "It'll be ready in an hour. Eat or come back later."

"We'll visit the marketplace."

They left, no one saying anything. What could they say? Marcas knew the man had guessed they weren't a married bunch, but he'd mercifully said nothing. "We'll get meat pies from the vendors. You can check the herbalist along with the street vendors, see if there's anything you'll need."

They headed toward the market, where colorful banners waved in the wind, but a voice caught him. "Matheson, hold!"

The three men turned around at the sound of their clan name, surprised to see one of their guards running toward them. The guard pointed to an area out of the way for a chat, and the lasses followed along. Marcas knew they'd probably heard his name called out, but they'd learn it soon enough on their own.

"Torcall," Marcas called out. "How do you fare? Why are you in Inverness?" Torcall was one of their best guards, always loyal and faithful to his sire. Would Torcall be the same if Marcas kept the lairdship? When they left, nothing had been decided for certain, there was too much work and worry to discuss it. He didn't know, wasn't even certain he'd take it, though his sire would tell him it was his responsibility. The difficulty of meeting everyone else's expectations weighed heavily on his mind.

Actually, thinking about taking over his father's place as chieftain of the clan was more painful than he'd anticipated. He knew the position was his rightful heritage and duty. Could he do a good job, though? He didn't know and didn't have time to think on it yet. He plugged along, his mind on his daughter and whether he'd find her alive and well.

"Laird," Torcall said, coming to a swift halt in front of the group. "Where have you been? Everyone thinks you've deserted your keep. Surrounding clans are awaiting the curse to end to take over our castle."

Marcas glanced at his brothers, then back to Torcall. "We had important business to attend to, but since you're a guard and we left you to protect the castle, why are you here? Did we not leave several of you there with orders? Our numbers are dwindling. I expected all remaining guards to stay and offer what protection you could until we returned."

"Aye, there are about ten remaining, but many are gone. We had no idea what happened to you three, if even you were to return. Even Gisela does not know where you traveled. She was sickly when you left and didn't remember. But you are well?" The man assessed the three lasses warily, not mentioning their presence. He was one of their stronger guards, still young and unmarried with time to devote to protecting Matheson land.

"We've brought three healers to eliminate the curse, so there'll be no need for anyone to take over our keep. We're getting supplies and heading that way on the morrow. Are you returning with us or going to another clan?"

"Nay, nay. I have supplies to get for Nonie. Which one of you is accepting the lairdship? Gisela said you had not decided yet." Torcall looked from Marcas to Ethan to Shaw, then back to Marcas. "'Tis supposed to be you, Marcas."

"And I will be," Marcas said, not consulting his brothers. Ethan couldn't handle it and Shaw probably wasn't interested since he was just past twenty, so it had to be his. After all, he was the eldest. There really was no reason to discuss it. He'd promised his sire long ago to lead when it was necessary. He'd just never guessed it would be so soon. He was only five and twenty, and four years separated the three brothers. Ethan was three and twenty and Shaw two years younger. Gisela was a year younger than Shaw.

None of them had expected their mighty sire to pass away from the heaves. He was too large, too boisterous, too strong. To see him wither away was a horrible experience. It had been two days later when Alvery, his loyal guard and second-in-command, had finally confronted the three brothers over who was to be laird.

All three had stared at each other, then his two brothers had brought their attention to him, Shaw's eyebrows raised in question. He'd accepted and that had ended the discussion. While he wished more than anything to tell Alvery they all needed to grieve before someone took their sire's position in the clan, he understood the clan had expectations. Marcas knew now he had to step up and claim his rightful heritage, but if he did a poor job, he'd quickly hand the position to Shaw.

"How are the others? Gisela? Kara? My wee laddie?" He knew right away by the look on Torcall's face that the answer wasn't going to be what he wished to hear. But he had to know.

Torcall stuttered, a sound that sent an arrow through his heart. "Gisela is healing. She heaved for days and we thought she'd die, but she survived. Her fever is gone, but she has no stamina. Can barely walk much each day, just to go to the garderobe. Nonie is much better and she cares for your son, Tiernay. He will live."

Hellfire. He didn't want to ask the next question, but he had to. "And Kara?"

Torcall stared at the ground. "She's gone missing."

"What the hell does that mean?" Ethan barked. "How could a wee lassie go missing?"

"It means we were all so sickly, busy helping

others, trying to keep as many alive as possible, and when we woke up one morning, Kara was gone. She disappeared in the middle of the night. We've looked everywhere."

"No one has found her body?" Marcas asked, a sliver of hope emerging in his heart.

"Nay, and we've looked everywhere." Torcall paused, but then said, "We need you, my laird. Glad to have you back, and with your guidance, I'm sure we'll find the wee lassie. Mayhap the healers can help everyone feel better. 'Tis no one left who has not had it. Except for you, Ethan."

"Our thanks for the information, Torcall. Find what you came for and ride back with us on the morrow. We'll leave at dawn. We're at the inn at the end of this road. Join us or meet us in the morn." Marcas couldn't loosen the tightening in his belly, the awful feeling spreading through him as he thought of all the things that could have happened to his dear daughter, the one whose smile could light up the entire keep.

Torcall nodded and gave a slight bow, stepping away, but then he whirled around and said to the lasses. "Welcome to all of you." Then he spun on his boot and disappeared.

Shaw clasped his brother's shoulder. "They have not found her yet, so mayhap someone from a different clan came and took her away, trying to save her. You cannot be sure yet, Marcas. And your son needs you, so we must hurry back."

He rubbed his eyes and said, "True. I'll be upset until I've searched myself. I'll check all the paths here in Inverness while we're here."

"Good idea," Brigid said. "I could picture someone taking her away from a curse just with the hope of saving an innocent child. 'Tis surely possible you'll find her. In the meantime, we'd like to go to the herbalist's stall. Hopefully there are several here still offering supplies."

She pointed down the way, and all Marcas could do was nod. "Do as you wish. And here's coin to get what you need. Whatever you need, get it and do not dwell on it. We need the healing supplies."

Marcas turned away, sick inside. He didn't know what to think, except that he would search all of Inverness to see if he could find dear Kara. She was only three winters old. She couldn't take care of herself. She needed someone to take care of her.

"Wait, please," he called out, a sudden urge to have everyone's input.

The three lasses returned while Ethan and Shaw waited to see what Marcas wanted. "I could use your input. I don't know if I can think of every situation, so please help me see all the possibilities. What are different reasons Kara might have been taken away? Assuming she did not wander off on her own in the middle of the night, something I think unlikely, she must have been taken. Any ideas?"

Ethan, the most analytical, said, "Stolen for ransom."

"More, Ethan, please. Why ransom?"

"To force you to give up your castle in exchange for her return."

"Good idea. Others?"

Shaw said, "Freda's mother took her because she missed her daughter."

He considered that for a moment. "Possible, but unlikely. I don't see her doing it quietly or not letting Nonie or Gisela know. Other ideas?"

"Someone could have stolen her because they wish for a daughter and Freda is gone now, so she is less protected," Tara said.

Brigid cast her eyes down, then lifted them. "Or because they lost their own daughter to the heaves and can't deal with it."

"Brilliant, cousin," Jennet said, "Someone could have left the clan to stay safe from the heaves, and since Kara lost her mother, she was an easy target for a grief-stricken mother to steal away and take as her own. They could then travel back to Inverness and blend in. No one would be the wiser."

This was something Marcas hadn't thought of, and he wasn't sure if he understood it. "But she wouldn't be at all like their daughter."

Brigid said, "When a woman loses a child of any age, she loses a piece of her soul. Some will do anything to make the pain cease, even an act as heinous as abducting a bairn not theirs. And in her heart, she might even believe the child to be her own, even change the bairn's name to the name of her dead bairn."

Perhaps he needed to do a thorough search of the area, Marcas realized, more thorough than he had thought.

Ethan said, "'Tis possible, Marcas, but I would bet they would cross Black Isle and try to blend in there. Too many people know Clan Matheson in Inverness."

He couldn't argue Ethan's reasoning. "My thanks for your suggestions. Please do as you wish and return within the hour."

His beloved Kara had been sick when he'd left, but not as sick as the others. His sweet one with long dark curls had just stared at him, her skin waxy, her eyes red-rimmed, only able to say the same thing. "Mama. Where's Mama? Papa, I want my mama."

He'd hugged her close and told her he was going to leave for a short bit and return. He'd thought this journey would take four days, yet they were already on day five. But they had the healers. Would they find anyone upon return who needed healing? Or were they too late?

It was good news that Tiernay, who he'd named after his sire, lived on. His son had been fed with goat's milk after his wife had died since there were no other women able to take over for her to meet the bairn's needs. Of the two other women in the clan who'd had infants, one had passed on and the other had returned to her own clan in Cromarty.

But Nonie had taken over for Freda, making it her mission to see that the wee lad, heir to the lairdship, would survive. Their housemaid had tended Tiernay so carefully and Marcas prayed he would live. One prayer had been answered. Or two. Gisela lived on with Nonie and Tiernay.

But what of sweet Kara?

CHAPTER FIVE

———◆———

BRIGID SAID TO her cousins, "I had to leave. I could not watch him grieve for his daughter. How horrible."

Tara said, "Whatever this is, we must be careful. We cannot catch this. I could not bear to lose either of you. Think carefully of all the supplies we'll need."

Jennet ticked off on her finger. "Mint, sage, thyme…"

"Thyme? Why? I agree with the other two because Mama uses both for any stomach ailments, but not thyme."

"Thyme handles the odor of sickness, and after all who've been sickly, the odor in the keep could be ghastly. I suspect we may have to do quite a bit of cleaning, so we'll also need lavender. Coriander for fever, chamomile for headaches. They all seem to go together. We have a bit of each in our healing bag, but not much." Jennet thought again. "What else, Brigid?"

"Mayhap borage and dittany."

"Good idea. Mama uses both," Tara added. They found two vendors selling herbs, surprised the booths were stuffed with nearly everything they wanted.

"You have not changed your mind about leaving?" Tara asked, cautiously looking over her shoulder for eavesdroppers. "This would be our time to get away. You have the coin to pay for horses, though I've no idea how many we could buy."

Jennet looked at Brigid, who sternly shook her head. "I can't leave him like this."

"Him?" Tara asked. "Isn't it *them*?"

"All of them, aye, but mostly because I feel we must take care of Marcas's bairn, their sister, and now they need help finding his daughter. I would worry about what happened to her if I never knew the truth of it." Brigid tucked the herbs into her sack. "At least we know of the clan name. Papa will be here soon. Until then, I say we stay and try to help."

Tara chewed on her lip. "Clan Matheson. Heard you anything of them before?"

Jennet shook her head along with Brigid.

One of the vendors said to them, "You must be healers. Stay away from Clan Matheson on the Black Isle. They say 'tis badly cursed. So many dead. They fear it will curse all of Black Isle."

Brigid nearly dropped the mint package in her hand. "That bad? We had not heard." She thought it best to learn what they could. "What causes the curse? Witchery?"

"No one knows, but more than half the clan are dead. 'Tis a sad situation for sure. No one dares approach them. Heard the laird and his wife died and the sons all left." The vendor just shook his head. "They said the eldest didn't wish to lead, that Clan Matheson will be no more. The three lads are probably cursed for sure."

"Many thanks for your help." Brigid blindly picked up the packages wrapped in twine, giving some to Jennet as she turned around, back toward the inn. She didn't wish to hear any more. They were in dire straits, yet everyone in Inverness spent time wagging their tongues about the clan's troubles. "Do you believe him?"

"That the sons are cursed?" Jennet asked, snorting lightly. "Nay, there are no such things as curses."

"My sister would tell you differently. She has unusual abilities, as you know. Riley's a seer and believes in helping the dead pass on. I'm glad she's not here. 'Twould be too much for her tender nature to be around this many souls recently passed."

"Riley could help them."

"Mayhap at a later time," Tara said, shaking her head as if to convince the others. "But do you believe that Marcas won't lead? That mayhap they wish to dissolve the clan? He said he was laird when we met that guard, did he not? Did I hear him correctly?"

Brigid paused to think. "Marcas did say something like it when the guard asked the three of them. He said he would be the laird." She wandered down the path, doing her best to stay out of anyone's way. Most people ignored them completely, so absorbed in thought it was as if the women didn't exist. "But do you not notice something odd in Inverness? Have you ever seen a group of people so sad, so quiet, so pensive?"

Tara whispered, "'Tis a most simple explanation. They're all afraid the curse will move outside of Clan Matheson." She looked over her shoulder to see if anyone had overheard her. "The Scot's believe in curses."

Jennet said, "I think you're right. Ethan is up ahead, and everyone is walking away from him."

"I noticed it when Torcall left. Everyone made sure to walk far away from him, too. The situation must be frightful." The women exited the area of stalls and goods and headed toward the end of the path where the inn sat in a less populated section of the burgh. Lined with inns and private manor homes, the street they returned to was peaceful, and it lent a bit of comfort to Brigid's inner being.

The women returned to the three men eating meat pies on a log in a small unoccupied courtyard beside the inn. When they approached, Marcas led the group to where no one would bother them, not far from the firth where they could sit in the grass. He held out two meat pies. "Mutton or beef?"

Brigid took a mutton pie and chewed slowly. "This is a large port. Lots of ships on the river. My cousin met his wife here and said it was one of the busiest ports. What do they carry on the large ships?"

"Mostly wool and furs. 'Tis a great area for fishing, and there is much wood for shipbuilding. That business flourishes here. We can get nearly anything we want when the ships come in. Spices are what we like most. Since the city sits on the River Ness, the ships can take goods into Scotland, too."

The others helped themselves to a meat pie. Brigid enjoyed hers. It was delicious, far better than the fare they'd been eating, and she had to wonder if there would be any food at the keep. "Did you purchase any foodstuffs? How well stocked were you before this started? Mayhap you should arrange for fresh vegetables to bring along with us. At least we could keep a nice broth for the sickly ones. Steamy broth is the best and the safest. No meat at first."

"We hunt for most of our food. I did get oats and barley, along with some root vegetables and onion. Enough for the number we have remaining. I don't know how often I'll be there or how long it will take to find my daughter," Marcas said. "Others will join me in the search and we can hunt along the way."

Brigid looked into the distance, the reflection of water shining through the trees. "What is that? A firth or a loch?"

Marcas said, "Come. I'll show you. We can eat on the bank if you like."

"We'll stay here," Ethan said. "You know I don't like the firth. But neither do you, Marcas."

"I'm not going swimming, Ethan. Don't worry about me. I'll be fine."

Ethan's worries seemed to ease, and Brigid decided she'd like to see the landscape.

She glanced at Tara and Jennet who gave her

small nods, encouraging her to go along with Marcas. Her sire had taught her to learn as much about her surroundings as possible, and this seemed an important opportunity. "I heard mention of Black Isle. Is that where we're headed?"

"Come and I'll show you." He led her down the path quite a way before he found a section under a tree above the water. "Sit here and look straight across."

He pointed to a soft spot of earth. She settled her wool gown underneath her and sat down cross-legged, not worrying about being dainty, as she had leggings on underneath. They were wonderful leggings, the same kind her mother had made for all the females in the clan.

The day was cloudy, but there was little mist, giving her a clear view of the water in the firth. Sparkles danced across its surface whenever the sun peeked from the clouds even a wee bit. Across the waterway sat a large sprawling area, and hills in the distance backed up a long coastline dotted with fishing boats and small buildings. They were up higher than she'd have thought, giving her a wonderful view when she glanced down the small cliff of craggy rocks beneath her feet. Getting to the water would prove tricky from their spot.

"You're looking at all of Black Isle. But it's not really an isle because 'tis surrounded by three firths: Cromarty, Moray, and this is Beauly Firth. 'Tis truly a peninsula, I'd say from my travels around here. We're in the Highlands but different."

"In what way is Black Isle different?"

"The rich soil. Clan Matheson has some of the richest soil. I'm told much of the Highlands is infertile for growing food, but we have no trouble. We're close to the sea and Inverness's merchant boats, as I was saying. We can get all we wish here for not more than a two-hour journey."

"'Tis quite beautiful from here. Are there many clans? Many villages?"

He sat down beside her and leaned back, resting his hands flat on the ground. "Our castle is well hidden in the woods of Gallow Hill, yet still close to shore, which is why everyone wants it. We have the richest fields, we are close to the water, and can fish from the mudflats when the tide goes out. There are other villages along the coastline, but few inland. 'Tis a good life. *'Twas* a good life until the curse came to us. We did not know if any other clans were ill, but I sent Ethan with some guards early on to check, which is probably one of the reasons he never took ill. I sent him to North Kessoch, Munlocky, and Avoch. No one else was cursed, just us. We stopped at Beauly when we left to find you, but no one was ill there either."

"'Tis most odd then."

"Why?"

"Because Aunt Brenna always said if the sickness is one that passes from person to person, then others will have it outside of your keep. People travel, give it to others. But if no one else has it, 'tis possible it could be something spoiled. Some meat, or an ill goat. A badly prepared butte of ale. We'll have to check the buttery, the well, even your animals. But we'll uncover the truth of it, I think. We've seen similar circumstances."

"And the last one? What caused it?" he asked, staring oddly at her lips, a look that caused a flutter deep in her belly.

"A bad butte of ale. There was a crack in the butte no one saw, and it turned bad. Made everyone sick, but I don't think such could be the case for you. The ale eventually soured, so people could prove it had been bad. How long ago was the first illness?"

"Two moons."

"Oh, my. We will have to do some serious investigating."

"What do you mean?"

"May I explain once we arrive at your castle? 'Twill be easier then." She stared back across the water, thinking of all he'd endured. "I'm sorry you lost your wife."

"Don't be," he said, abruptly, sitting up straight. "Forgive me. It shouldn't have come out that way. I am sorry my bairns lost their mother, and though we didn't have strong feelings for each other, she didn't deserve to have her life cut so short."

Brigid wished to ask him more but didn't. She hoped that if she waited, giving him time to think, he'd tell her more. What could cause a husband not to be upset at the loss of his wife?

"We had problems. We were a match, not a love match. She was from Avoch, and it was a good match to keep peace. There was no love. And I found out about six moons ago that after she gave birth to Tiernay, she started seeing another man back in Avoch. Someone she'd loved long ago."

"I'm sorry," Brigid said softly. "That must have been hard to discover. He came to your keep?"

"He never used to, but she traveled home with the two bairns, spent a fortnight with her parents, then returned. Shortly after, he visited a time or two that I never knew about, bringing gifts from their clan to ours. He was careful to come when I would be in the lists training our men, apparently. I discovered the affair in a different way, but Freda was unhappy she was caught and begged me not to tell her parents."

"Did you forgive her?"

"Nay. We were never in love, but we did respect each other. I cared for her. She was a good mother to our bairns, but I couldn't bed her after I found out. She begged me to keep her secret." He exhaled. "I've said too much. Forgive me for rambling. I think we should return." Then he stood up abruptly and held his hand down to Brigid to help her to her feet. She stood. Yet he didn't let go right away, his gaze locked on hers.

A heat passed between them, searing her skin as if they were touching beyond their hands. It was the oddest experience she'd ever had with a man.

"Brigid, I'd appreciate if you'd not repeat what I told you. I went too far…about Freda. The rest is fine, talking about Black Isle and our castle in Gallow Hill, but I shouldn't speak of the dead in such a way."

He dropped her hand and made a motion for them to walk back through the trees.

She moved to follow. As they kept step, she silently considered his words. Her heart skipped a beat when she realized: he hadn't loved his wife. Why?

CHAPTER SIX

———◆———

THE COUSINS AND brothers sat around a table in their chamber, eating a second meal of mutton stew and crusty brown bread. Marcas had requested special circumstances because of how everyone had looked at them in the market area. He and Ethan had both noticed how everyone had kept a distance from them.

They were responding to the believed curse of Black Isle. He wouldn't subject the lasses to that rudeness.

But something else had overtaken his mind, even beyond the facts of the Inverness townspeople's reaction, and his sorrow at Kara gone missing. Marcas couldn't get past the guilt over confessing what he had to Brigid. How could he have shared everything with her?

Well, almost everything.

"Can I ask a question and receive an honest answer?" he asked.

Brigid nodded, glancing at her two cousins, who nodded accordingly.

"Is your sire the one with the reputation of being an excellent tracker?"

"Aye. One of the verra best."

"Is he truly that good a tracker? Will he follow you here within a sennight or fortnight? I'm trying to gauge how long we'll be able to take advantage of your healing skills before he brings an army along to whisk you away."

Jennet looked as perplexed as the other two. Glancing at Brigid, she asked, "Did he say sennight? Fortnight?"

Brigid glanced at the men, trying to hide her grin.

Tara chuckled, briefly choking on a piece of her bread. "Uncle Logan will be here within a day. Two at the most. If it were strictly up to my father or Jennet's sire, mayhap they would take several days, but not Brigid's sire. He'll come ahead of the big army of warriors, but they'll be along behind him, I would wager."

Jennet continued with another casual observation that lent credence to Tara's comment, though Brigid could tell she tried to contain her amusement. "Though Uncle Logan has adopted other lasses and loves them all equally, Brigid is still his wee bairn, his youngest before the adoptions. He won't bring many warriors, but if he feels the need, he'll stop at Clan Grant, our closest ally, and bring two or three hundred behind him. That could slow him a day."

The three men paled. Ethan whispered, "Clan Grant? Did you say Clan Grant, the one with over a thousand warriors? The biggest in all the land?" His gaze traveled from one face to another, but no one said anything to appease him.

"What the hell have you done, Marcas?" Shaw asked. "Though bringing warriors will cause no problem—there's no one left to fight save for mayhap ten men. We'll all be dead—those of us who survived the devil and the curse will be killed at the end of Grant blade."

Ethan stuttered, "We'll concede quickly under those circumstances." He darted a glare at his brother as he took another timid bite of his stew.

No one said anything for several minutes, all six working away at their food.

Marcas had to do what he could to protect his clan, his castle. "And what say you, Brigid? When your sire arrives and you speak with him, will you tell him to attack?"

Ethan leaned forward in his chair, his eyes wide. "Will he take your advice, whatever you tell him?"

"My sire will listen to me. When the three of us inform him that we wish to help, that there is a curse that could take us all if we do not find the cause, he'll be more apt to listen. He'll do what he can to help."

Tara asked, "Do you think he'll stop at Clan Grant?"

Brigid shook her head. "He won't because he could lose the tracking, though if he does, I'm sure it will not be for long. Sometimes he stops for information. He might consider that Alex's sons know more of this area since Connor met his wife in Inverness."

Shaw snorted. "He does not know we're taking you to Inverness."

Tara leaned closer to him. "Aye, he does."

"How the hell would he know that?"

Brigid glanced over at Jennet. "Because one of us left clues."

The three men looked equally confused. Ethan asked, "What kind of clues?"

"Jennet dug letters into the bark of a tree telling him where we were going."

Shaw guffawed. "And you think your sire is such a good tracker he'll find your miniature letters? In a million trees in the Highlands, he'll know exactly which to look at?"

All three lasses had smug expressions on their faces, then broke into giggles. "You don't know my sire," Brigid said. "Or my mother. They've been doing this for a long time. Also a reason why they won't stay at Grant land for long. *If* they stop."

"Why wouldn't they stop?" Marcas asked, hoping the women were wrong. He could use the extra day before they were attacked by a wild sire.

Jennet explained, "Sometimes tracking is only clear for a day. Once it rains or snows, you lose many of the tracks. It took him a few days to catch up with us when we were abducted before, but the weather complicated it."

Shaw pushed his chair back. "You've been taken from home before?"

"A while ago," Brigid said. "Jennet and I were stolen away in the middle of the night when we were young, around six or seven. I did not handle it well, but Jennet, well, she played one of the finest tricks I've ever seen."

"And what was that?" Marcas asked.

Brigid glanced over at her cousin, who gave her a short shake of her head. "Mayhap best we keep some secrets, my lord. But you might enjoy hearing about my sire and when he's at his best."

"Go on. I'd love to hear," Marcas asked, tearing off another hunk of bread.

"My parents and my adopted sister Molly, along with her now-husband Tormod, tracked us. My mother helped with the tracking, but she was hurt, so it was up to Molly to find where we were hidden. Poor Jennet was held with a dagger at her throat while another man grabbed me and took me behind the building. Molly fought him off and helped me get back to Jennet. Finally our sire arrived, and he did what he does best."

"And that would be?" Marcas asked, but then said, "Even though I'm aware you may tell me an outright lie."

"My sire is an expert at trickery, at making you believe one thing while he does another. I watched while I hid behind a tree. My father made himself the target, positioning himself perfectly while he taunted the bastard, giving Molly the aim she needed from behind him to hit the villain with her arrow. The villain so busy with the knife at Jennet's throat and watching my father, he never saw Molly behind him. Papa knew she could hit him easily. She's one of the finest archers ever, but she needed a clear shot that wouldn't hit Jennet. But as Papa continued to speak to our captor, he got the daft man to turn just so, giving Molly the target she needed. Once my sire had him turned just right, Molly fired, hitting him directly in his flank, the deadly spot, killing him. When he collapsed, his hands were locked on Jennet and it took forever to free her, but she remained calm. Unlike me."

"You weren't calm? You're as composed as can be now," Shaw said.

"Not at six summers. I cried and screamed until our captors wanted to knock me out. Jennet is the only reason I managed to survive. She's always been the strongest person I know, which is why…"

"Why what?" Jennet asked, turning to face Brigid with an odd look on her face.

Brigid's face flushed, but she didn't back down. "'Tis why I owe you an apology, cousin. I shouldn't have said you were a healer when they came in our keep. 'Twould have been better if I was the only one taken. My apologies."

"You need not apologize because whether you had said that or not, I would have come along, even followed you." Jennet continued to eat, no expression of emotion on her pretty face while Brigid looked close to tears.

Why the hell was Marcas so drawn to her? If he could, he'd have lifted her onto his lap, kissed her forehead, and rubbed her back just to calm her down. She was too strong to cry. In his heart, he truly believed that.

But then, Gisela had often told him that crying was not a weakness.

Brigid squeezed her cousin's shoulder and said,

"I could always count on you, couldn't I?"

"I feel honored to be along with you two," Tara chimed in. "This will be quite an adventure. My father will be shocked to hear I was taken along with the Ramsays." She smiled, and Marcas noticed Brigid laughed with her.

Brigid had been embarrassed about her mistake of including Jennet in their journey, but her cousins had done what they could to make her feel better. Their efforts appeared to be successful, and her warm green eyes smiled at the other two lasses.

He and his brothers had never acted like that together. Perhaps he'd be wise to attempt to learn from the women.

———◆———

Logan stood in a clearing, staring up at the trees, then pacing its periphery, looking for clues. "Gwynie, I haven't had this kind of fear in a long time."

His wife consoled, "I know, Logan, but we'll find them. If they could leave enough clues for us when they were six, I'm sure they found ways to leave clues on this journey, too."

Kyle Maule, head of the Ramsay guards, joined the two, dismounting. "I would say they were definitely here. We found evidence of three or four horses, but the other part that caught me was this." He led them to an area in the trees where the bushes were thicker. "Look." He pointed to the ground where someone had apparently been digging.

"I'll agree about the horses, but what the hell does a hole in the ground mean, Kyle? I'm not liking my first thoughts that go with it. What the hell were they doing? Trying to bury someone?" Logan, his long light brown locks blowing in the wind, gave Maule the intimidating stare he knew wouldn't work. Logan felt he had to practice it because he didn't know what was coming. And he surely didn't like not being in control.

"Healers, Logan. They dig for roots and herbs. Jennet and Brigid are healers. I think they were here."

Logan hadn't even considered that. He scratched at the stubble on his chin, deciding Kyle could be correct. "Well done, Maule. Have your men keep searching for other clues." They'd brought twenty Ramsay guards along to search for the lasses.

Logan and Gwyneth's only son, Gavin, said, "Papa, you have the pieces of cloth that were left for you. They were here."

His mother barked, "But they don't match any of their clothing. We don't have a weave like that. I know I've seen it, but I can't recall. I hate getting older. I cannot see as well, and I cannot recall like I used to. Good thing we brought Merewen along to shoot the bastards in their bollocks for me." Then she looked at Sorcha, who was just joining them from the woods, her husband, Cailean, behind her. "Sorcha, you'll have to shoot the bastards in the bollocks if Merewen won't do what I ask."

Merewen paled. "You want me to do what, Gwyneth?"

"Never mind. When the time comes, I'll explain it." Gwyneth paced in circles, staring at the bushes, then the ground, trying to absorb everything in sight. "We haven't seen any of those pieces of fabric in a while." She spun around to stare at Logan as her face lit up. "I remembered who has that weave!"

"Who? Hellfire, just say it, Gwynie." Logan stopped to await her answer, his hands firmly planted on his hips.

"Jennie. 'Tis a Cameron weave for sure."

Gavin asked, "Why would they want Aunt Jennie?"

Logan sighed, the full implication clear. "Not Jennie. Tara. They stole the three healers."

"I don't think anyone considers Tara and Brigid the healers. Jennet possibly, but not Brigid."

"So what are you saying? Why would they steal those three away?"

Gavin said, "They're all young. Mayhap they're stealing brides."

"That suggestion might have some merit if they stole from one keep, but they went to two different ones. And so far apart? Nay. The only thing Cameron and Ramsay lasses have in common is being healers." Logan paced, trying to figure out exactly what had happened.

Sorcha said, "Right before they were abducted, Jennet and Brigid delivered a bairn. Did you know that?"

Logan spun around. "Mayhap the villains knew that. Could they have learned of such and followed the healers back to the keep? If so, then they were definitely after healers."

Gwyneth played with her long plait, tossing it back and forth in her hand. "Do you suppose…"

"What, Gwynie? Just say it."

"Logan, what if they thought they were stealing Brenna and Jennie? If that was their intent, then mayhap they aren't alone. That is a Cameron weave. I'll bet Tara is with them."

"I'll not say you're wrong, Gwynie," he said, pacing again.

"Three of them—that does make me feel better, Logan," Gwynie mumbled, still lost in thought about something. "Do you think Aedan is out searching?"

"We'll spend the night at Grant Castle. 'Tis only a couple of hours ahead, and I'd like to see what Alex knows, if there are any new marauders in the area. I don't bet these are average reivers who stole the lasses. These were men with a purpose. Mayhap Alex knows of something happening in the Highlands. None of our neighbors are clever enough to get inside our keep. And none of Grant's neighbors are either. When we get there, I'll have Grant send a messenger to Cameron to be sure."

Logan scratched his head, wishing he could think of something more useful. He looked at his wife, every bit as beautiful in her leggings and tunic as the day he married her. "What has you so preoccupied?" Logan asked. "There's something more you're not telling me. I know that calculating mind of yours. It's a fine one, especially when it comes to your bairns."

"When they were kidnapped before, years ago, by Bearchun—there was another way the lasses got clues to us. What was it, Logan?" She paced again, her brown hair now streaked with strands of gray well hidden in the tie at her crown and plaited down her back. "The direction they headed in. Somehow we figured it out from their tracks. Think, Logan. Think! What the hell was it? We aren't that old yet."

"I'm sorry, Gwynie, but I don't recall."

Gwyneth chewed on her lip while the other three continued to look over the area after Kyle returned to his men. Then she suddenly jumped and ran to the trees, going from one to the next to the next, staring at the base of the trees.

"What the hell are you doing now, wife?"

"Scratching!" she panted. "I remember now. Jennet scratched messages to us in the trunk of the tree. I'm looking for scratches." The five of them leapt to search the area, looking for this new type of clue that the lasses had been there.

As they searched the copse, a seemingly endless task in the forests of the Highlands, Gwyneth felt glad that this was a clearing, narrowing the number of trees the girls could have accessed. "There are enough other signs they were here that we should search all of these trees," Gywnie said, circling one and bending over to stare at the lowest part of the bark.

"Like this?" Merewen called, pointing at the base of an oak. Running to her side then kneeling down to take a closer look, Gavin joined her.

Sorcha looked over Gavin's shoulder. "Mama,

you're right. There it is. Merewen found it."

"What does it say? What?" Gwynie pounded on Gavin's shoulder, peering over.

"I think 'tis an H." Merewen and Gavin leaned closer.

Logan looked too, thinking it could indeed be an H. "That doesn't say anything. And what the hell would an H mean? Didn't you tell me before that Jennet scratched S for south or something like that? H is no direction. What the hell could it mean?" Hell, he'd kill all the grass in the clearing from his pacing before he was done.

Merewen shouted, "Not an H, but an I. I, then N, then V, then another letter that could be an E, then nothing. Mayhap she was interrupted."

Gavin sat on his heels, contemplating the letters, but the answer suddenly came to Logan.

"Inverness. They're going to Inverness." He grabbed his wife and kissed her hard on the mouth. "Hellfire, but that Jennet is a smart one. Nice job, Gwynie."

Logan moved outside of their small clearing and bellowed, "Maule, gather the men. We're off to Grant land for the night, then to Inverness."

CHAPTER SEVEN

———— ◆ ————

BRIGID HUDDLED INSIDE her mantle as they approached Eddirdale Castle, home of Clan Matheson, the next afternoon. She rode with Marcas again, fortunately. She'd leaned back into his heat, and he hadn't seemed to mind at all. Now that they were nearly to his home, she felt the need to sit up straight and not touch him.

He had only recently lost his wife, even though she'd been seeing another. Brigid couldn't help but wonder if the clan had known about her indiscretion. Not that it would matter, Marcas was still laird. If they'd have known, the villagers might have stoned her, or something else less obvious, to let her know their feelings.

The night had been uneventful. They'd eaten porridge and honey in the dining hall below stairs once they were all up, partaking quietly because a few others had been present, also. Once they finished, they headed back out.

A small part of her was now afraid to see what they would find. Would the keep be deserted? Overrun by others who took advantage of the brothers' absence? Her stomach roiled in turmoil the closer they came. While reason told her that her aunts were both fine healers whose teachings would prevent the cousins from becoming ill, a small fear she knew would sit in the back of her mind until they uncovered exactly what had caused the sickness in the first place.

Would she become ill? Would she lose one or both of her cousins?

A sudden need for the comfort of her mother and Aunt Brenna washed over her, leaving her feeling bereft. Determined to survive if only to see her parents again, she worked to quell her fears and vowed to carefully uncover the issues at the Matheson keep.

And do what she could to help Marcas find his daughter.

The gates were open, one guard standing near the wall. "Marcas? 'Tis truly you? You've returned?"

Torcall had ridden back with them and called, "Found them all in Inverness."

"And who are the three lasses? You have not brought them to the curse, have you? You've told them?"

"Aye, Alvery," Marcas said as they approached the curtain wall. He stopped his horse where Alvery stood. "These are the three healers I've brought to fix everything. Two are the daughters and one a niece of the two most renowned healers in the Highlands. This is Lady Brigid, the fair-haired lass is Lady Jennet, and the one riding with Shaw is Lady Tara."

"Welcome, ladies. There are not many of us

who survived, but those who have are mighty tough." Alvery was an older man, but he had kind eyes and broad shoulders, evidence he could still wield a sword.

"Have you found Kara yet?"

"Nay. We have a search patrol out again."

Marcas didn't hide his disappointment at returning to a still-missing daughter. "Tiernay and my sister?"

"Both are well."

"Before we head to the keep, tell me how many are left, Alvery."

"I think a dozen at last count. Nonie, Gisela, Tiernay, Jinny, and six guards. And now you three."

"Anyone sick at present?"

"Nay. Which one of you is laird? If I may ask." Alvery definitely looked uncomfortable, but it was a fair question.

"I'm taking over the lairdship," Marcas said.

Alvery continued, "Pleased to hear it, Chief. No one is sick at present, but four of the guards had a small bout again right after you left. Though they were not as sickly as before. They healed in two days."

Brigid didn't like the sound of that. She glanced over at Jennet to see if she'd been listening, and she clearly had. Her dear cousin had a way of narrowing her eyelids whenever she was analyzing a situation, which was exactly how she looked now.

They headed toward the stable, and a lad came out to get their horses. "Greetings, Chief," he said, looking from one to the next as if he wasn't sure who to direct his comment to.

"You are better, Timm?" Marcas asked, dismounting and lifting Brigid down, settling her carefully onto the ground.

"Aye, much better. I'll take care of your horses, Chief."

"Brigid, can you walk, or do you need assistance?"

"Nay, my ankle is much better. I'll not be running any races, but I can walk to the keep on my own. My thanks to you." Hell, but the man looked even better in the morning.

Alvery nodded. "Och, I forgot the laddie. Add Timm to our numbers. We're growing again, lads."

Marcas explained, "Alvery has been with Clan Matheson and our sire for years. Every male is considered a lad to him. Glad you are both better. I'll escort the lasses inside, then return to get an update on everything."

Marcas led them across the courtyard, an area so quiet Brigid could actually hear every tweet from the birds. The sound was something she'd never hear inside the Ramsay walls. She spotted a community well off to the courtyard's side, with several buckets nearby. The castle was built of stone, as most castles were, one center square section and two adjoining partitions attached on either side. A hut for the smithy sat off the courtyard, the buttery next to it, and the armorer on the far side of the buttery. A larger hut on the opposite side she guessed housed the weavers.

But all was quiet as if no one were there at all.

The sense brought a sadness to her she couldn't shake, such emptiness in a place that should be full of life, of clan members working together for a common goal, enjoying each other's company, working the fields. Instead, an eeriness settled over her, and a slight shiver coursed through her body, though she did her best to ignore it.

They moved up the steps, and Marcas held the door open for the three lasses to enter, Shaw and Ethan behind him.

The great hall was nearly deserted but for a fire, an infant playing on a blanket a safe distance away from it, and an older woman bent over a washbasin while another woman worked some dough at the table.

The two women stared in shock at the trio of lasses, but when their gazes fell on Marcas and his brothers, their faces burst into smiles. The woman washing clothes dried her hands and picked up the chubby bairn who was sitting and chewing on a knotted piece of fabric.

"Greetings, Nonie." This Marcas said to the woman who held the bairn. He reached for his son and received a big smile showing off new bottom teeth, then placed a light kiss on the child's forehead. "These are the healers I've brought to help us, Lady's Brigid, Jennet, and Tara."

Nonie offered a small curtsy to the three, her gray hair tied back in a plait with wisps flying free around her face. She was of average build, her face strained.

"And this is Jinny, our cook. She is a fine cook

when things are the way they should be." Jinny was fuller in the hip, as many cooks are, and her eyes were kind. She was clearly a hard worker.

Jinny also greeted the ladies meekly, but with a smile. Marcas leaned forward and inhaled the scent of the infant in his arms. "Sweet Tiernay. You are a strong laddie." The boy rewarded him with a bright smile.

Brigid thought Tiernay was a beautiful wee laddie, the wisps of his brown hair covering the top of his head just reaching his ears. He still held the chunk of fabric, biting down on it while smiling up at his father.

"No word on Kara yet?" Marcas looked from one woman's face to the other, but they shook their heads in denial.

"Marcas! Brothers! You're all home and hale. Praise be to God for that." A beautiful woman came flying down the staircase to the left of the door. Her hair fell down her back in thick, brown waves. Her clothing made her look overly thin, but Brigid guessed she'd probably lost quite a bit of weight from the sickness. She raced over and gave a swift hug to each of her brothers before she turned to the three ladies.

Shaw introduced them to Gisela, but then said only one more word. "Kara?"

Tears misted Gisela's eyes right away, and she shook her head. "I'm so sorry. She was asleep with me on a pallet in front of the fire, but when I awakened, she was gone. We looked everywhere. I don't understand. I really don't think she would have gone off on her own."

Ethan said, "Kara is incapable of opening the keep door by herself. She left with someone."

Gisela calmed right away and stared at her brother. "My word, but your wisdom is much needed here, Ethan. You are absolutely correct. And she was much weaker than she was before, so she never could have opened it." She stared at the door, working her way through this new development.

Jennet said, "Pardon my intrusion, but she would have to be tall for a child of only three years to reach that door handle."

Gisela stared at her. "You are Lady Jennet? You speak much like Ethan, recognizing things I should have but overlooked. Nay, I recall her trying one day, saying she was going for her papa, but she could barely touch the base of the handle. And the door is too heavy for her tiny frame. Someone must have helped her outside. I have gone over and over it, so many times, yet I come up with no memories that help me understand what happened. The lass could not have gone off on her own, could she?"

"We'll call a meeting of everyone once the guards return from patrol. I wish to hear that no one in this keep opened the door for her," Marcas said. "If you don't mind, I'll leave you ladies inside to warm up while the three of us go back outside to assess the situation and see what else we can learn." He handed Tiernay back to Nonie, giving the boy a quick kiss atop his head.

That movement pulled on something inside Brigid she didn't recognize, a feeling of admiration that went deeper than how she would react to a fine archer or a swordsman. No, this was different. She had a sudden urge to kiss him, to see how it would feel to have his arms wrapped around her.

A few years ago, she'd experienced longing, even desire, for some lads in their clan, but her sire's reputation always frightened them away. But here, no one knew her father. No one yet feared Logan Ramsay. Her instant reaction at home would be to tamp down any feelings of interest in a man, but here on Matheson land, she didn't have to.

Gisela said, "Of course. I'll get you each a cup of warm broth. Please warm yourselves by the fire."

Marcas and Ethan set the two healer bags on a trestle table along with their purchases from Inverness.

"Has the broth been well heated?" Jennet asked.

Jinny said, "Aye, my lady. I always cook the broth with the bone for at least an hour."

Jennet said, "Then I would love a cup. My thanks to you."

"And some bread and cheese?"

"Aye, that would be lovely," Tara said, a smile lighting up her eyes.

The three women took chairs near the fire, hanging their mantles on nearby hooks next to the hearth. Brigid stood in front of the heat for a minute, hugging herself and allowing the warmth to travel through her, which made her sigh, not caring who heard her.

Nonie went to set Tiernay down, but Brigid

quickly asked, "May I hold him?"

Nonie said, "Of course. He's verra good natured." She handed the bairn over to Brigid and said, "I'll help Gisela with the food."

Brigid had always been drawn to bairns, at least until they started walking and could get themselves into trouble. This wee laddie would be happy to sit on her lap, or so she hoped. Gisela, Jinny, and Nonie had all gone into the kitchens, leaving the three cousins alone.

Jennet quickly said, "We must agree not to eat anything that hasn't been cooked. It's Mama's golden rule when there is much sickness around. And no ale either."

Tara added, "And we'll start boiling the water. Even what I use on my face and to freshen my mouth in the morning. Mama says heat, heat, heat when one is sick." Then she scowled as if she had recalled something. "Except the windows. Mama likes fresh air."

Brigid said, "So does Aunt Brenna."

Tiernay stopped biting for a moment and turned to look at Brigid, "Mama?" he cooed.

Brigid thought her heart would surely break. But Jennet quickly reminded her why she needed her quick mind around. "Do not start crying over that, Brigid. He probably calls everything and everyone Mama."

As if on cue, Tiernay turned to Tara and repeated himself. "Mama." Then he held the fabric toy out to her as if he wished to share it. He promptly announced, "Mama."

"Aww," Brigid said. "He surely is a cute one, is

he not?"

"They all are to you, Brigid," Jennet drawled.

Tara giggled. "I feel the same, Brigid. He is adorable. I love how he smiles. He is fortunate enough not to remember he lost his mother." She dropped her voice to a whisper. "What do you think could have happened to Kara?"

Jennet said, "There's no conjecture. Someone clearly led her astray. The only mystery is who would have done it. Marcas needs to have a meeting and ask everyone. Find out who was here and who wasn't."

"And we need a meeting to ask our questions, too." Brigid settled the bairn back against her chest while he shook the fabric up and down before biting on it again. "He must be teething."

"Look at his drool." Tara couldn't take her eyes from him, so he continued to smile at her.

Jennet said, "We'll convene in a chamber, make our own plans, and ask for a meeting on the morrow. 'Tis my suggestion. Hopefully we'll get the chance to ask them questions before your sire arrives, Brigid."

She shrugged. "Papa won't stop us from helping them in this tragic time. You'll see."

"Only if he brings your mother along. She's the one with the soft heart." Tara reached over and rubbed the bairn's head, gaining herself a smile.

"And Mama will bring Gavin and Merewen along just for their archery skills."

"I'll agree with that. Since Linnet is expecting, Gregor won't come along, but I'll wager Gavin and Merewen will."

Jennet stared into the flames, not speaking.

Brigid was about to ask what had her mind so involved, but Gisela returned. "Here we are. I've brought you each a cup of broth, and Nonie is arranging a platter of bread and cheese. I cannot wait to hear all about you three and express my deepest gratitude for being so willing to help us out."

Jennet rolled her eyes.

CHAPTER EIGHT

———◆———

MARCAS MADE HIS way back out to the gates to speak with Alvery. There were definitely issues they needed to see about. While he'd have been pleased to sit next to Brigid and settle Tiernay on his lap for the next hour, he had obligations to take care of if he was to maintain the lairdship.

He hoped he would do a good enough job to gain the respect of his clanmates.

His father had prepared Marcas for the day he would take over, but the man who'd been their laird for more than two decades had been as strong as a horse, and no one had thought he'd be replaced for another ten years. Nor had Marcas thought he could withstand losing both his parents at the same time.

The clan had been waiting for him to become the new chieftain once his parents had passed, but there was a small faction who'd doubted he could do it. After all, Marcas had been the one who had upset the healer so much she'd left the clan, which happened just before they'd been inflicted with the curse. He'd said he had a good reason for the way he acted toward her, but he hadn't shared it with anyone. Nor would he yet. The entire situation was too embarrassing.

Thus, once the curse came, he became a hated man. He lost his parents, then his wife, and many others. Most of the clan blamed him. He understood, but even after taking the abuse and beratement, he insisted he hadn't sent their healer away. She'd made the choice herself. There was just one hidden aspect of her departure he kept to himself, never offering an explanation as to what happened or why. He planned to keep it that way.

"Ethan, check wee Timm and see how he fares. Get the count on our horses, please. Then report to me at the gatehouse."

Ethan headed off to the stables to speak with Timm.

Shaw said, "At least we have Gisela and Tiernay. Gisela looks much better, and the wee laddie seems like he's never been ill."

"Aye, I'll not argue on that." Marcas stepped inside the small hut near the curtain wall to speak with Alvery. Torcall was also still inside. "Alvery, an update, please. Speak up when you have information to add, Torcall. You were here, also. What of the dead? How many? And how many deserted the clan?"

Alvery sat down on a stool. "Chief, we've buried all the bodies in a field behind Gallow Hill Woods. We notified Beauly Priory in hopes they'd send a priest or a monk to bless the new graveyard. We wished to bury them nearby, but some of the villagers insisted they remain far away. However, many of those people have now passed on, so I suppose it did not matter."

"In a field is fine. How many at last count?"

"Three and thirty, including your parents. Another twenty ran to neighboring clans. I expected to see some of them sent back, but most were accepted. Some went to Clan Ross, some to MacHeth, and a few to Clan Milton." He shrugged. "I could not stop them."

"We shall rebuild soon enough. Once we know the cause and word travels, we'll draw them and more. We have empty cottages inside the bailey now, and most are empty behind the curtain wall in the village. We have some of the most fertile fields in all of Black Isle. Our root vegetables are plentiful, and we have many fruit trees. The villagers who left will return once they hear the curse is gone, and the healers will find the culprit and eliminate it. Any livestock taken ill? Any dogs?"

"Nay, all are well. Four calves were born in your absence. And three goats, I believe—they are so plentiful we rarely count them. All surrounding folk stay away in fear. No one will steal from us for a while yet."

Marcas arched a brow at his faithful guard. "Yet?"

Alvery sighed deeply, then looked up at him. "Word is two clans plan to overtake the castle once they discover the curse is gone."

"Is that so?"

"Aye, a couple of guards who left came back

to advise us after they had gone hunting in the woods. Felt guilty they'd left, I guess, so they stopped to let us know what they'd learned. I thanked them and invited them back, but they said not yet."

"Which clans are eager to invade?"

"Milton and MacHeth."

"I don't believe MacHeth would attack us. I'll go speak with their chieftain. His sire was good friends with our sire. He won't do it, I tell you." Marcas looked at Shaw to see if he agreed.

"Probably would be a good idea to visit them, Marcas. We'll let them know we have healers present, that there have been no new deaths. Let him know we don't intend to give up easily."

Ethan joined them and said, "We've plenty of horses, and three are ready to foal. Did no one take horses when they left?"

"Nay, most would not. Afraid they were cursed. The ones who left walked with just their belongings."

The sound of hoofbeats on the path carried to them. Marcas looked out and saw his patrol returning. He stepped out to greet them and the others followed. His gaze searched each guard, looking for any sign of his three-year-old. He saw none. He closed his eyes, wondering what the hell could have happened.

The four men dismounted and led their horses to the stable where Timm awaited them. The guard named Mundi came forward and said, "Welcome back, Marcas. Or is it Chief?"

"I'll be taking over the lairdship. Any sign of my

daughter?"

Mundi shook his head, the expression on his face letting Marcas know this was hurting his clan, too. "Nay. But we did find something. We encountered an old man who said he saw a woman walking with a toddler, and the lass wasn't agreeable. Kept saying she wanted to go home. He said she was headed east. Could have gone to any of four clans."

Shaw said, "How many of our women left?"

Alvery said, "I wish I hadn't been ill, and I'd tell you. I simply lost track of exactly how many, but several left."

Ethan asked, "How many had lost a bairn to the curse? Seems a woman might be quick to steal another if she lost her own, just as Brigid suggested."

Marcas stared at his brother, stunned by that thought. "Ethan, I'd wager you to be correct. That answer makes the most sense."

Shaw said, "Aye. Someone had to open the door. They must have crept in when Gisela was asleep and ill, stole the lass away, and went to join another clan. If you agree with this conjecture, Marcas, it has important implications."

"What?" He had many of his own, but he wished to hear from his brother first.

"Kara is alive—we just have to find her."

Ethan added, "You'll not find her at night. The best time would be to travel into the clans while the sun is high and the clan members are working. Mayhap at the burn washing clothes. You'll not see a wee lass about at night."

Marcas had to agree with his brothers. He needed to find out exactly when his guards had patrolled, not just where. "Tell me everything about the areas you've patrolled. Where, when, everything."

Mundi said, "Chief, we've checked every area close by at least three times. Farther out, we've covered twice. Mostly during the morning hours. We searched the woods thoroughly at night because at first we were afraid she was lost. She's not there. Your suggestion sounds feasible to me, though. I'll bet another woman stole her away. We lost some bairns."

Marcas said, "No patrol this eve. We'll have a meal together, all of us, to allow the healers I brought to ask questions of you all. Shaw, you're in charge of the men. Plan to go to the clans and ask about new arrivals on the morrow."

"You don't wish to go? And if we go, they may spread word that the healers are here and the clans can plan their attack." Alvery looked from one brother to the other. "How will we fight them off? 'Tis less than a dozen men left."

Marcas smiled at this. "Nay, there'll be more. Probably late on the morrow or the next day. But I promise you we'll have enough to help us hold the castle. We'll have thirty hard-fighting warriors."

Ethan said, "I agree."

"Where will you find so many fighting men by then, Chief?" Mundi asked.

"I won't have to find them. They'll find and assist us. I promise."

"He's gone daft," Alvery said to himself. "'Tis like wishing on a star."

"Nay, he's not," Ethan said. "I agree with him."

"Who will come and help a cursed clan?" Torcall asked. "They've all run from us."

"The Ramsays. Clan Ramsay will have the best warriors and archers here in less than two days." Marcas had a sudden burst of hope in his heart. Kara was alive and the healers would end the curse.

He just had to get Logan Ramsay to help him.

———— ◆ ————

Gisela stared at Jennet and asked the group, "Did she just roll her eyes?"

Brigid said, "Probably. She does it often when she's doesn't agree with a statement."

Gisela directed her next comment to Jennet. "Why your disagreement, Lady Jennet?"

"Because we are not here because of willingness to help out." Jennet pursed her lips, not lifting her gaze to Gisela but instead staring into the goblet she drank from. She swirled the liquid in small, rhythmic circles, never spilling a drop. "And you need not be formal with us. No titles, please."

"But we are willing to help out now," Brigid added, glaring at Jennet.

"I don't understand."

Brigid cleared her throat and continued, after casting another quick glare at Jennet, "We were kidnapped in the middle of the night. Marcas stole me and Jennet. Ethan and Shaw stole Tara. They thought they were stealing our mothers, who are both renowned as the best healers in the land."

"Clan Cameron and Clan Ramsay? They kidnapped all three of you?" Gisela paled and stood from her chair, pacing. "Then your clans will be attacking us soon. We have no warriors left. Only six, ten at best. We're doomed." She sunk back into the chair.

"Nay, do not worry. I'm Brigid Ramsay, and my parents are Logan and Gwyneth. They are the ones who will track us here and will seek me out first. Once they understand the situation, they will help you, just as we will. But trust us that they will be here soon."

Jinny and Nonie joined them, Jinny carrying a basket of fruit and cheese. Nonie said, "Why don't we show you to a chamber? The three of you can sleep in the same chamber, can you not? We have one we just cleaned, with several pallets. All the linens have been changed."

Tara said, "That would be lovely. I could use a rest. I haven't slept well. I usually don't when I'm traveling."

Brigid handed Tiernay back to his auntie, and he smiled at her, mumbling, "Mama."

Nonie led the three upstairs with their belongings. Brigid was grateful they had just repacked their bags after their last journey and had extra leggings to wear. Her mother had trained her well. Always have extra leggings. She'd also rolled two woolen tunics into her bag just as they'd been interrupted.

Nonie led them down the passageway, carrying

the basket she'd taken from Jinny, explaining along the way. "We have plenty of foodstuffs even though we threw out any food we thought may have soured. Take a rest and we'll have a nice stew this eve. We have it simmering in the kitchen, full of root vegetables and beef. We cooked fresh bread this morn and put a small loaf in the basket for you to share. And we can arrange a tub brought up for you later, if you'd like."

"Aye, before supper would be lovely," Brigid said.

"We'll have it ready for you. Just let us know in the kitchen."

When Nonie opened the door to the large chamber, she immediately moved over to the window and pulled the fur back. "Tis a lovely day. Allow the fresh air in while you eat, then rest. We've been told all who have survived will convene together to answer your questions at the late meal. Our chief has ordered us to do so. We'll have it ready in a few hours. Rest until then. We'll send the tub in an hour."

"Our thanks for your gracious hospitality, Nonie," Tara said.

"And here's a bottle of wine the laird and his wife had hidden in the cellar from London. Cannot be tainted, so drink hearty. There are many bottles there. The laird's mistress loved her wine."

Then she left with a small curtsy as she closed the door behind her.

Brigid fell onto the bed and said, "I'm tired, but I'm hungry, too. You should each take a hunk of bread or I'll eat it all."

Jennet quickly grabbed a piece and handed it to Tara. They sat and chewed for a bit, then each filled a goblet with the open bottle of wine. Brigid took a long swig after her last bite of bread and reached for the cheese. "What say you, Jennet? I know your mind is deliberating on all your questions. Have you any immediate thoughts?"

Jennet finished her chewing slowly and stared out the open window. "I'm not sure. The illness has been here a long time. From the numbers Ethan gave, I don't think it was something that passed from one person to the next."

"What about the well?"

"We'll need to check that."

"Check how they handle the goat's milk."

"Ask about the ale and check the buttery for bad buttes."

"Check how they prepare the meals."

The three talented women's minds moved like lightning as they bantered off of each other's thoughts.

Jennet thought about Tara's last question and answered, "If Jinny has always been the cook, then nay, we may not need to see how she prepares meals. But if she has only been cook for a few moons, then aye. 'Tis a great thought that a change in the cook could affect the overall conditions of the clan. Some cooks try to take spoiled food and throw it in a broth, thinking no one will know, but if 'tis badly spoiled, no broth can save it."

"I get the impression Jinny has been cooking for a long time," Brigid declared.

"Why?" Jennet and Tara asked in unison.

"Because this bread is delicious. I don't think a new cook could be this successful already."

"I think you're correct, but we'll ask nonetheless. And we need to know all the symptoms," Jennet said. "I'm tired. I'm taking a nap." She moved to the pallet closest to the window, removed her boots, and huddled beneath the furs. "These linens are fresh."

Brigid leaned back into the bed she was on, where her head found a soft pillow, and she moaned with pleasure. "Better than the inn."

"And the ground for two nights." Tara settled into a pallet, too. "I do not sleep much on the ground. I awaken at every hoot of the owls."

Brigid got up and hooked the furs tight over the window, then said, "What do you think of Marcas? Is he strong enough to lead his clan?"

Tara rolled onto her back and said, "Aye. Why do you question it?"

"Because he's so young."

"But look at Jake and Jamie Grant. They stepped in when young. And so did Torrian."

"But they all had their sires to help them," Jennet added. "You are taken with him, Brigid. How did it happen so soon when he stole you away from home?"

Brigid sighed, hugging herself as she moved back to her bed. "I don't know for sure."

"As long as it's not because you feel sorry for him." Tara put her hands behind her head, staring up at the ceiling. "But I understand part of what you're feeling. 'Tis the first time anyone has expressed interest, and I don't have to worry about the whole clan watching me."

Jennet sat up and turned to stare at Tara. "You are taken with Marcas, too?"

"Nay. Shaw. I like Shaw. Mayhap 'tis because I was so close with him on his horse. What say you, Brigid?"

"'Tis when it started. I don't know why I feel the pull. Because he's different, because my sire is not watching, because of the way his hair curls on the ends, or the way he always smells of mint leaves…"

Tara giggled. "You are falling in love with him. He's a handsome man. I don't blame you. I understand all those reasons."

Jennet settled onto her back, her hands folded across her belly. "I don't understand any of them. Go to sleep."

No one said another word, but Tara winked at Brigid. Brigid sighed. At least she wasn't alone in her attraction to one of these new men in their lives. Despite the fact they'd taken the three women captive. But Brigid had felt the hardness of Marcas's chest, the strength of his arms when he'd carried her to the burn, his scent of mint and pine.

She closed her eyes, thinking of a man with long dark wavy hair and gray eyes. Brigid fell asleep in a matter of minutes, a strange need deep in her belly, something she'd not had before.

Brigid wanted Marcas's attention.

CHAPTER NINE

———•◆•———

LOGAN SHOUTED TO the two men greeting him, Connor and Jake Grant. "Is your sire here? I need your help." Coming to Grant Castle to tap into the wisdom of the Grant lairds would prove a wise move, he was sure of it.

"He's here, Uncle, and Uncle Aedan just arrived. You heard about Tara being stolen at night?"

"I guessed, because so were Brigid and Jennet. 'Tis exactly why we stopped. I wanted more information. Hoping to spend the night if you'll have us before we're off to Inverness."

"Of course you're welcome. Just in time for the evening meal. Venison stew." Jake was co-laird with his twin brother, Jamie. Connor, though the tallest, was the youngest of the family.

Sorcha whispered to Merewen, "And fruit pies, I hope. Their cook makes the best."

Cailean said, "Stop your drooling, wife. You'll embarrass me."

Logan dismounted just outside the stables, reaching for Gwynie, who was directly behind him. "Go inside and rest. I know these journeys are more difficult for you than they used to be."

Gwynie snorted, a sound he still loved. He was drawn by her sarcasm. She held onto his shoulders a wee bit longer than necessary, letting him know she was not as strong as when he'd met her. Then she proudly straightened up and said, "I'll go inside for a moment to greet everyone and eat something. Then, when you're finished in the solar with Alex and his sons, you'll find me at their archery field."

"You always liked their field. Better than ours?"

"Nay, but in the Highlands with the view of the mountains in the distance, 'tis quite beautiful." She gave an audible sigh. Then she clutched her husband's hand, returning to her more serious self. "I need to be prepared. 'Tis our youngest you speak of, Logan. I'll kill the bastard who dared touch her."

He leaned over and nuzzled his wife's neck. "That's my lassie."

Gwynie promptly snorted. "Lassie. Logan, you're turning daft."

She would tell him otherwise, but she still enjoyed his compliments.

They headed inside, greeted by Maddie, Alex's wife, and Kyla, their eldest daughter. Alex's booming voice came from the back of the hall as he exited his bedchamber. "Something else is wrong. Aedan is here and now you. What happened?"

Logan said, "Some bastard stole my bairn and niece out of their beds, 'tis exactly what happened."

"You mean the same way you stole my sister

Brenna away years ago?"

"Aye, and it worked out for the best, so don't hassle me about something from long ago, old man. What have you heard?" The two were best of friends, but they loved challenging each other.

Aedan came down the stairs, his son Brin behind him. "I'm listening."

Alex pointed to the solar just as Jake and Connor came in, followed by the rest of the Ramsay group. But Logan wasn't quite ready to enter the solar yet. He grabbed an ale and observed the gathering, motioning to Alex that he'd follow in a few moments.

Logan had always enjoyed stepping into the Grant's great hall, full of people he loved. It especially pleased him to see how close the cousins were—Kyla and Sorcha, Gavin and Connor. He waited and watched, simply because it gave him the satisfaction to see what he, his brothers, and Alex Grant had built over the years.

They were the greatest of allies and could always count on each other for support, no matter the problem. And support came in many ways— warriors, archers, coin, even food. It pleased him that this alliance held strong.

Maddie approached Alex and said, "Go in the solar with Aedan and Logan. I'll get the others fed and chambers arranged. 'Tis past supper, but I'm sure they're all hungry. I'll send a platter in."

She gave Logan and Gwyneth a quick hug, then turned to leave when Alex said, "I'd prefer that you bring the platter in, if you please."

She nodded, then conversed with Gwynie,

Kyla, and the new arrivals as Logan followed Alex into the solar, Aedan behind him.

"Fill me in, Logan," Aedan said. "Tara's missing and I brought a dozen guards." Jake came in behind the party and closed the door.

Logan added, "Someone stole both Jennet and Brigid out of their chamber. Actually, out of our healing chamber, but straight from our keep nonetheless. We have no idea who, but we've tracked them north, and we believe Tara is with them."

"I hope you speak true, as I'd feel better if Tara was not alone. Any idea who?" Aedan sat down, his face drawn, something Logan rarely saw. The man had a calm demeanor not often rattled, even though his clan protected Lochluin Abbey nearby.

"Nay," Logan said, standing up to pace. "We tracked four horses, and we found fabric dropped in a trail along the way. All our lasses would know to do this, but 'twas a weave I didn't recognize. Gwynie recognized it as a Cameron weave."

"Why north?" Alex asked. "You must have your suspicions of the culprits if they're headed north."

"Nay, but if you recall, Jennet left us messages when Bearchun kidnapped them so long ago, so we searched in a clearing where we knew they were. Sorcha found scratchings in the bark that looked like an I, and N, a V, and part of an E."

Alex's eyes lit up as he processed this information quickly. "They're headed to Inverness."

"Inverness?" Aedan asked. "Why? What clans are that far north?"

"Quite a few," Jake answered. "Ross is the largest,

but there are branches of MacKenzies, MacHeths, Mathesons, Miltons. But I can't fathom why someone would take our three lasses. 'Tis an odd arrangement."

"Healers. They need healers for some reason. How they deduced which ones to take captive, I don't know. But Brigid and Jennet had just returned from delivering a bairn, so that could be why they were taken. How they knew Tara was the healer, I have no idea," Logan said.

"I have to agree with you, Ramsay. I don't know why else anyone would choose those three lasses. Too coincidental to be anything but a need for healers. The only question is why," Alex said, thrumming his fingers on the desk. "No matter. How many guards have you, Ramsay?"

"A score with another score coming behind us. Maule is here, and some archers. More guards coming."

"You're welcome to as many as you need."

Aedan said, "Mayhap I'll go Northwest to Braden's. See if there's any word there. I think it best we do a thorough search."

Logan sat down, giving in to the fatigue in his body. He was getting too old for this, especially sleeping on the ground, but he had to find his dear Brigie. He forced himself not to think of the possibilities that could happen to three young, beautiful lasses. "I don't think we'll need any more, but if I send a messenger, dispatch warriors quickly. As you know, Grant, when healers are stolen, 'tis usually a rare need for them. I'll determine that before I kill the bastard who stole

Brigid."

"When are you leaving?"

"I'll leave on the morrow with my group, first light. And whoever the daft bastards are, they better hope I find them first. It won't be pretty if Gwynie beats me to them."

CHAPTER TEN

———————◆———————

M ARCAS STEPPED INSIDE the keep in the
middle of the afternoon, surprised to see it
empty. Tiernay often took a nap at this time, but
where were the others?

He heard the sound of light footsteps descending
the staircase and spun around to see who it was,
then froze. Brigid descended the stairs in a pair
of snug and tight-fitting trews, which showed off
her long legs, a tunic covering her hips.

The attire was scandalous and made Brigid
the most erotic vision he'd ever seen. Her hair
was tousled as if she'd just climbed out of bed,
her cheeks pink with heat. She was the most
gorgeous woman he'd ever seen.

What the hell had happened to him? This lass
was a siren unlike any he'd ever met before.

"Brigid? Are you hale?" He didn't know what
else to say.

"Aye. I hope you don't mind me wearing the
leggings my mother makes for all the females in
the clan, but you didn't allow us to grab extra
clothing."

"I'm sure we have some extra gowns for you

somewhere, but if that is what you wish to wear, I'll allow it."

She stepped directly in front of him and smirked. "You'll allow it? Would you rather I have nothing on?" Her voice had dropped to a husky tone that went straight to his loins.

"Nay," he mumbled. "Leggings are fine. No one will see you. I've just never seen anything like it on a woman before." The leggings, as she called them, were suggestive and erotic and enticing and everything he liked, but he could hardly say any of it.

"My mother will surely have something to say to you if you ever repeat that to her."

"Repeat what?" She wore a wide smile, something that made her even more beautiful.

"That you'll *allow* it. My mother is quite unusual, believes a woman is as talented as a man. In fact, she believes many are more talented." She lifted her chin as if it were a challenge.

He wouldn't argue with her, even though she, the trews, and her following comments were the most audacious in all the land. He had a sudden inkling he'd just met a trio of women who would make him question that thought and many more.

Especially Brigid. His gaze locked onto hers, and they stood for a moment, neither of them speaking. All he wished was to touch her, tug her close, and feel those delicious curves against his body.

But he couldn't.

"Mama designed the leggings to be worn by anyone who is an archer. They allow us to shoot better."

"You are an archer?" Would this woman ever stop surprising him? He did his best to hide his shock, but he doubted he succeeded. But talented women archers? Perhaps they played at it. He surmised. Though he had heard something in Inverness many years ago about a female archer. Could it have been her mother?

"Aye, I'll be honest and say I'm a fine archer. Mama insisted. Too bad you didn't allow me to bring my bow." Her long lashes fluttered as she flipped her hair back. "I need to plait my hair again. My apologies."

He didn't mind one bit. He hated it when lasses plaited their hair all the time. He found hair much more appealing when left to its own accord. The way Brigid's hair fell into wavy curls down her back made him wish to touch the silky strands so much he forced himself to take a step back. Perhaps there was a reason so many lasses plaited their hair. "'Tis fine. Will you walk with me? I have an important question for you."

"Of course."

He went to the door and grabbed her mantle from a peg there, helping her into it before he opened the door, allowing her through first.

"Where are you taking me?"

"I'll show you. Gallow Hill Woods. 'Tis quite beautiful when the leaves are budding. There's a lovely waterfall my wife always liked. But I take you because the question I have is something I need to ask you in private. I want no ears listening."

"All right."

He led her across the courtyard and out a door in the side of the curtain wall. "Are your cousins archers, too?"

"Nay, only me. At least, I do not think Tara is. Jennet is definitely not an archer. She has probably the finest mind of anyone I know, but she hates archery. She has learned to use a dagger."

"Truly? Lasses don't need to learn archery or how to use a dagger." They walked across a glen, passing a group of huts that were mostly empty, and into a thick copse of pine trees. Here they saw groves of oaks and sporadic elm and ash trees.

Brigid's gaze stayed on the empty huts. "This is where your village lies? Those are Matheson empty huts?"

"Aye, and we built here because the fields behind them are the most fertile. The villagers tend the fields, pick fruit in the fall, and grow root vegetables and some barley. We also have sheepherders that travel into the center of the isle."

"Your fields lie dormant?"

"The root vegetables have been planted, but not the barley. We were fortunate the curse happened when it did. We've had rain, so the plants should grow. Ethan likes to check on the plantings."

"So none of your women are archers? None are trained with daggers?"

"The women bear children and raise them. They cook and weave."

"They are capable of other things, if you would try. Perhaps you could have female archers."

"We don't have *any* archers. We lost the only two we had to the curse. That should be something we change. Perhaps I could convince you to stay and train some of my men." He cast a sideways glance to see her reaction to his comment.

"But not your lasses?"

"Lasses don't need to be archers." Somehow, he knew he was about to get a strong reaction from Brigid over this comment, but it was his goal. He could listen to her for hours. Her views were different, intelligent, and enlightening. If his sire were here, he'd ask him about training women archers.

"But my sire would disagree with you. All lasses must know how to defend themselves. Of course, my mother and sister carving out roles as two of the finest archers in all of Scotland have helped him see it."

"You mean they are finest for women."

She laughed. "You will enjoy meeting my parents. They are quite different. My mother and sister are both better archers than my sire, so nay, I don't mean for women. My mother has been the best in the land for years, though her eyesight fails her a bit now."

"Watch your step," he said, pointing to a log across their path. He stepped over it first, then offered her his hand. To his surprise, she took it. His heartbeat sped up, simply. He was so drawn to this woman. Why? What was so different about her? Was it the novelty of the new, or was it something else?

He dropped his hand once they settled back on

the straight path.

"So you wished to ask me something." She glanced over at him, running her hand through her hair and tucking it behind her ears, the glossy brown strands floating down across her breasts and nearly to her waist. Hellfire, another look he liked.

He had to fight the image that wished to monopolize his thoughts—the lass with nothing on at all, her long locks falling down over her breasts, her nipples protruding through the strands. Heavens above, what was she doing to him?

He stopped to face her because he would not muck this up. He saw a tree stump a distance away and said, "Please sit." She did, and he sat on another.

"Any word on your daughter?"

"Aye, someone like her was seen with a woman heading down the path. She was said to have been wee and wishing to go home and struggling. We think it was Kara. She could not have left the keep on her own. My men have searched the area thoroughly and there's been no sign of her, no soiled raggies, nothing. So on the morrow, some of us will travel to search the nearest clans, to speak to those around who may have seen her. But 'tis not why I brought you here."

"Go ahead. Ask your question." She folded her hands in her lap and waited for him to continue, her back erect, her carriage as regal as any lass he'd ever seen. And yet her intelligence, her fierceness. This lady was far different than any he'd ever known. He had to force himself to focus.

"How long before your sire is here? I'm asking your honest opinion about this."

She stared up at the treetops for a few moments before dropping her gaze back to his. "I would say the day after morrow."

"And how many warriors will he bring? Your wisest guess, if you please." He held his breath awaiting her response. He needed those warriors.

"Between one and three score. He'll bring my brother and his wife, also fine archers, mayhap my sister and her husband. And probably thirty warriors, though they may arrive over two days. When he tracks, he goes faster and into areas that large numbers can't go through."

"I wish to ask you a favor. I know we stole you away from your clan, but would you consider asking your sire to help us fight off our attackers? If so, I'd be forever grateful, and I promise to make amends with him for what I've done after we secure the keep. I want to make up for my lack of discretion in my activities. Worry about my bairns made me a bit daft, I'll admit, and perhaps I didn't think it through carefully, but now you are here, I believe I made the right decision for Clan Matheson."

"What attackers?" Her face changed from a smile to a frown, as her head tipped sideways and her eyes narrowed. She reminded him of a mother about to protect her pups.

"Word is that once it is believed the curse is gone and there is no more sickness, two clans will attack to overtake our castle. They are planning as we speak. I only have six guards left. I need help, and I'm asking for Clan Ramsay's assistance in this. I've made some mistakes, but I'm here to do my best with the lairdship and fight for Clan Matheson. Will you help me?"

Brigid got up and paced the small clearing, staring at the ground with her hands behind her back. Hellfire, she was a beauty, but he could hardly keep himself away from her.

He got up and stood in front of her, a hand's breadth away. "Please. If you wish me to beg, I will."

They stood there for a long pause, staring at each other. He took in her sweet scent, the deep green in her eyes, the white teeth that chewed on her lower lip. A small breeze caught them, and a tendril of her hair blew across her face. He couldn't stop himself. He reached up and tucked the silky strands behind her ear.

His touch startled her, but he caught a slight tremble in her and reached for her hand to still it. "You are cold? We can return if you like. I think you've given me your answer." She wasn't answering as quickly as he'd have liked, but he gave her a few moments to gather her thoughts. If she had to think so hard about it, he believed he knew her answer. She would deny him. He'd totally misjudged her. He'd had this odd feeling that she returned his interest, but perhaps he'd been mistaken.

When he wrapped his hand around hers, he was surprised to find her hand not cold at all, so he let go and walked away. She was unwilling to help him. What the hell would he do now?

"Aye, Marcas."

He stopped, then spun on his heel to face her. "What did you say?"

"Aye. I'll ask my sire to help you."

———————◆———————

How could she tell this man she'd do anything he asked of her at this moment? By the heavens above, he was gorgeous, his long, mahogany-colored waves falling to his shoulders, and having him this close nearly undid her. Her thoughts seemed to scramble around him, forgetting he'd even asked her a question.

But he had, and her heart told her he'd been through enough; the loss of his heritage was not something she would support. She'd ask her parents to help him, do what she could to locate his daughter, try to uncover what caused the curse, and go home.

Back to her life of boredom.

But until then, she'd stand atop the curtain wall and shoot down his enemies, hold his son again, and use her best healing skills to find out what plagued this clan. In the midst of all that, she'd do what she could to help him find his daughter. There was much to do on Black Isle.

"You will?" he asked, stepping closer, brushing his thumb across her cheek. "You know I'll forever be in your debt if you do."

His touch nearly caused her knees to buckle, but she held strong. "No need. 'Tis the right thing to do. Taking advantage of a clan after the tragedy you've had to deal with is cruel. My sire will help you."

"I will be truly grateful. Come, I'll walk you back."

They took their time, and Brigid had to admit she was entranced with the beauty of his land. "Do I hear a waterfall nearby? I love any burn."

"I'll show you. There is a glen where the rumors of a faerie door flourish. I know not if they are true, but it is said the isle had a special connection with faeries in our land." He led her down a separate path, underneath some pines, and into a small clearing, the sound of rushing water growing stronger. He held branches back for her, and she ducked under a low pine, stepping into an area that did indeed feel enchanted.

"Marcas, 'tis beautiful." The budding wildflowers and the bird songs made it a very special place. There were two separate waterfalls, filling the area with the soothing music of the stream cascading down over the stones. It was the kind of sound that made you wish to never leave the area, just to listen and be taken to a different world where birds frolicked and butterflies danced across the water.

"Why is it called Black Isle?"

He laughed and said, "Everyone asks that and no one knows for certain. We have numerous ideas. One is because of the dark, fertile soil we have. Our fields, the ones behind the village where some of our cottages sit, though they're mostly empty now, are some of the richest in the area. Another odd event that happens every year is that when it snows, the white doesn't stick. When the ships come into Inverness, they often ask why the peninsula is black and the land is white around it."

"Why doesn't the snow stick?"

"I don't know. No one has ever understood it. We have thick forestry that prevents snow from landing in some areas, but 'tis not everywhere." He looked up at the clouds overhead, said, "We should probably go. I'll tell you all about Black Isle on our trip back to the keep."

She loved listening to his animated conversation. He truly did love his land, which made her wonder why he'd been considering not taking his rightful heritage. In fact, she was paying so much attention to him that she tripped over a tree root, and he caught her, her face so close to his he could have kissed her if he wished to.

They froze, both staring at each other, and she noticed his eyes were mostly gray but had a bit of blue in them, much like her cousin Connor's. However, his gaze wasn't on her eyes, but her lips, and she had the sudden wish that he would kiss her.

A bird squawked overhead, and the moment broke as he lifted her to her feet and apologized. "Forgive me. I don't know what came over me."

She didn't know how to answer, but instead fussed with her hair and her tunic, smoothing wrinkles that weren't there.

"Lady Brigid, I am too forward with you. I shouldn't be. I hope you'll forgive me."

A boldness came over her that was most unusual,

but she pressed forward. "There's nothing to forgive. I am pleased by your attention. No lad has ever dared come near me because of who my parents are, so I have to admit I enjoy being this close to you." She nearly added that it wouldn't happen once her father arrived.

He stopped, cupped her face, and said, "You would welcome my kiss? Because I have this urge that will not leave me." He gave her a crooked grin but waited for her answer.

"Aye." A fluttering deep in her belly nearly made her jump away, but the thought of being truly kissed by a man, and a handsome one at that, set her heart beating faster, and she stayed.

His lips touched hers tenderly, just the slightest contact, before he lifted his head to gaze into her eyes. He was gauging her interest, if she were to guess. The sign of a true gentleman—he was giving her the chance to back away.

No way in hell.

Instead, she leaned forward, wanting more, and his lips descended on hers, his tongue pressing at the seam of her lips until she parted them and he delved deep inside, inciting something she'd never felt before—desire. Innocent in the kissing game other than harmless pecks, she imitated whatever he did to her, their tongues now in a dance that sent a fluttering deep in her core. He gave a low growl and tugged her close, her curves melding against his hardness, and she reveled in this new sensation. But more surprising was the way the fluttering and the heat traveled through her, from her belly to below, something as unfamiliar to her as this new, overpowering need for fulfillment.

Being wanted, being devoured, playing with the forbidden.

He ended the kiss rather abruptly, but she was pleased to see the hunger in his gaze, telling her he'd enjoyed it as much as she had. His thumb brushed across her lower lip, and he whispered, "We better return. You are way too enticing for me, lass."

They walked back hand-in-hand until they reached the curtain wall, the heat of his skin searing into her. But, alas, it ended when he let go and opened the door. He started to escort her back to the keep, but she stopped him and said, "I think if we're truly going to help you, you need to locate something for me."

He turned to her. "Anything. What do you need?"

"A bow, a quiver, lots of arrows, and a target to practice on."

CHAPTER ELEVEN

LOGAN RAMSAY CURSED when he came out of the inn but headed directly to his wife, now standing next to her horse with a bucket of water. Cailean, Sorcha, Gavin, and Merewen stood not far from Gwyneth. "They were here. Three men and three women."

"Did they know the men?" Gavin asked.

"Aye. From Clan Matheson of Black Isle, near North Kessock."

"Then off we go," Gwynie said, dropping the pail and mounting her horse again.

Logan held his hand up. "Not yet. Hear me out. They had more information than I wished to hear. No one is inside, so why not get a warm bowl of stew while we have the dining area to ourselves and I can tell you details?"

Gavin said, "Sounds like a wonderful idea. I'm starving."

Merewen drawled, "When are you ever not starving, Gavin? You eat more than anyone I know."

"Except Cailean," Sorcha said, glancing at her muscular husband.

Logan loved having the group with them, and he admitted it was the best decision to protect his daughter. Cailean, the son-in-law he enjoyed harassing, was a strong and intimidating hulk of a man. He was tall, large, and muscular, and an expert swordsman while the rest were all skilled archers. Gavin could do either, so he always came along, too. His bairns had all married well. Maggie and Molly, his two adopted daughters had also acquired good matches. In fact, Logan expected to see Maggie and her husband, Will, shortly behind them. He'd sent a message to them in Edinburgh that Brigid and Jennet were missing.

Once inside, the group settled in front of the hearth around a large table, then the serving lass arrived carrying loaves of warm bread while they helped themselves to ale on the sideboard. Next came steaming bowls of lamb stew thick with carrots, peas, beans, and parsnips flavored with parsley and onion.

Cailean growled when the food came out. He took one bite and reached for Sorcha, leaning over to nibble her neck. "'Tis most delicious."

Once they were alone, Logan explained what he'd learned. "The three lasses were kidnapped by the brothers of Clan Matheson. The laird is the eldest brother."

"Why?" Gwynie asked flatly.

"Clan Matheson is on the other side of Beauly Firth, opposite Inverness and the first castle you come across when you travel the southern coastline of Black Isle. They say Black Isle has been cursed."

He let that settle for a moment while he took a bite of his stew. It was a mighty fine stew, evidence they were in Inverness, where ships carrying spices often came from Europe. The Norse had a heavy influence here, of which the Grants were well aware since Connor had found his Norse wife, Sela, here in Inverness.

"What kind of curse?" Gavin asked.

"A sickness of the heaves and fever. It's killed more than half of Clan Matheson, including the laird and his wife, plus the eldest son's wife, who just gave birth to their second child in the past year. His daughter and sister were both taken sick, so word is he's gone daft. But the innkeeper also heard from others that the new laird and his brothers went in search of more powerful healers. All conjecture, but you know how word travels when so many die."

Gwynie asked, "And they were sharp enough to go after Brigid, Jennet, and Tara? All three? Wise chieftain."

Logan said, "Nay, they set out to steal Brenna and Jennie. Two brothers went to Cameron land and the eldest snuck into Ramsay land alone and left with two lasses."

Sorcha giggled. "I wonder how long before they figured out they didn't have Aunt Brenna."

Gavin added, "And Jennet must have been a joy along the way."

Kyle came inside to join them. Logan filled him in quickly and they waited for his reaction. "I thought someday 'twould happen just as you did so many years ago, Logan. Healers' reputations travel quickly, and as you know, desperation drives men to do unusual things."

No one made a comment on Kyle's observation. True, Logan had done the same to save his brother Quade many years ago when Quade had been near death, and the oddest part was that the healer had ended up marrying his brother. Brenna Grant had healed his niece and nephew also, for which he'd been eternally grateful. Now she had the best reputation in all the land, along with her sister Jennie Cameron, both trained by their mother and grandsire.

Sorcha took a bite of carrot and said, "Three lads, three lasses…" She waggled her brow at Merewen.

Logan scowled at his daughter. "What the hell does that mean?"

"It means it's a bit difficult for your daughters to find a husband because the men are all afraid of you. Mayhap Brigid will find hers in Clan Matheson. She's of age, Papa, though you'll not admit it."

Logan nearly jumped out of his chair, but Gwynie already had a strong hold on his arm. "Sit down. If what was said is true, they need all three healers. Mayhap they can uncover the problem. Jennet loves those kinds of puzzles, so my guess is they did not try to escape."

"I agree," Merewen said. "Once they learned the truth, they probably agreed to help. They're both softhearted when it comes to healing, especially Brigid."

Logan ran his hand across the stubble of his beard. "Hellfire, you're right. Those men lost half their clan, their chieftain, and his wife, along with their son's wife, the innkeeper said. He explained how the surrounding clans are just waiting for the curse to be gone. Once they're no longer afraid to enter the keep, a few clans plan to attack and take over the castle and rich fields. It's just a matter of who will dare go first."

Sorcha said, "Papa, we have to help them."

Gwynie said, "Aye, we do. But I also don't wish to get sick either. I say we spend the night here and give the lasses another day to uncover the cause of the sickness."

"But they've had sickness and death for nearly two moons according to the innkeeper."

"'Tis good news. You know what Brenna says. 'Tis not the catching kind if 'tis around forever. Something else is wrong."

Gavin said, "Da, they'll figure it out. I say we stay here for one night on a bed. We may not want to stay in the keep when we arrive at the castle. You don't know what the condition of the place is with that many dead. True, some may have survived, but did they stay or run? Do they still have a cook?"

Merewen drawled, "Fitting that you're most worried about them having a cook, Gavin."

Kyle said, "I agree with Gavin. If there were any left who didn't catch it, they've probably gone to another clan by now, taking their family and belongings with them. Once the word *curse* became involved, folk started running, is my guess. We don't know how many were left when the three brothers returned."

"Please, Papa?" Sorcha asked. "Say you'll help them?"

"I'll agree. But we leave on the morrow. I'll not wait any longer."

Logan had to know if there was any truth to what Sorcha had said. Was his wee lassie in danger of falling in love?

CHAPTER TWELVE

————————◆————————

BRIGID ADJUSTED THE skirt on the dark gown Gisela had found her. It was such a dark blue color that it was nearly black, but it would work. They were a similar size, so while it was a bit snug, it would still be better than a dirty gown. Refreshed after their tub baths, the cousins had all found clean clothing Nonie had left and got ready to head to the hall for evening meal.

When they arrived, the group was just getting seated. Marcas motioned for the three healers to seat themselves at the trestle table with his brothers. The group sat around three tables, though Marcas left the dais intentionally empty.

Once they were seated, Jinny and Nonie brought out a variety of stews, meat pies, and bread. A tray of cheese had been set on each table. Tiernay sat on Gisela's lap happily gnawing on a hunk of bread crust.

Little was said during the meal, mostly talk about weather and furnishings, how much food they had, or the men's success hunting.

When the fruit tarts came out on platters, Marcas stood and the group quieted. "I'm sure you all know how fortunate we are to have three of the finest healers in all of Scotland here, but I insist we continue on our quest to ascertain what caused the sicknesses and death here. I don't believe 'twas a curse but an error in judgment, some food or animal that made us ill. So I ask you all to stay, listen, and answer their questions thoughtfully." Then he motioned the healers to stand.

Jennet, Brigid, and Tara stood and moved to where they could be seen by all three tables.

Jennet started. "How many of you were taken ill and survived? If you were sick in the past two moons, please hold your hand in the air."

All but Ethan held their hand up. Brigid glanced around and asked, "All of you? All but Ethan?" All nodded or made some gesture of assent.

Tara asked, "Were you equally as ill as members you lost, or just a wee bit sickened?" She went around the hall so each person could answer. Most had been very sick, but not all.

Brigid asked another question. "Were any of you taken ill more than once?"

Six hands popped up.

"More than twice?"

Four of the six stayed in the air.

Jennet looked at Jinny and asked, "How long have you been the cook here, Jinny?"

Jinny glanced at the three brothers, then timidly answered, "Nearly two summers, my lady."

"Have you found any new herbs in the garden or dug up any unusual greens to add to stews for flavoring?"

"Nay, just the same I've always used, and spices from Inverness. Salt, parsley, the usual ones brought in. Onion."

Tara asked, "Will those who were ill please stand?" They stood as a group and awaited instructions. "If you don't drink ale, please sit down."

Three sat. Tara motioned for them to return to standing. "If you don't drink goat's milk, please sit down."

Half of the group sat down.

She motioned for them to sit again. "How new is the well you've been using?"

Shaw replied, "About nine moons, but the first sickness wasn't until two moons ago."

"And no one from the other clans have reported the same sickness?"

"'Tis correct. I've asked many. No deaths due to heaving." Ethan stood up to explain more. "I stopped at Beauly Priory, and the monks said they have been called for few burials and none due to heaving."

Brigid looked at Jennet. "Can you think of anything else?"

Jennet said, "Just one. Please make sure every bit of water you use from the well is boiled first and for several minutes. 'Tis verra important."

Jinny nodded. "Aye, my lady."

Marcas stood and said to Alvery, "Please take your posts again. I don't wish to be caught by surprise when the Ramsays or the Miltons arrive."

The guards took their leave, a few grabbing another ale before they left. Jinny and Nonie cleaned up, and a young lass came from the kitchens to assist them. Jinny blushed and said, "I asked my daughter to come help us. She'll be staying for a while." The girl was visibly pregnant. "She lost her husband. He fell from his horse and snapped his neck."

Marcas said, "My sympathies to you, lass. We're pleased to have you join us. Many thanks to you, Jinny, and to your daughter. What is her name?"

"This is Edda."

"My thanks for allowing me, my lord." She gave a brief but awkward curtsy, given her pregnant state.

"You are always welcome, Edda."

Once the tables were cleared, the three brothers, Gisela, Tiernay, and the three healers were left. Shaw said, "So, Marcas, have you discovered how long before the Ramsays arrive to hang us up by our bollocks?"

Marcas didn't hide his smile, but said, "Two more days is our best guess. Ethan and I will venture to Clans Milton and MacHeth on the morrow, looking for Kara, then we'll be back in time to greet the Ramsays."

Jennet said, "And you need not worry about being strung up by your bollocks."

"Why not? I heard the Ramsays are ruthless that way, especially Logan Ramsay," Shaw said.

"'Tis not Logan Ramsay you need to worry about. 'Tis Brigid's mother."

The three brothers looked at each other, clearly confused. "Why her mother?" Ethan asked.

Jennet said, "Because her mother is the finest

archer of all, and she prefers to shoot men in their bollocks, not string them up."

The three brothers looked at each other and broke into gales of laughter.

"You cannot be serious," Marcas said.

Tara said, "Oh, she's serious. Ask about a man named Bearchun. He kidnapped her dearest niece, Jennet's eldest sister, and Gwyneth pinned him to a tree with an arrow in his bollocks."

Marcas and Shaw roared even louder, while Ethan quieted. Marcas moved over next to Brigid and set his arm over her shoulders. "You jest with us and I think 'tis funny. Do you not?"

Brigid shrugged and started to giggle. He was so cute when he laughed, and he had the most gorgeous smile. She'd never seen him like this, and she liked it. The more he laughed, the more she laughed, and before she knew it, the two of them and Shaw were caught in bouts of hysterical laughter.

Marcas stepped away from her and bent over at the waist, still laughing, partial words coming out of his mouth. "Pinned…to a…to a…treeeeee…" He laughed and laughed until he fell into a chair. Shaw and Brigid were still laughing with him when Jennet stepped in front of him.

"Why do you laugh so?"

He slowed his laughter while his hands came to rest on his middle, and he managed to get a phrase out, "Just the image. How could you think of something like that?" Then he chuckled again.

Jennet said, "I didn't have to think of it—I saw it. A few moments after it happened, I was nearby and the arrow was still in the juncture between his legs, blood covering his private area."

This new development sobered Marcas and Shaw immediately, or perhaps it was Jennet's serious expression. Shaw looked at her and asked, "You do not jest, do you?"

"Nay. I rarely jest about anything. Tara does, and Brigid does, but I do not. 'Tis true. The Ramsay contingent, with Brigid's sire in the front, threatened the man and begged him to tell where we were. They'd tied us up and left us in a cottage, but the devil told Brigid's mother we were in a crate buried in the ground with a tube to let air in. Told them they'd never find us. That set Aunt Gwyneth off a wee bit. She fired two arrows and pinned him to a tree where he died a few minutes later. But not before he revealed the truth."

The three men paled as they stared at Brigid. Marcas whispered, "Your mother?"

Brigid nodded. "You have one more day before they arrive. Use it well."

CHAPTER THIRTEEN

————— ◆ —————

MARCAS RODE UP to the gates of Clan MacHeth, rubbing his knuckles along his jawline. He and Shaw had already gone through Clan Milton and saw no one suspicious. He'd questioned the laird and the guards at the gate, but no one had seen any new young lass.

When he arrived at the gates of Clan MacHeth, he shouted up to the guard atop the wall, "I'd like to confer with your chief."

"You still cursed, Matheson?" the man yelled down to him.

"Nay, my brother and I had it a full moon ago. No one has been sick of late, and I have three healers to help us if it returns."

"You shouldn't have sent your first healer away." The man climbed down the staircase inside the wall beyond their view, then came under the portcullis to speak with them. "Wait here. I must check with the chief."

Marcas nodded, looking at his brother and shaking his head in frustration. "They think we're going to kill them all."

"Let it go, Marcas. The point is to get inside and

look. 'Tis all we're here for."

Marcas knew Shaw was absolutely correct. Nothing else mattered. Kara was on Black Isle somewhere. He could feel it, but where?

Harald, the second-in-command, came to the gates to greet them. "Matheson, you're back. I heard you left. Sorry to hear about your parents and your wife. You have not been ill?"

"Shaw and I were both ill, but we survived. 'Tis not why I'm here."

Harald ushered the two into the gatehouse, sending the one guard outside. "How can I help?"

"Have you seen a woman who brought a young lass with her? One who was not her own?"

He frowned. "Nay, not that I recall. Why?"

"My daughter has disappeared. She's three winters old and was taken from our keep at night when my sister was ill and slept."

"You've searched the area? I don't need to remind you of the wild animals we have roaming here." Harald had red hair and a full red beard, and he brushed it often with his hand, grooming it like a cat.

Shaw said, "She has neither the size nor the strength to get out of the keep on her own, nor to get out of the gate. Someone had to have taken her."

"I haven't seen anyone, but they say there will be a market at Rosemarkie in a sennight. You could check there. How many clan members have you lost?"

Marcas didn't like the way the questioning was going and felt suddenly suspicious of the man he'd considered a friend. He crossed his arms and said, "Are you one of the clans planning to attack and take over our keep?"

"Nay, but I heard Milton was. I'll help you if you need it. You know our sires' alliance goes back a long time." Marcas noticed they were starting to draw attention, as more guards approached the guardhouse. The men's voices had carried out the door and alerted the curious, so Harald stuck his head out the open doorway and barked, "You have naught to do?" The onlookers shuffled off.

"My expectation is we will have some support. I have three healers from Clan Ramsay and Clan Cameron, and the Ramsays are headed this way. If we are fortunate, they'll help us protect our land."

"Logan Ramsay? You know him?" Harald whistled, a sure sign of respect. "That man has a reputation, as does his wife. You'd be fortunate to get him on your side."

"Nay, I've never met him, but his daughter says he'll assist us."

"I hope so. I wouldn't want Ramsay warriors attacking. Hell, Matheson, but your life has taken a bad turn. Your sister lives? Ethan?"

"Aye, Gisela, my son Tiernay, the three of us, Nonie, and the cook Jinny. About a dozen guards."

Harald stepped outside and stared up at the birds flying overhead, motioning to lead the brothers back to the gates and their horses. He brought his gaze down to the two of them. "We'll help however we can. I'll put the word out about your daughter, and I'll ask at the market. Brown-haired like you?"

"Aye."

"One more question, if you don't mind," Shaw said. "Have you heard of anyone heaving in other clans?"

Harald shook his head, hands on his hips. "Over the last moon, I've been to Rosemarkie, Cromarty, and Munlochy, and I asked at each. No one has had the curse you did, but everyone heard of it."

Shaw said, "We better get back, just in case someone decides to attack."

"Send for me if you need help." Harald clasped Marcas's shoulder, then turned back.

They weren't any closer to finding Kara than the day before.

———————◆———————

After the men cleared out of the great hall the next morn, Brigid, Tara, and Jennet sat at the table finishing their porridge.

Brigid said, "I'd like to hear what each of us considers most suspicious. It wasn't as clear as I'd hoped, but I think we can agree 'tis not a sickness that passes from one person to the other, thanks to Ethan's careful numbers and the fact that it started over two moons ago."

"Agreed," the other two said in unison.

Tara said, "I'll go into the kitchens and check the herbs and anything else they have. It could be those. We also have to ask Ethan about his habits, since he's the only one who hasn't been sick."

"Aye, we can catch up with him at the midday meal," Brigid said, setting her chin in her hand, her elbow against the table. "Jennet? Your thoughts of the most likely culprit?"

"I'm going to check the buttery and see if they have any cracked buttes. Then I wish to check the goats, see if any are sick. Bethia says sickness can travel from animal to human sometimes." Jennet stood up, dressed in her favorite pair of leggings. In fact, the women all wore leggings because though no one knew for certain where they would be investigating, the chance of staying clean in a gown was slim. They knew they had to study the well, check out the animals, and examine the plantings outside. Who knew what else they would get into? "What about you, Brigid? What do you think is the cause?"

"I think Tara's idea of searching the kitchens is good, as well as yours, but I'd like to take a look at the well."

Jennet said, "Then I say we all leave and meet back here in two hours. We'll search everywhere in the castle. Eddirdale Castle has secrets we must uncover. And we need to do it before Uncle Logan arrives."

They separated, Brigid going out the door while Jennet headed to the cellars and Tara moved toward the back door and outdoor kitchens. The well was off to the side near the curtain wall, and Brigid was surprised to see someone there, looking inside, half his body tipped over the stone circular protection.

When she moved closer, he stood up quickly, shock on his handsome face. His hair was fair, and he donned a wide smile as soon as he saw her, flipping his long locks back over his shoulder as though a natural move for him. His eyes were blue, and they stared at her as if she were the most special creature on Black Isle. His face was stunning. It was so handsome it nearly left her speechless.

"My, but I've found a lovely beauty on Matheson land. I've not seen you before. Where are you from?" The man moved from the well and stood directly in front of her, a hand length away. Such closeness made her uncomfortable, but Brigid held her ground and only took a half step back. "And the closer I get, the more beautiful you are. What is your name, and where are you from?"

"I have not seen you here before. Mayhap you should introduce yourself first." Brigid said, folding her hands in front of her and stepping further back.

"My name is Morris, and I need to get to know you better." He reached for her, tugging her close until they were face-to-face. "We don't have many beauties like you on the Black Isle. May I steal a kiss?" He closed his eyes and pursed his lips, aiming for hers, but she pushed him back.

"Nay, you may not. You are incredibly rude. What clan do you hale from?"

"I am the man of many clans. I travel from one to the next because I like to keep moving. I just needed a fresh drink, so I thought I'd stop at the Matheson well since there aren't many people left here and I wouldn't bother anyone. But now that I know you are here, I may join Clan Matheson just for you."

Brigid had to admit she was flattered. No one would have dared approach her like Morris on Ramsay land. And he was a fine-looking man, with a smile that was whiter than any she'd ever seen. Long blond hair, deep blue eyes that locked onto her and didn't let go, and a scruffy beard made him quite appealing.

Brigid had the oddest feeling that, since she'd just been thoroughly kissed by Marcas, mayhap she was about to receive more kisses. "Are you not afraid of the curse?"

"Nay, they say no one has died in a fortnight. But when did you arrive? You're new. And pretty. And young. And everything I've been looking for in a wife. Mayhap I'll be stealing a bride soon."

He winked at her, but she didn't encourage his playfulness. "My sire wouldn't be happy if you stole me away."

"Who is your sire?"

"Logan Ramsay." She waited for the name to settle on the man, looking for any change in his demeanor, but she didn't see much.

"I've done nothing wrong. I'd be pleased to meet him and ask his permission to take you as my wife."

Brigid crossed her arms and said, "Mayhap you should ask me first."

"Women are beautiful and do a wonderful job as mothers, but men make the best decisions." He looked at her from the top of her head to the tips of her toes, giving Brigid the vague feeling he was undressing her. "Lasses in tight trews are my favorite. You are quite appealing in that lad's clothing you wear."

"Hmmm. I can't say I'll agree with that foolish comment about men making the best decisions. Some make the worst." Bearchun and the Buchans popped into her mind, the two villains her clan had had past interactions with. Those run-ins could have been disastrous. Those men made the worst decisions of anyone she'd ever known. The one who had made the mistake of abducting lasses of the age of seven had regretted it multiple times.

Morris winked again and said, "I didn't expect you would agree, but I must go, much as I enjoy our interesting conversation." Morris leaned over and whispered in her ear, "I will return for that kiss another day, because I will have you."

Then he left her, heading out through the gates. No one stopped or greeted him. She'd have to ask about him when Marcas and Shaw returned.

Heading back to the well, she reluctantly admitted to herself that she liked this attention from men. Strictly because of her father, brothers, and cousin, the laird, everyone stayed away from Jennet and Brigid. Jennet didn't mind, but Brigid did. In fact, she hated it so much that when they'd visited Loki Grant at Castle Curanta, she'd begged Kenzie, Thorn, and Nari to kiss her just so she had some experience. All three had denied her, but then one night when she was in the stables tending her horse, an arm darted around her waist and tugged her into a corner, kissing her quite thoroughly. It had happened in the dark when she'd least expected it, and the person wore a hood to hide himself.

But it was the husky voice of Kenzie who'd said at the end, "Your wish is granted, lass. Now find yourself a husband."

No one had ever said a word more on the subject, and she hadn't run into Kenzie once before they left. But on her way home, she'd thought about the kiss, and the feelings that had unfurled deep within her, and her fingers reached up to her lips on their own accord, her traitorous mind causing a trail of other thoughts to follow.

It hadn't made her want Kenzie as a husband, not at all, but at least now, when her first true kiss happened, she'd had some experience, something to use as a comparison.

Marcas did not kiss at all like Kenzie, and she had liked his way very much. How would a kiss from Morris feel? She had a sudden urge to chase after him to find out. In fact, she found it rather freeing that there was no one here who would care if she kissed anyone. Jennet and Tara were otherwise occupied, and the other few on the grounds would hardly be interested.

She let out a deep sigh and forced her concentration back to the task at hand.

The well.

She leaned over, trying to guess what Morris had been looking at, but she failed to see anything at all. She took one of the buckets and attached it to the rope, dropping it into the well to see how much water was in it and how far it reached before stopping. It was quite a while before she heard it land with a wet splash. The good news was there was water in the well.

"My lady, my lady!" Timm ran to her side. "'Tis too heavy for you, my lady. I'll help you lift it."

She smiled, giving in to his honor and allowing him to help her, which was silly because she was taller than him, though not by much. Yet her mother's insistence on her becoming a skilled archer had built a hardness into her arms most lasses never saw. "I'd be pleased with your help, Timm."

They both leaned over and pulled on the bucket. She allowed Timm to give it his strength but kept hold of the rope and guided it to the ground as they raised the bucket. He picked the bucket up when it reached the edge and proudly lifted it out, handing it to her. "Here you go, my lady. Let me know if I can be of any more assistance."

"My thanks to you, Timm." He bowed slightly, then hurried off, but just then something dawned on her.

"Timm, wait, if you please." She set the bucket down and followed him, though there was no one else in the area to overhear their conversation. Making it to his side, she said, "I wish to ask you about someone. His name is Morris and he just left. What know you of him?"

"Morris?" The lad thought for a moment, scowling. "I don't know of anyone named Morris. You know Marcas, so could not have been him. Mayhap you just heard the name wrong? I can think of all the guards, but none with that name, and even so, many of them are gone, my lady."

"Morris? Tall, with long blond hair, he said he

often travels from clan to clan. Says he belongs to all of them."

"Nay, no one like that. And I was in front of the stable. I never saw anyone take their leave. You must have misunderstood him. He must have been another visitor I didn't see. Alas, if you have any more questions, I'll be in the stable, my lady."

"Have you been drinking this water lately, Timm?"

"Nay, not since Marcas returned. He said it must be boiled first, so I go to the kitchen for my water. And goat's milk in the morning." He hurried off to finish his job. Timm reminded her of the many lads who had ended up at Castle Curanta, though she had no idea if he was an orphan or not. Perhaps he'd just become one and Marcas wished to keep him here.

She looked at the water in the bucket, surprised to see it was quite clear. She knew from their own wells that when a well began to dry up, it carried more sediment. Aunt Brenna had always advised boiling any water they drank, though most people were not drinkers of water unless on a long trip.

Aunt Brenna and Aunt Jennie had also insisted on boiling any water they took in a skein, though others thought it odd. Yet Uncle Quade had always said they'd had less sickness since Brenna had become the mistress than before. He swore their clan had less sickness than any other clan.

Brigid laughed when she thought back on the methods her dear auntie had used to convince others her ways were best. One of the guards,

Mungo, years ago, had jested about her ways. Then one day, she'd brought over a bucket of water to him and said, "Have a drink, Mungo."

He was as leery as anyone would be when approached by their mistress. Since she'd cured Quade's two bairns of an odd ailment, they knew she was wiser than most. Mungo had reached to take a drink, but first held the bucket up to stare at it, looking for something hidden in the water.

Quade stood behind her, his arms crossed and a wide smirk on his face. "I wouldn't drink it if I were you."

"Where'd she get it?" Mungo asked.

"From the burn. I watched her."

"Why shouldn't I drink it then? I've been drinking from that burn for years."

Quade looked at her and nodded, but Aunt Brenna surprised all of them by saying, "Give it a try then, see if it tastes different."

Mungo scowled and took a small swig—and spit it out before swallowing. "What the hell? It tastes like someone took a shite in it."

Quade burst into laughter and said, "Not someone. Something. She took it from the spot right next to the horse droppings at the edge, half in, half out."

"Not fair, Brenna!" Mungo shouted, but Uncle Quade gave him a look.

"Mistress Brenna."

"Do you see my point, Mungo? Just because water looks fine doesn't mean there isn't something in there that could make you sick. My mother believed wee bugs lived in water that could make us ill. She showed one to me once. It was so small one could barely see. Other bugs aren't at all visible to us, so I always boil first. And so will anyone at Clan Ramsay."

Uncle Quade nodded. "'Tis true. My bairns will only have boiled water in their food."

And thus started the rule at Clan Ramsay. Aunt Jennie, being Aunt Brenna's younger sister, brought the same rule to Clan Cameron.

Brigid took a ladle out of the bucket people used for drinking and poured it on the ground, looking at its clarity in the sunlight. There was nothing in the water.

Nothing one could see.

Jennet came out of the keep and joined her at the well. "Anything unusual?"

"Nay, nothing other than an odd male getting a drink from the well then disappearing."

"You didn't recognize him?"

"Nay, and neither did Timm. He told me his name was Morris, but Timm doesn't know anyone named Morris. He said he spends his time traveling from clan to clan." She wiped her wet hands down her tunic. "Did you find anything unusual in the buttery?"

"Nay. All looked to be safe casks, but you know what Mama says. When testing, taste just a wee bit if you can't find the guilty part. It will not kill you but may make you heave once. Then you know."

Brigid remembered a time when her aunt had done that even though Uncle Quade had argued. She'd tasted a touch of goat's milk and it had been contaminated. She heaved the next day. Then, when all were checked, they'd found one new serving lass who didn't believe in washing out the buckets for milk from one day to the next. "So did you taste the ale?"

"I did. Just a wee taste, so keep an eye on me. You need to taste the water from the well without boiling. If I do it, we won't know which one it is."

Brigid thought for a moment but realized it was the best plan.

She refilled the cup she'd used to check the clarity of the water and took the tiniest sip. "What's the worst that could happen? Heaving once is not going to kill anyone."

CHAPTER FOURTEEN

———————◆———————

MARCAS AND SHAW had looked everywhere. After stopping at the two closest clans, they'd searched the coastal area, all the while praying they wouldn't find a body floating in the firth or washed ashore. But they hadn't seen evidence of one anywhere. Then they'd gone through the forest, taking a few wolfhounds with them, but again—nothing. They'd stopped at every hut along the way and asked the villagers, but no one had seen a stray toddler anywhere. He was starting to lose hope. Who could have taken his dearest daughter?

He'd thought that somewhere along the way, a clue would surface—a lost wee boot, a tip from a clan about a woman who'd lost a bairn, a sound of her voice from somewhere.

His mind went to Freda, thinking how she would be if she were still alive. She hadn't loved him, but she'd adored their bairns. While he and Freda had not developed a loving relationship, it had been initially built on mutual respect, something on which he'd insisted. And once she had Tiernay, the relationship had changed yet again to something less than respectful. But now he understood. She'd been in love with another man. Once he'd learned that, his marriage was mostly ended. What a sad ending it had come to, Freda dying before she could go to her lover.

He didn't regret their time together because she had given him something that was invaluable. It was the one part of his marriage that had given him more happiness than he'd ever expected, his wee bairns. How much he'd loved Kara, her smile whenever she saw him, how she'd always held her hands out to him and say, "Up?"

He'd always given in, picking her up and holding her tight, breathing in the sweetest scent ever. Sometimes, he'd place her on his shoulders, and she'd hang on to his hair and giggle. All the hair pulls in the world from her could never bother him. Then, when Freda had given him the gift of a wee laddie, his heart had nearly burst with pride.

But shortly after that day had happened, the day he wished to forget, the day that forced him to make decisions that could still have long-lasting effects for his clan, the kinds of decisions that he would regret for days, his entire life had changed.

Nay. He shook it off. He had no regrets.

They left the last clan in Munlochy, and Shaw made a statement, not a question. "'Tis time to return. We don't wish to be out here when the Ramsays arrive, in case they decide to kill all our men. We can continue our search after their arrival."

"I'll agree. We must return."

They'd gone for nearly an hour without speaking when Shaw pulled his horse abreast of Marcas. They were in an area that required slower travel, so it was an ideal time to talk.

"What's bothering you, Shaw? I sense something." Marcas had always considered Shaw his best friend. While Ethan was closer in age, Marcas rarely confided his most private thoughts to him because Ethan was special. Everything in Ethan's world was easy to judge. He went by the rules instilled in him by their parents, their church, and their country. Emotion was difficult for Ethan, so it was never part of a decision.

Marcas needed emotion as a large part of his decision making.

"You," Shaw stated, powerfully, then lifted his gaze to his brother.

"Me? Why are you upset with me?"

"Because I'm not blind, Marcas. I see what passes between you and the healer named Brigid, and 'tis wrong. Your wife was buried less than a moon ago, and already you're flirting with another woman. I couldn't say anything about it at the keep, but since we're alone, I'll speak my mind. You should have visited your wife's grave instead of flirting with the healer."

Marcas was furious. If they weren't under time constraints, he'd jump off his horse and haul his brother over to a clearing so he could beat him until he was daft. But this wasn't the time. He could still give him a tear down without revealing the truth. "How dare you judge me! After all that has happened, I view Brigid as a small bright spot in my life. After all that has transpired, I think I deserve a wee bit of happiness. As do you. You should go after what you want. I see the way you look at Tara. Let her know. Just because I acted on something you wish you had the courage to do doesn't make it wrong."

"I saw you pick the flowers back near Cameron land. Flowers to put on your wife's grave because she loved flowers so much."

Their voices had reached a pitch that was clearly more than conversation. Marcas felt like screaming at his brother, his so-called best friend.

"Why the hell didn't you put them on her grave?"

"You're wrong. Dead wrong. They were not for Freda but for Kara. But I've since tossed them, because will she ever see them? Mayhap not."

"Why didn't you put them on Freda's grave? It would have pleased her to know you were thinking of her. She deserved at least that much from you."

Marcas stopped his horse to yell at his brother. "She doesn't deserve anything from me! She was a traitor to our clan, a liar, and a cheat. Freda deceived everyone, including me. You want the truth? I'll give you the truth, but you have to swear you'll never repeat it. The only honor I bestow on her is not revealing her transgressions. And it is only because of our bairns that I keep it to myself. I don't wish for them to have bad memories of their mother."

"Marcas, what the hell are you talking about? Liar? Cheat? What the hell?"

Marcas said nothing, instead staring at Shaw. He waited to see how long before the truth dawned on him.

The change in the arch in Shaw's brow told Marcas he'd finally solved the puzzle. "She cuckolded you?"

Marcas took a deep breath and muttered, "Aye. 'Struth."

"Who? And how did you find out? Did you catch him? Why didn't you cut the man's bollocks off? You're heir to the lairdship." The shock in his brother's face didn't surprise him. He hadn't suspected Freda's infidelity. No one had. She had everyone fooled.

"I've never met the man. He is not from Clan Matheson. At first, she wouldn't tell me what clan, but it didn't matter, did it?" Marcas scratched his head, a delay on the next part because he wished to make sure, doubly sure, that he wanted to reveal all to Shaw. Could he trust him?

As if he could read his mind, Shaw said, "You can trust me, Marcas. I'll keep your secret. You've held this inside for a while already. Tiernay is clearly yours because he's the spitting image of you."

"And he has the spot on the back of his neck like I do. He's mine. 'Twas a short time ago I found a strange concoction on her chest in our bedchamber. She forgot to put it away. I'd seen it before, recognized it as the healer's type of sack, a bagful of herbs, so I brought it to Ellice. I set it on the table and just asked, 'Why?'"

"This is why you sent Ellice away?"

"Allow me to finish the story. I did *not* send Ellice away. Ellice took one look at it and burst into tears. She apologized and explained that Freda had begged her. That she was in love with another man and now that she'd given you a son, she didn't wish to have any more children. She wanted to carry on her affair without any way of getting caught."

The truth suddenly dawned on his brother— Marcas recognized the look in his eyes. Shaw said, "A bag of herbs to prevent pregnancy."

"Freda came in while I was there. Ellice was sobbing, and Freda just stared at me. She said—" He stopped, wondering if he should continue or leave the story as it was. But he needed to be completely honest. "She said, 'Marcas, we are not a love match. I agreed to this marriage for my sire's sake, but I regret it now. I was in love with another man before we were even betrothed. I promised my father I'd give you a son, but no more. Make up whatever reason you wish, but I wish to return to my clan for a short time to make sure what's in my heart is true.'"

Marcus continued, "Ellice had stopped her crying and was mopping her tears. I remember I looked at Freda and said, 'So you asked Ellice to betray her laird and her clan? You knew she would do your bidding as my wife, but all in the clan would view this as wrong. She had no choice, Freda. Why not go to your own healer?' Ellice had whispered, 'My apologies, my laird.'"

He shrugged. "I told Ellice I did not hold her responsible. The act was on Freda's shoulders. I remember Freda looking at me, crossing her arms, pursing her lips in defiance. 'Go, Freda.' I told her. 'I don't wish to see you. Go to your mother, then to your lover. But my bairns will stay. You may take Tiernay since he's still at your breast, but Kara will remain until you return.' It was the only way I could be certain she would return. She hadn't argued, instead just packed her bags to leave for her home. Ellice left with her. I did not send her away. She left on her own accord, following my wife."

"This is why?" Shaw said, his mouth agape. "This is why Ellice disappeared, why you and Freda were no longer getting along?"

"I could not accept her indiscretion. When she returned, she confessed she was in love with another and would be leaving me. According to Freda, her sire would be visiting to talk with me and our sire. She said she would give up the bairns to be free of me."

"Marcas, you must have been so angry. I cannot believe you didn't share this with me sooner. Why not?"

"Because I wasn't just angry, I was hurt. I needed time to think on it and get over her in my own way. Then the curse came along and took her." Marcas stared at his hands. "I never wished for her to die, but I'll not put flowers on her grave. Her lover can do that."

Shaw let out a huge breath. "Understood," he said. "You've had more than your share of tragedy and disappointment."

"I hope you'll consider that when I treat Brigid

as a breath of fresh air. She is exactly so to me. Brigid gives me hope. I've never loved before and don't know if I ever will. Am I capable of loving a woman? I'm not certain, but I'll never be forced into another marriage. If I ever marry again, 'twill be my choice."

"Yet you allowed everyone to blame the curse on you, saying we were all taken ill because you sent Ellice away. Why didn't you correct them?"

"Because I don't wish our children to ever know the truth. Bairns should believe their mothers to be wonderful and honorable. When they're older, they may learn it elsewhere, but they'll not learn it from me."

"Had you told our clan, mayhap they would have blamed the entire episode on her instead of you. They could have known that the curse was because your wife took another, and that Ellice left with her."

"I considered all that, but I wasn't sure."

Shaw said, "I am. Your clan would have stood behind you. Now, first we must find Kara. Then we have another task ahead."

"What?"

"I'll find the bastard your wife was sleeping with."

"I don't know anything but his name and his clan."

"'Tis enough," Shaw said. "I'll find him."

Marcas thought before he revealed the detail, but then decided his brother would have his way. "Hamon."

CHAPTER FIFTEEN

———◆———

BRIGID AND JENNET stepped inside the keep, surprised no one was around yet. "I'm going upstairs to our chamber for a moment." Jennet said, "I'll meet you in the kitchens. I'm assuming you're going to chat with Tara since you have the place to yourselves."

"Aye, meet us there. I'll see if she had better luck than we did." Brigid brushed a stray hair away from her face, moving to the dying embers in the hearth's fire to warm her hands before heading to the kitchens.

She stepped outside before opening the kitchens' door. Her father had told her that long ago their kitchens had been in a separate building, but when Aunt Brenna had arrived, she insisted on a passageway from one building to the other, so serving lasses weren't forced to walk outside in the elements during the worst weather.

Some people still didn't mind their bread wet, apparently.

Tara was the type to so deeply focus that she never heard Brigid's approach until Brigid stood directly next to her. "Have you found something?"

Tara jumped, startled by her cousin's approach. Even though Jinny and Edda were nearby chopping vegetables and meat for a stew, she had been so involved in looking at the greens that she hadn't expected Brigid at all. "Sorry, I didn't mean to startle you."

"Doesn't bother me. I'm used to it. Brin loves to do it apurpose." Tara smiled fondly when she named her only brother, who was several years younger than her. "While one or two of these are new to me, we've used all the others on multiple occasions. But this one..." She picked up a small object that looked like a red covering over a hard shell. "Jinny calls this nutmeg. She said the outside covering is a different spice called mace, and the inside is nutmeg. It has a nice flavor. She says she's been using it for years and gets it from France."

"That's probably not the piece she's used for years," Brigid said, taking the spice and holding it in the air to get a better look.

"Oh! Come try this. She showed me this odd concoction that looks exactly like salt but it tastes the opposite. I wondered if this could be it." She pulled out a bowl with a white granular substance inside. Tara stuck her fingertips inside and pulled them out, several granules sticking to each surface.

"What is it?"

"She called it sugar. I've not seen it before. Claims 'tis sweeter than honey and they get it from Spain. She uses it in her pies and any sweet sauce she has. They can't get it all the time, so she saves it."

"Sugar? 'Tis an odd name. I've never heard it before either. From Spain? They've used it before?"

"Often. Taste it."

Brigid sniffed the odd substance but gained the courage to stick her tongue to the granules on her finger. She was surprised to find them melting in her mouth, leaving a sweet taste behind. "Oh, 'tis most sweet. Oh, my." It gave her such a strong sensation she wondered how it was used. "I hope they don't eat it like this, do they? It would be too strong."

"Nay, she said she heats the sauce, and it melts before she stirs it. Sugar sweetens the flavor in the sauce."

"And she's used it before?"

"Often." Tara stuck her tongue out and cringed at the sweet taste. "So odd."

"I don't think you've found anything, and neither did we," Brigid said, noticing Jinny and Edda having their own conversation and ignoring them. "So, have you eyes for Shaw?"

Tara's gaze widened, but then she broke out in a big smile. "Aye, and I'm hoping he'll kiss me soon. No one ever kisses the laird's daughter."

"'Tis so true. I have no luck on Ramsay land because they're afraid of my sire, my uncle, my brothers, or my cousin, the laird. I hate it!"

Tara lifted her chin and scrunched her shoulders up. "Now is our time. I say we kiss while we have the chance. Has Marcas said anything yet?"

"Nay, but…"

"He kissed you already?" She let out a low-pitched squeal. "Oooooh."

"Stop it, Tara. 'Twas only a kiss, but…" Brigid glanced around to make sure the other women were unawares. "I surely did like it."

Tara offered another wee squeal, then washed her hands, dried them on a linen towel and grabbed Brigid's. "I'm happy for you, but we need to find Gisela and talk to her."

"About what?"

"I have an odd feeling about Marcas and his wife. I'd like to hear what Gisela thought of their relationship before the curse." Tara's voice had dropped to a near whisper.

While Brigid had to agree with her and would gladly ask Gisela whatever she could, she couldn't help but wonder what prompted Tara to pursue this. "Why, Tara? I know from both you and Riley, there is usually a reason for whatever you do. Why ask Gisela?"

Tara tugged Brigid behind her, out through the passageway, and back into the hall. Before going through the last door, Tara turned to face her. "Because I see the way he looks at you. He looks like a man for the first time in love. Like he's just discovered the feeling and has never experienced it before. Yet he was married, and so recently lost her. He seems to carry so little grief over her, settling all his sorrow on Kara. It's not wrong, but it makes me want to ask a question or two about them."

Brigid nodded, her gaze searching Tara's, wondering her own thoughts about Clan Matheson, its laird, and his family. Marcas had not been laird until recently, but he'd been married with the expectation that he would be heir to the lairdship. Yet she'd heard comments that made her believe he hadn't always been willing to take over the lairdship after his father's death.

What had happened?

"Shall we look for her? Do you not agree?" Tara asked, pausing for Brigid's answer.

"Aye, I'd like to hear her view of her family."

They moved inside the hall and were pleased to see Gisela in a chair near the hearth, Tiernay at her feet, pulling himself to a standing position using a stool. "Good laddie," Gisela said, clapping at his talent.

"Learning to walk?" Tara asked, leading Brigid over to speak to Gisela.

"He's trying, but not quite yet." The bairn took a step, then fell to the floor with a thud, landing on his well-padded bottom. A grin crossed his features as he reached for a fabric toy to put in his mouth. Nearby lay another toy that made noises whenever he shook it, something that made him giggle.

Brigid looked at Gisela and thought she caught a tear in her eye. "Are you all right, Gisela?" she asked, sitting in a chair behind Tiernay. Tara taking a seat across from her, the women forming a semi-circle around the lad.

"Aye, better than a while ago." Gisela's lower lip trembled. "I miss my parents, and I feel sad Tiernay has lost his mother. And wee Kara…I so hoped Marcas would find her, but if he had, they would have returned by now."

Tara asked, "What was Tiernay's mother like? What was her name?"

"Freda. Her name was Freda. She adored her children, and—" Gisela stopped after a halting delivery, so many emotions crossing her face Brigid had no idea what she was thinking.

"I'm sorry you lost her," Brigid said. "You all must be having such a hard time with so many losses."

"Nay, 'tis not that. Oh, I...how shall I..." Gisela closed her eyes, kneading her hands. After a moment, she spoke, "Freda was a sweet woman, but she wasn't for my brother. Sometimes I fear I'm being punished because I had such hard feelings toward her, feelings that were wrong. I should have been more generous."

Tara said, "I have never heard of anyone being punished like your clan has for any special reason. 'Tis not a curse. Freda and Marcas didn't get along?"

Gisela sighed, and a different look crossed her face, one of resignation. "I'm going to be honest with you, because I need to be. I never liked Freda for my brother. She was a good mother to Kara and Tiernay. She loved them truly, but she was never kind to my brother. I felt bad for him because he was stuck in an arranged marriage and tried to make the best of it, but she did not. She was harsh toward him, and I hated her for it. I couldn't hide it in the end. But something changed between them, and their marriage went from worse to awful. I tried to talk to him about it, but he didn't wish to hear it. He deserved better."

Gisela leaned over and kissed Tiernay's head. "Then, she died, and now I wonder about curses and so many things I don't know what to think next."

Tara said, "Nothing you did caused a curse on your clan."

"Freda was a curse on our family," Gisela retorted.

Brigid had no idea how to respond to that. But Gisela's words had had the oddest result. Her feelings toward Marcas grew stronger. She needed to step away before she opened up about her feelings to Gisela, something she thought would definitely be wrong. This was not the time, especially since Freda had passed such a short while ago. "If you all don't mind, I'm going to go practice my archery, just in case I'm ever needed."

Jennet came down the staircase just then, so Brigid approached her. "We found nothing. I think we wait to see if either of us is taken ill. Until then, I'm going to the archery field."

Jennet said, "Go. We may need your archery skills soon. Your sire will be here, but not until the morrow or after."

Brigid left, finding her way to the small archery field outside the castle after grabbing a bow and quiver from the stables. Timm chased along behind her, calling out, "May I watch for a bit?"

"Of course," Brigid smiled. She began to set herself up, arranging everything the way she liked. She had her leggings on so clothing wouldn't interfere with her aim. She squared up and found her target, locked in, and fired her arrow. It struck nearly center. She fired one off another two shots before pausing.

Brigid smiled inwardly at her success, pleased she hadn't lost her skills yet, when she heard two voices behind her. Timm said, "You are the best. 'Twas the fastest shots ever." Then he disappeared back into the stables.

Ethan came closer. "You did that? You have skills as an archer?"

"Aye, I was trained by my mother and my sisters."

"You have a fine eye, especially for a lass." Ethan kept his hands folded in front of his body, his gaze on the center of the target.

"Ethan, may I ask you a few questions?"

"What about?" He took a step back, letting her know she was starting to make him uncomfortable, but he stayed. Apparently, he trusted her, so she pushed forward.

"I need to understand why you never got sick. What do you think it was?"

"I don't know," he answered.

"What do you drink most? Ale? Mead? Goat's milk?"

He shook his head. "Water. From the burn. And I cook it first."

"Cook it?"

"I always put the water in a pan and cook it over the fire. Then I add a bone and let it simmer."

"So mostly broth?"

"Aye. I prefer warm broth. But only from the burn in the forest. 'Tis fresher there. I did not like the old well, so I stopped using it. Sometimes I take goat's milk, but not always."

"My thanks for the information."

"'Tis my honor to assist the healers. I've always been interested in the healing arts. But I must go back to my post on the wall until Marcas returns."

After Ethan left, Brigid made several more shots from different angles while she thought over all he'd said. Since he was the only one who'd never taken ill, it followed that the disease had to come from one of the things he never drank.

That left the water from the well, goat's milk, any uncooked water, or ale and mead the primary suspects.

She picked up her arrows and filled her quiver, lining up for a few more shots when a pair of arms surrounded her. Her arm swung out and caught her embracer in the chin.

"Ow," a familiar voice said. "I didn't mean to startle you."

She turned. "Well, you did, Morris. Please don't sneak up on me." Secretly pleased he'd returned to see her, she nocked another arrow, then fired three off in fast succession, all finding their target.

"'Tis quite a skill you have, my lady. You nock an arrow faster than anyone I've ever seen." He sauntered over to her, staring at her target, as she set her bow against the trunk of a nearby tree. He moved over to stand directly in front of her, his gaze locked on her mouth. "I came back because I could not get you out of my mind."

"Truly?" She guessed he was lying, but she thought she'd play his game for a wee bit.

"I came back because I need that kiss. And to find you still in those leggings is more than I could have hoped for."

"If you ask nicely, mayhap I'll allow it." This close, she could see his long lashes, a shade darker than his fair hair. His beard was also a shade darker, and right now a shadow across his strong jawline and firm lips.

He took a step closer until she could feel the heat of his breath, the color of his eyes darkening. "Will you?" His voice came out in a husky whisper, and she couldn't help but give him a slight nod.

His lips melded with hers, and he wrapped his arms around her, pulling her tightly against him, which she found she didn't like. But she focused on the kiss, his taste, parting her lips to give him access deep inside. His tongue took over, teasing her until he tightened his grasp, his hand falling to her bottom and holding her so close that she could feel his erection against her.

This, too, was something she didn't want. Why, she wasn't sure, but she knew she didn't like his kiss or feeling his hardness next to her. Was it because of Marcas or just because they didn't suit? The reason didn't matter at this point. She had to get away from him.

She pushed against him and he released her. "Oh, but lass, I wasn't finished yet. I have so much more to show you."

She crossed her arms and said, "But I was finished. I'm returning to the keep. Where did you say you were from, Morris?"

"I didn't. Mayhap you'll meet me later this eve. We could look at the stars together. It promises to be a clear sky." He waggled a brow at her, but she wasn't interested.

"I must refuse you. If you'll excuse me, I need to practice a few more shots." She turned around, giving him her back as a hint.

"I suppose 'tis time for me to move on. Though I could stand here and watch your softly-rounded backside for a while if you don't mind."

"I do mind. Be off with you."

"You are right. I've been here too long. Think of me in that way. I'm everywhere."

She bent over to pick up all her arrows and then turned around to see where he was, but he was gone.

Timm stepped out of the stable a short distance away and said, "I heard your voice. Were you speaking with me, my lady?"

"Nay, Morris was just here. Did you not see him?"

Timm said, "I saw no one."

The man had disappeared. Like a ghost in the wind.

CHAPTER SIXTEEN

———— ♦ ————

MARCAS ENTERED CLAN Matheson through the front gate with a frustration he didn't often have. When had he failed so wildly at a quest before?

While he hadn't found Kara, he knew he needed to get back to wee Tiernay. Even though the lad wasn't able to speak thoughts of missing his mother, he had to notice something had changed. He had no Freda or grandparents, either. Grandmama had loved to hold him on her lap.

Marcas felt exactly the same. Before he had been able to walk, Tiernay's wide smile called to Marcas whenever Marcas passed him. He loved holding the wee one on his lap while he played with his toys.

Ethan yelled from the curtain wall as they approached. "No luck finding Kara?"

Marcas shook his head, tired from their relentless pace to cover three clans before returning. "Any visitors yet?"

Ethan said, "None, Chief."

He hardly minded Ethan's title for him. Ethan was a rule follower, so he would insist on calling

Marcas by his title simply because their sire had taught him to do so. No reasoning would convince him of anything different.

Glad they'd made it in time for the evening meal, even though it was nearly dark, he hoped to see everyone still here and no one else sickly. Once he dismounted near the stable, Timm came out and grabbed Marcas's horse. "Timm, are your sire and his men here?"

"Aye, they are. They're inside eating. They didn't find Kara either." Alvery was Timm's sire.

For some odd reason, he wasn't surprised by their failure, too. "And for supper?"

"A fine venison stew."

The thought of hot stew sent his belly rumbling, so he waited for Shaw, then headed inside. All quieted when he entered. He shook his head. Gisela got up to greet him, "We'll find her, Marcas."

The men washed up briefly in the kitchens, then took a seat. Ethan asked, "Anyone coming to steal our castle?"

"Nay, not yet. Word is Clan Milton has been watching, but MacHeth said he'd come to assist us if we need it. I was grateful for his support and hope he is true to his word."

The bread was passed around, along with a bowl of berries. Jinny brought them each a bowl of stew, which Marcas dove into with pleasure. They'd eaten little besides oatcakes on the road. Once he swallowed his food, he looked at Brigid and asked, "No Ramsays yet, lass?"

"Nay. I told you, on the morrow. It may not be

until nightfall, but he'll be here."

"Any ideas on what caused the heaves?"

"Nay, but we're studying and testing. We'll examine theories on the morrow."

Ethan asked, "Chief, will you take me fishing on the morrow?" It was one of Ethan's favorite activities, but he hated going alone and considered his two brothers the best fishermen of all.

Marcas groaned while Shaw chuckled.

Tara asked, "Why is that funny?"

Shaw couldn't stop his chuckling. "Because Marcas hates to swim."

"Why? I thought everyone loved to swim?"

"Not Marcas. He got caught out on the mudflats after staying too long when he was younger. He had to swim in a long way, as we yelled for him to hurry, but he got trapped in a boggy area. When he stepped onto the sandy bank of the firth, he looked like a swamp monster."

Ethan said, "He had weeds in his hair, stuck to his clothing, everywhere. He frightened me."

Marcas shrugged. "'Twas a long swim in. I thought there was a monster connected to some of the weeds. I was afraid I would be pulled under. I don't like weeds near my feet or swirling around my legs."

Ethan's chest puffed out a little. "He still takes me fishing during low tide, but he searches for the sandflats, not the mudflats. We get good trout and sometimes flounder. And we're always back before the tide changes."

"You're a good brother to Ethan," Jennet said, surprising Brigid. Jennet glanced at Ethan, an odd look on her face Brigid didn't recognize. This was an unusual journey for the three of them. She'd never seen Jennet give a look to any male.

After dinner, when they stepped away from the tables and the dishes were removed, Marcas sidled over next to Brigid and asked, "Would you do me the honor of a jaunt to the parapets?"

"Aye," Brigid said.

He led her up the stairs, down to the end of the passageway, then tugged a heavy door open and held it for her, a whoosh of wind blowing her hair back. She giggled, falling back against him, and he set his hand around her waist, which she liked, but she didn't stay long, instead pushing away and walking up the short staircase to the parapets.

With Marcas, she was happy and excited, an entirely different feeling than she'd had with Morris. More importantly, she trusted this man, unlike the fair-haired stranger with sweet words.

When she stepped outside, she sighed at the view across the firth, the mountains in the distance, and the clouds appearing close enough to touch. "'Tis beautiful, Marcas."

"That direction is Gallow Hill Woods, my favorite forest, though we have many on Black Isle."

"Enough of that. Tell me what you learned. Anything at all about Kara?"

He hung his head, leaning his arms on the edge of the wall. "Nothing. Though we were not allowed in Clan MacHeth."

"Because they're guilty of some kind of

subterfuge?"

"Verra possibly, aye. They could know something about Kara, or they could know something about the curse. More likely the laird worried about us bringing the curse to them. You've heard nothing of your sire?" He stood to his full height, looking to the west. "I hoped we could see their approach from here. If he brings an army of four score, we'll be able to see him."

"Nay, he'll not bring that many yet. The extra guards could be along in another few days, but my sire prefers to sneak about. He and my mother were spies for the Scottish Crown many years ago. He can get in and out of areas quickly without being seen. He stole my auntie from Grant Castle and was never caught!"

"I hope he has a generous heart. Not finding my daughter does not put me in a fighting mood."

"The loss of your parents and wife must cause you a great deal of pain. Even if there was little love between you." She rested her hand on his forearm and he stared down at her, the gray eyes pulling on some odd string inside her that made her wish to follow him anywhere.

"I may as well tell you all. There was no love between us, but it was worse. I caught my wife using herbs to keep herself from ever carrying again. I confronted our healer and she confessed. My wife admitted to being in love with the man she'd always wished to marry and told me she'd never be in my bed again and had been using the herbs since Tiernay was born. Once I learned that, I knew we'd never have relations again, but she was also quite adamant she wished out of our marriage, though 'tis never done. She went home with Tiernay and left Kara with me, two moons ago. She met with her lover again and made her mind up. She came back to Matheson land just to settle things. Her sire was planning on coming to talk with me and my sire. She wished to leave and move back home, dissolve our marriage. But her sire never made it. She became ill the next day."

"Oh, Marcas." Brigid's hand moved up to his back, rubbing lightly. "How terrible to have that memory, to have learned that about her. Did you know the man she loved?"

"Nay. I have no idea what he looks like. They say he was here to see her after she was sick, but I never saw him. Then I stopped allowing visitors as the sickness spread."

"I couldn't imagine learning something like that about my spouse. So 'tis the reason you had no healer?"

"Aye. Our healer left with Freda when she returned to her clan. I believe Ellice felt a great deal of guilt over betraying me, which would explain why she left so quickly. I don't know if she is still with Freda's clan or not."

"And no one knew why? They must have questioned you, especially after the illness started."

"They did. But I said nothing. I didn't want my bairns to ever learn the truth of their mother. 'Tis not what bairns need to hear, so I quelled it all."

Brigid leaned over and kissed his cheek. "You're an honorable man, Marcas Matheson."

"Please don't hate me when I tell you how

much I like and respect you. 'Tis the truth. For you, I feel things I've not felt before. And I'm at a loss as to how to handle it."

She stared at him, brushing his locks back off his collar. Then her eyes widened.

"What's wrong?"

"My belly. Something's wrong." Her hand went to her waist and she turned away from him.

Moments later, she heaved over the side of the parapets.

Three times.

CHAPTER SEVENTEEN

———— ◆ ————

MARCAS SCOOPED HER up when she fell, wanting to get her to her cousins before he determined how badly she was hurt. Besides heaving, she must have passed out. She'd banged her head on the stone wall while falling, and he could already see the swelling in her scalp.

She was not awake.

He managed to get the heavy doors open while he carried her, and when he finally reached the balcony, he leaned over the railing and said, "Brigid is ill. She has the curse, and she hit her head."

Gisela said, "Bring her into the sick chamber down here. She'll need to be watched all night long."

He did as his sister suggested, going down the staircase and following her into the chamber while she lit the torch, giving them much-needed light. Tara and Jennet were right there, pointing to a pallet to set her on and rushing to gain their tools.

"What could she have done to make her heave?" he asked. "No one else has been sick.

I thought we were finally finished with it." He paced the small area, so upset to see Brigid now sick. Everything he did, everything he touched, seemed to come back to haunt him. He'd brought her here with the best of intentions, and the poor lass was heaving because of his actions.

This was all his fault.

Jennet, looking far from innocent, muttered, "I might know something of it."

Tara said, swatting her cousin's upper arm, "Out with it. What did you two do?"

"We made a pact. I tasted a butte of ale that may have been tainted, and Brigid tasted the well water. She took the tiniest of sips." Jennet looked a bit guilty after the look her cousin gave her. Then she glanced over at Marcas. "The good news is we know what the culprit is—the well."

"Are you two out of your mind?" Tara shouted, her hands going to her hips as she glared at Jennet. "Look at her!"

"My mother has done the same before. 'Tis the only way to be certain."

Tara rolled her eyes. "Now we must treat her. Marcas, leave us and we'll change her clothing, get her settled."

Marcas looked at the pale face of the woman on the pallet and started praying. He hadn't done so in a while. But Brigid...he couldn't lose her. Then he left, barking at his brothers on the way through the hall. "'Tis the well. We must cover it, and someone tell Nonie and Jinny that any water from it should be tossed out."

Edda hurried into the kitchen while Marcas

and Shaw headed to the courtyard.

Ethan had a most excited look on his face, something Marcas hadn't seen in a long time. "Why do you look so happy, Ethan?"

"Because we've found the solution. It may not be the best for Brigid, but she's a strong lass. She'll heal if she'll not have any more water to drink. The well is the cause of all."

Shaw said, "We'll use water from the well in the woods. 'Tis still good."

They did what they needed to do before Marcas made his way back into the hall. He had to see her, see that she was hale. He'd be inconsolable if anything happened to Brigid.

He knocked on the door and stepped back, waiting until someone answered before entering the chamber. Tara stood by.

"How is she?" he whispered.

"She'll be fine. We've bathed her and put her in a night rail for the eve. She's awake and asking about you."

"May I see her?"

"Of course," Tara said, grabbing Jennet's hand and tugging her out of the chamber.

Jennet cried, "Why do I have to leave?"

"Never mind, just leave them alone," Tara said, making sure Jennet followed her out the door and didn't turn back.

Marcas stepped inside, waiting for his eyes to adjust to the light of the torch. The chamber was still dark, but he found Brigid quickly and knelt down beside her. "You will heal?"

She nodded, the dark circles under her eyes

telling him she was still quite ill, but still he had hope. Brigid sat up a bit and said, "My apologies. What I did was foolish, but we know the problem now. I'm sorry you had to be a witness to my illness."

"Lass, I've seen worse. Do not think on it." He paused, trying to come up with the best way to do what he wished to do. "May I join you?"

She didn't speak but held up the coverlet as her answer.

"You may think me daft, but I have to hold you. I need to see for myself, listen to your breathing, feel your heartbeat to convince myself you'll be fine." He climbed in behind her and snuggled his front to her back, wrapping his arm around her and moving her close to him.

He took in her scent of lavender and closed his eyes, sighing, resting his head in the crook of her neck. "I panicked," he whispered. "I feared the worst."

She tried to speak, but he put his finger to her lips. "Please, save your efforts. Allow me to say what is on my mind."

Brigid leaned back against him and whispered, "I can do that."

He was glad she had her back to him. If he gazed into her eyes, he'd lose control for sure. "I wish to try to explain what is in my heart. I may not be able to, but I will make my best attempt.

"When I first encountered you on Ramsay land, I didn't think there was anything special about you. How wrong I was. I admit my heart was hardened to everything around me because I was wrapped in fear and self-pity. It took time for me to see you for what you are, one of the finest gifts I've ever been given."

She rolled onto her back and gazed into his eyes, her own misting from some emotion. Her finger traced his jawline, then dropped back onto her torso. "Marcas."

"Nay, I need to say this. I didn't understand what love was. I understand love for a child, or love for a parent or sibling, but this love between a husband and wife, a man and a woman, had eluded me. I thought it false, but as I watched you work, watched your relationship with others, listened to your laughter, I began to understand." He kissed her forehead. "I have feelings I don't comprehend, but I don't wish for them to end. I need you, Brigid Ramsay. I need you in my life, and when this is all over, I'll beg you to stay so we can get to know each other better. I don't know how that will work once your parents arrive, but I see hope when I look at you."

"Oh, Marcas." She cupped his face. "I would love to kiss you, but I don't wish to make you ill."

"I don't need to kiss you as long as I have you near."

She leaned against his chest and he snuggled into her. "This is all I need," he whispered. "But I don't know enough about you—your favorite color, favorite food, favorite pastime."

"We have so much time to learn those things. But for now: blue, fruit tarts, and the Ramsay festivals."

He chuckled. "I can't wait to hear about the

Ramsay festivals. There must have been archery involved. Will you give me archery lessons? I could use a few."

She nodded, stretched, yawned, and leaned against him again.

Before he knew it, she was asleep in his arms, and he watched her, taking in everything about her. Her long eyelashes, her soft skin. The strong jawline. A slight smile crossed her face, and he hoped she was dreaming about him.

He knew he should get up and allow her to sleep, but he didn't want to let her go. Ever.

———— ♦ ————

Brigid woke the next day in her bed, a big bucket by its side. She sat up, and Tara stared at her from across the chamber where she fussed with their clothing. "You will live?"

"Of course I'll live. Why would I not?" Once Brigid sat up, she understood exactly why Tara had asked that question. She had the pounding of a smithy's hammer in the middle of her forehead, and her stomach felt as if a dolphin in the firth, showing off its flipping skills. But she'd felt worse before, so she forced herself to sit up. Looking around the chamber, empty except for Tara, she asked, "Where's Jennet?"

"Jennet has gone to see what she can uncover about the well. She wants to see if she can find any reason the water is bad and talk to Marcas about digging a new well in a different location."

Memories began to percolate in Brigid's mind. Vomiting over the parapets. Feeling her knees buckle. Heaving into the bucket at some time or another. She couldn't help but study her night rail and the linens on the bed, just to see if she'd heaved on anything. There was a large linen square nearby that she must have been using.

Vomiting in front of Marcas. "Nay…" Then lying in his arms last eve, listening to his words that had made her feel so special.

"What's wrong?" Tara asked, rushing to her side to feel her forehead. "You don't have the fever, do you? I kept the furs away just for that reason."

"Nay, I don't have chills. My stomach doesn't feel like heaving. I just feel weak, but I don't remember how I got here." Her hand went up to rub her forehead as she set her feet on the ground, forcing herself to stand. That's when she felt the sore spot in her hair, and her hand moved to that area, encountering a bump the size of a duck's egg sticky with blood.

Tara appeared next to her in a flash. "Be careful. I'll not have you fall again while I'm watching over you."

"I'm not dizzy at all. But I still should remember coming to bed. I recall Marcas here last eve, why not before that?"

"'Tis because Marcas carried you here. Your knees buckled up on the parapets, and you fell, hitting the corner of your head on the stone wall." Tara reached up and felt her bump. "'Tis no bigger."

"So I slept all night?"

"And through the morning. The sun is dropping."

"I have to go to the hall and see how things are. Have they found Kara?"

"Nay, but you should stay in bed. You were verra sick."

"Please, help me find something clean to wear. My leggings are clean. I think Nonie washed them. And the tunic. I wish to talk with Jennet."

"I brought your clean outfit in. I'll help you."

"Many thanks to you, dear cousin." She moved around the chamber slowly, but once she realized how weak she was, she made sure to hang on to something as she made her way over to the chest where Tara had set her clothes. "Papa will be here soon."

"Shaw said they received word of a small contingency headed this way. Around a dozen. Men and women were sighted, so it must be your mother and father. My sire probably met them at Grant land and is waiting there. He cannot keep up with Uncle Logan." Tara held the leggings up for Brigid to slip into one side while she steadied herself holding Tara's shoulder.

"Jennet never took ill?"

"Nay, but she told us about your silly arrangement. 'Twas risky for both of you. You were lucky you weren't more sickly. Look how many died from ingesting that water."

"It was the smallest of sips. My auntie used to do it whenever she couldn't figure the cause of a sickness. And clearly, it worked. 'Tis the well, not a curse." There, she'd said it. And since she and Jennet had uncovered the truth, there was no reason to consider the clan cursed anymore.

"That small taste sure sickened you enough, though. Imagine if you'd had more."

"Imagine if I'd kept drinking it like so many here." Finally finished, Brigid ran her fingers through her wild curls and asked Tara to do the impossible. "Is there any way you can make my hair presentable?"

"I'll try." Tara braided Brigid's long waves and then tied the plaits in a bun on top of her head. "There. Just in case you heave again. You should have some warm broth. Nonie was steeping barley with honey in it for us. I'd like some, too. I'll help you over to the hearth."

Brigid didn't care how she looked, but she had two immediate needs. One was warm broth, the other was to see how Marcas would react to her now. He must have been disgusted to see her heaving, although she'd done her best to lean away from him in the dark.

They made their way across the hall, and she could see people were already gathering for the evening meal. "I guess I did sleep a wee bit."

"More than that, but you needed it, obviously. Other than your pale face, you look much better. I'll go in front of you down the staircase, and you can lean on my shoulder if you must."

Brigid did as she was instructed, and everyone quieted in the hall. All eyes lingered on her as she descended. Jennet rushed to her side. "You are better? We were foolish. I was verra afraid for you when you sickened."

"I'll be fine, though I'll not be running any races at the festivals yet."

Jennet smiled and gave her cousin a small hug. "But now we know what the cause was. We checked the well and Marcas covered it with a canvas so no one can use it."

"But they need cooking water and washing water."

"We're boiling everything, and there's another well near the forest that has always flourished and never run dry. Jinny is boiling and boiling and boiling. And Alvery said he'll have the men dig a new well soon, mayhap behind the keep." Jennet smoothed some stray strands of Brigid's hair back. "Would you like some broth?"

"Aye, though I'd also like to sit by the hearth. Where is Marcas?"

"He and Shaw went out on patrol, hoping to find your sire," Jennet explained. "They want to invite him in before he attacks." Then she disappeared. Brigid hoped she had gone to find her the warm broth.

Tara led Brigid to a chair directly in front of the fire, covering her lap with a thick fur. Jennet was there quickly with a cup. "Here, this is sweetened with honey. You'll like it."

Brigid had a few sips of the steaming liquid and felt immensely better.

"Don't rush. Let it settle before you swallow any more," Tara said.

Jennet pursed her lips and crossed her arms. "She needs the fluid. Let her take what she needs."

The two fussed over her much like her mother had a long time ago. She didn't mind at all. Brigid smirked and glanced from one cousin to the other. "'Twould be a challenge having both of you take care of me for long."

Tara waved her hand. "I'll leave you with Jennet. I'm hungry, so I'll eat at the table."

"My thanks, dear cousin."

Tara leaned over and gave her a hug. "It pleases me to see you healing."

Jennet didn't even get the chance to sit down when the door burst open and Marcas entered. As soon as he set eyes on Brigid by the hearth, he was by her side, kneeling down, the concern evident in his face. "You are hale?"

"Better. My apologies you had to see me like that."

"Do not apologize. I am just glad to see you better."

She had to ask the one question she feared. "Of those who died, did they get better first, then worsen?"

"Nay. Usually they passed within two days of the heaving, and they never stopped. My father lasted longer, but he was one of the few who improved, thought he'd completely healed, and then took ill again. The ones who passed quickly rarely sat up to discuss anything with me. You will heal. Jennet said you only took a wee bit."

"'Tis true. I should heal completely."

"Even though 'twas foolish, at least we found the source. That much pleases me greatly."

"Did you see any sign of my sire?"

"Nay. We looked, but he is nowhere to be seen.

He hides himself well."

Brigid smiled. "Aye, he does. You'll not catch him."

CHAPTER EIGHTEEN

L OGAN PACED IN a circle, waiting for his party to return after seeing to their needs. It was nearly dark, and he wished to be on Matheson land this night. They'd passed Tarradale Castle, settled on the western coast of Black Isle, and found a forest clearing he guessed to be about two hours from Eddirdale Castle. He had no idea what he would find on Matheson land. A battle? Three healers held hostage, fighting to get away? Locked in a tower like Elizabeth Grant had been?

Or would he find a clan riddled with death of an unknown origin? That thought made him give careful consideration to how they would approach this castle. After all, there were three of his loved ones inside the keep, presumably.

One of them was his dearest Brigie, the lass with the giggle that could always warm his heart. He swore no other had a sound like she did, her laughter bubbling up from an innocent heart full of love and compassion.

Who would be worthy of marrying a lass like that?

Gwynie stood not far away, bow in hand in case

of trouble, something she did out of habit after all these years. His wife was still a beautiful woman, her hair slicked back into a plait starting at the top of her crown. Sometimes she plaited it as she had for the journey, other times she let it swing free, his favorite. She had some gray streaks, but it still was a silky chestnut color.

Gwyneth had never put on much weight as other women did as they aged. She kept busy, always training the youth of their clan to use bows well. And they'd been blessed with plenty of grandbairns, something Gwynie said made their world even more special. He had to agree with her. Molly and Tormod had four, and Sorcha and Cailean two. Gavin and Merewen had none yet, but they would. Maggie and Will had just had their first, a wee lassie. Will doted on his daughter more than any other father Logan had seen. Gwynie recalled every name and the day each was born, something he couldn't do, though he always recognized his grandbairns for the special blessing they were. Cailean had been a surprise to both he and Gwynie. Both of his lasses he treated like princesses. Will doted on his daughter, but she would be brought up in the forest and live in caves like her parents did. Not Cailean's wee lassies. Sorcha loved watching them together, especially the day she'd caught the lassies dressing Cailean in their mother's gowns. They'd all had a good laugh over that one.

As his family began to return, Logan was drawn from his thoughts. He stopped his pacing to speak. "Our lasses are close, Gwynie, and I don't think they've been harmed. They were taken to heal." His gaze scanned their surroundings, something he always did when off Ramsay land.

"I won't disagree with you, Logan. I can feel they're not far. But will you be upset if my old bones wish for a bed to sleep in this eve? I don't care if they're still heaving. I need a bed."

Logan moved over and nuzzled her ear. "I'd like one, too. Will you share with me, Gwynie?"

A scream caught both of them.

"Sorcha!" Gwynie took off in the direction of the scream, Logan right behind her.

"MacAdam, find your wife!" His bellow carried through the trees so the others would help wherever they were.

The couple crashed through the brush like a buck leading its mate from hunters, following the sound of their daughter fighting off some bastard, her curses and kicks audible from a distance. The fool didn't know he was about to have his bollocks ripped in two by his wife. "Gwynie, can you see her?"

"Nay, but I hear them." She came up next to him and pointed in a different direction. "That way through the trees. I hear a bairn, a lassie, and a man, as if two are fighting and the other is watching or being held. I'm not sure which voice is Sorcha's."

They burst onto the scene at the same time Gavin and Merewen came from the opposite side, Kyle behind them. Cailean had a strange man on the ground, his knee on the man's chest and his sword tossed to the side, a dagger held at the man's throat.

"Please don't kill me. I didn't do anything," the man said with a wheeze, his hands flailing and his eyes crazed as he stared up at his captor.

Logan scanned the area, surprised to see Sorcha holding onto a lass of about three or four summers, dirty but healthy. The lass cried, her head on Sorcha's shoulder and her thumb in her mouth. "I want Papa."

Logan didn't see anything else in the area, no other strangers, so he came up behind Cailean and looked over his shoulder at the man, still begging for his life. The fool apparently thought Logan would save him, because he appealed to him instantly. "I didn't do anything wrong. He paid me to watch her for a few hours. 'Tis all I did. He'll return soon."

Cailean's voice came out in a growl that surprised Logan, "You touched my wife. No one touches her." Logan nearly sighed with pride. He'd taught him well, but as proud as he was, he knew they needed to find out the truth first.

"Lad, let him up. I want to know what he knows before you kill him and spread his insides across the land."

The man whimpered, but Cailean let his hand off his captive's windpipe. "Move and I'll slice your bollocks off."

The man, clearly intimidated by Cailean, shook his head frantically. "I'll tell you anything. What do you want to know?"

"Who is the lass?" Gwynie asked.

"I don't know. Mayhap from Clan Matheson?

They've all been heaving, so I'm told. I was traveling from Inverness to Avoch, delivering a missive, but he stopped me and asked if I wished to make some coin, that I just needed to watch her for two hours. He could be back anytime."

"Who is he?" Gavin barked.

"I don't know. I'm not from around here. It was just extra coin, but I didn't know she'd be so young. The bastard had tied her to a tree. I untied her, but she never moved."

"Let him go, MacAdam."

"You're sure?" Cailean asked over his shoulder.

"If you see the bastard who tied her up, you better keep your mouth closed or we'll come for you. You'll be easy to track because you'll be leaving a trail of pish all the way." Cailean let him up and he ran, running through the brush until he found his horse and left without a glance backward.

Gwynie moved over to the lass. "Greetings, sweeting. The bad man is gone. He'll not scare you anymore."

She shook her head emphatically.

"Nay? He's not bad?" Sorcha asked.

"'Tis anoffer bad man. He's mean to me. My legs hurt from the rope, but he took it off." Her wee finger pointed after the man who'd just left.

Logan lifted her gown to look at the wee one's ankles, not surprised to see them bruised and bloodied. He also caught a whiff of urine that nearly knocked him out.

"I'm dirty. He wouldn't let me go in the woods. I had to go on my gown." The look of remorse on her face reminded him of a wee lass named Gracie who'd been in the same predicament many years ago.

"What's your name?" Gwynie asked.

"Kara."

"Kara. 'Tis a beautiful name. Have you a second name? Do you belong to a clan?"

She nodded at that question. "Clan Maphson." Her thumb returned to her mouth as she tugged on a lock of her hair.

"Well, sweet Kara. How would you like to play bouncy in the water?" Logan asked.

She nodded, popping her thumb back out of her mouth.

"Take her gown off, Sorcha." She did as instructed, and he took the lass, swinging her back and forth until she giggled. He headed back to the burn they'd used before, and when he found a spot on a rock, he bent down and set her bottom in the water. At first she scowled, probably because it was cold, or possibly because of the sting on her open wounds, but he swirled and swirled her, dipping her down until the worst of her was cleaned. She giggled and frowned, depending on her most recent feeling, but she never let go of him, her big brown eyes locked on his.

"Papa, I could have done that, but you're so good with bairns that I prefer to watch you." Sorcha looked at her sire clearly enjoying the wee lass' laughter, then at her mother who shook her head while she watched his antics.

"He was so much better than I ever was with

you, Sorcha."

"MacAdam, take your tunic off."

"What? What the hell for?"

"Just do it. The lassie needs something dry to wear, and the plaid is too rough for her bottom. No one will care you aren't wearing a tunic."

"Cailean, just give it to him. You have another in your saddlebag. I packed it."

Cailean did what he was told, handing it over to Gwynie. Sorcha smiled and winked at her husband's physique while Logan held Kara up, allowing Gwynie the room to wrap the tunic around the lass, tying it in a knot behind her.

Sorcha finally stopped admiring her husband and said, "Papa, I cannot believe how good you are with her."

"Your father is excellent with bairns. He did the same for Gracie when she was two summers, and he took care of both Torrian and Lily when they were sickly."

"Better?" Logan asked the wee lass.

"Aye. My sanks to you."

"Merewen, go grab the salve I have in my saddlebag and I'll dress her wounds a bit," Gwynie offered.

"Take me home?" the girl asked.

"Who's your papa?" Logan asked. "What's his name, Kara?"

"His name is Papa."

Logan said, "Does he have another name?"

"Aye."

Logan wondered if her clan even knew the lass was alive after all the deaths they'd reportedly had. "What's Papa's other name?"

She beamed up at Logan and proudly said, "Chief. Nonie said his new name is Chief Maphson."

Logan looked at Gwynie but said nothing. It was Gavin who whispered in his ear. "Bargaining chip."

That was indeed true. If the Mathesons wished to argue, he had something quite valuable now.

The laird's daughter.

CHAPTER NINETEEN

———————— ◆ ————————

MARCAS FELT MUCH better after seeing Brigid in a chair sipping broth. "The color is coming back to your cheeks," he said after Jennet left them alone for a few moments.

"I'm so embarrassed," she said. "I can't believe I got sick in front of you."

He couldn't help but chuckle. "Do you know that a year ago I might have been bothered by it? But after all I've seen, yours was quite minor. I could tell by the look in your eyes when you turned that you wished to become a firefly and leave, but instead you somehow passed out and hit your head. My apologies I did not catch you."

"I think you must have or my injury would have been worse. I could have gone over the parapets, too." She took another sip of broth. "I know I've been sick because this barley broth is heavenly."

"Jinny makes it with love. 'Tis why you're enjoying it. Keep drinking." He leaned toward her and kissed her forehead. "As for going over the edge of the wall, I would never allow that to happen. But for now, I'm headed out to look for your sire. Word has reached me there is a strange group of men and women in the area, but we could not locate them. It's nearing dark, and I suspect they'll be here soon."

"Strange? Someone you don't recognize? But you did say the party includes women, which means my mother is probably with him." She had to admit she hoped her mother was with her sire. There was something about being ill that still made her wish to have her mother nearby.

"I say strange because he disappears. If any other band of warriors comes from the Highlands, they don't attempt to hide. I hear the Grant contingency will run down anything in its path. Not so with this group. I've been unable to track them either. I'll have to talk to your father and ask him how he does that."

"He's a fine tracker. I can't say if he'll tell you or not."

Marcas stood and clasped her shoulder, wishing he could wrap her in a warm embrace, but he did not. Much as he hated to let her go, he had to. Where had he ever met a woman so wise as this one? But he had to go out to the gates.

Just in case.

What the hell was Logan Ramsay planning to do, anyway? Would he mount an outright attack? If so, Clan Matheson's small number of men wouldn't do much to hold them off. He had to admit, while he'd been in charge of training their men in the lists before the curse hit, he'd lost many of his strongest swordsmen. Shaw was still powerful, but Alvery was an old man. Torcall was solid, but still, he knew the outcome wouldn't be good.

And if they were sneaking in with the chance of stealing his daughter back, then Ramsay would have to come right into the great hall to do so. Although no one would stop him if he did.

Marcas made his way to the gate and yelled up to Torcall, now overlooking the area. "Anything, Torcall?"

"There might be. I see a few horses approaching, and I don't think they're going to follow the trail. I think they're coming here."

"Plaid color? Ramsay is dark blue."

"Can't tell, Chief."

Marcas climbed up the staircase to the top of the wall, then peered out over the night. There wasn't a cloud in the sky, fortunately for them. The moon lit the area nicely. He scanned, just able to make out the group on horseback. The first two were men, followed by three women. A small contingency of guards surrounded the group. Two men came behind the three women, and then his vision caught something that caused him to nearly choke.

A bairn.

He swore there was a bairn riding in front of the first man. He held his hand across her protectively, but the person was less than half his size.

Something lodged in his throat that threatened to make him heave everywhere. Could it be Kara?

He whispered, "Torcall, is that a bairn on the first horse?" His gaze searched the rest of the group, all wearing the same dark plaid, which he thought blue, but it was difficult to discern in the dark. The Matheson plaid was also primarily blue, but it was more turquoise with green. The men were monstrous looking, large and muscular, especially the one riding next to the man with the bairn. He was fair-haired and looked like he chewed nettles for entertainment.

"It could be a bairn, Chief. Or it could be trickery, meant to bring you out, meant to make you think it could be Kara. Tread carefully."

A voice called out as they approached their closed gate, "Tell Chief Matheson we have terms to discuss. I have something he wants."

That was all Marcas needed to hear. "Open the gate," he barked. He flew down the staircase just as the gate lifted, rushing through the opening and shouting before he stopped. "State your name and business."

Waiting took an interminably long time. But the man in front finally said, "Ramsay. You have something I want. Bring my daughter out now. And my nieces."

Then the next sound unmanned him.

"Papa! I'm home!"

Marcas never heard another word. "Kara?" He ran, ignoring the shouts of the Ramsay men, ignoring the one who dismounted and stood in his way, the others who dismounted and aimed their bows at him.

"Kara?"

It didn't matter. He would risk death to hold his daughter again.

"Kara? 'Tis truly you?"

His eyes misted, but he swiped the tears away to see if it was his dearest daughter. She was the one he used to croon to, the one who'd made his heart burst with just a smile, the one who looked at him now and said, "Papa, I wuv you."

"Kara." It was her. Truly her. He took one look at the man standing in front of the horse, his arms crossed and ready to fight, and pulled his fist up at the last moment to punch the man square in the jaw. Nothing and no one would keep him from his sweeting.

The man was indeed a monster because he didn't move much, but he backed up when the man on the horse said, "Leave him be, MacAdam. He only wants one thing."

"Greetings, Papa." The man on the horse lifted her down to Marcas, and he grabbed her, hugging her so tight he had to force himself to ease up on her tiny frame. He cried tears and carried no shame.

"Ah, hell." The man on the horse climbed down and helped the woman next to him dismount. But Marcas still couldn't speak.

"Papa, these are my friends. They took me away from the bad man. I didn't like him."

"What bad man?" Marcas looked back at the man who stood in front of him, nearly eye-to-eye. "My thanks to you for bringing her back to me."

"We'll tell you all once you tell me if my daughter and my nieces are here. The name is Logan Ramsay."

Marcas nodded, a clump in his throat that he

fought down, ending his tears. "They are all here, all hale, and you have my apologies. I needed their help. I welcome you all to Eddirdale Castle, home of Clan Matheson. Please join us inside."

The man named MacAdam said, "What about the curse? Are you all sick? Are the lasses sick?"

"The curse will be no more. Your daughter, Lord Ramsay, discovered the culprit: our freshly dug water well. I have not harmed nor imprisoned any of them, though Brigid voluntarily tasted the water and became a wee bit ill, but she's better now. You're all welcome for a meal and to spend the night. We have plenty of room in our castle."

"I told that lass to stop doing that," the woman said. "That child will kill me yet." The woman was lean and beautiful, and Brigid looked much like her, so Marcas suspected it was the infamous Gwyneth Ramsay standing in front of him, bow in hand.

Logan said, "We accept your hospitality. You have stables?"

"Aye, with one lad who will care for your horses. We have plenty of stalls, just not many stable lads left." Marcas led the way, calling out to Timm, who greeted them right away.

Ramsay said, "Kyle, send a few of our men in to help with the horses. They'll sleep out here, though they'd appreciate a meat pie or a trencher of stew if you have enough."

"We have plenty. Have your men join us in about half the hour."

Marcas couldn't let go of Kara yet, her voice babbling but calming as she took in all that was around her. He had to wonder what had happened to her, but for now, he'd settle with seeing her bathed, fed, and in proper clothing. She wore some odd garment he'd never seen, but she seemed in good spirits.

A group headed out the main door of the keep and barreled down the steps straight toward them, probably sensing the Ramsays had arrived or hearing Kara's voice. Jennet and Tara came out shouting. "Uncle Logan! Aunt Gwyneth?"

"Where's Brigid?" the woman he guessed to be Gwyneth shouted.

"She's coming," Jennet replied.

Marcas had turned around and faced the keep. He stopped to observe all that was taking place in their quiet castle, the noise reminding him of past times. Of happier times.

Brigid had just stepped outside, making her way slowly toward them as any regal person would do, her head held high, her walk one of nobility. She wore a dark gown that Gisela must have found for her.

"Papa, she's pretty. She looks like a queen."

"She does, doesn't she, princess?"

Brigid spotted him, and her eyes fell on Kara, and she hurried toward them. "You found her? This is Kara?"

"My name is Kara and this is my papa."

Brigid kissed her forehead, looked at Marcas, and whispered, "I'm so happy for you. You have your bairns back and they'll be together. A family again, and if not perfect, nearly there."

"I think I have your sire to thank," he said,

pointing off to the group behind them.

Brigid stared at him wide-eyed. "They finally made it."

Her mother rushed over, leaving Jennet and Tara with Sorcha and Merewen. "They did not hurt you?" She reached for Brigid's hands and studied her head to toe, as if afraid she was missing something. Then her eyes narrowed. "You're different. Are you sure you were not hurt?"

Kara, not knowing Gwyneth spoke to her own daughter, said, "Aye, my legs still hurt." She held one up to show her father. "See, Papa? Bad man tied me up."

Marcas did his best to control the fury that raged inside him when he saw the condition of his daughter's tender skin, but he said nothing. He'd have time to learn all.

Gwyneth introduced herself and said, "We did not harm her, nor were we sure who she was, but we'll tell you all if you'll lead us inside. I'm not used to riding a horse this far. I could use a chair and a hearth, if you don't mind."

Logan came over and wrapped his arm around Brigid. "Who do I kill?" he teased. Then he looked rather guiltily at Kara and said, "I mean, who do I thank for taking such good care of you?"

Marcas quickly introduced himself. "Marcas Matheson, Laird of Clan Matheson. Please join us for a repast and I'll explain myself. If you'll allow me to enjoy my daughter's return, we can meet in my solar on the morrow. We have plenty of chambers to keep you all warm inside on beds instead of the ground. I know I have atonement owed to you."

"Fair enough." Logan swept his arm out and the group proceeded inside, making their way to the fireplace and some to the trestle tables while Jinny and Nonie cried at seeing Kara again.

Nonie said, "My thanks to you. Oh, the dear Lord has blessed us this day."

Gwyneth said, "She needs a bath. We dipped her in the burn when we found the terrible condition she was in, and I put some salve on the ankles. She was tied with rope to a tree right before we found her."

"He was a bad man, Nonie." Then Kara pointed to Gwyneth. "Winnie saved me."

Nonie whisked her up the stairs while Jinny grabbed Tiernay to follow her. Edda and Ethan brought platters of food. Shaw said, "I'll see to the tub, Nonie."

The group all pitched in to make everyone comfortable after introductions were done, but Brigid looked exhausted. Marcas moved over to her and said, "If you're tired, please feel free to find your chamber. I promise to be honest, and Jennet will be here with Tara. Do you need anything?"

"Nay, seeing you with your daughter was enough for me."

"I'll even escort you to your chamber, if you'd like. I know you're a wee bit weak. Then I'll check on my bairns."

He noticed the uneasy glance she cast toward her father, but Marcas felt he needed to do the right thing for this lass who had risked so much to heal his clan. Surprised she finally nodded, he ushered her to the stairs, following her.

"Brigid, where the hell are you going? And why is he with you?" Logan's bellow carried across the hall loud enough to stop everyone from what they were doing.

Marcas stared directly at him. "Since she's been ill at the expense of healing our clan, 'tis my duty to see she makes it to her chamber safely. The curse did attack her somewhat, and she is still weak because of it. I'll not have her taking a fall on my staircase. Once I depart, she is free to lock the door behind her if she chooses. Then I will attend to my bairns. I will return shortly."

Logan locked gazes with Marcas as he approached the staircase, but Marcas's hand went protectively to Brigid's lower back. He stopped to make his point clear. He'd heard much about this man and respected his work as a spy and the strength of his clan, but no one else would take over Clan Matheson. "With all due respect, because you are her sire, I honor your position, but you'll not give me orders in my own home." He turned away from Logan and gave a wee push to Brigid. She continued up the staircase.

"Papa, I promise he'll not be in my chamber. My thanks for coming after me, but I'm exhausted. I need sleep."

"That I'll agree to."

"I will get your fire going," he said, making sure Logan heard him. "Then I'll leave immediately."

When they reached the top of the stairs, Marcas

glanced back down and noticed her father had backed away, though his eyes still remained on the two. Marcas followed her to the door of her chamber, then stepped inside and said, "I'll throw logs on your hearth to warm the space."

"My apologies over my sire." She sat down on her bed with exhaustion written across her face.

How he wished he could make everything better for her with a wave of his hand. But she was strong if nothing else. She'd be back to her usual state on the morrow if he were to guess. She did need a good night's rest.

"No need to apologize. He has every right. I would do the same in his shoes. But you are my first concern right now and you need your sleep." He finished with the fire, then moved over to her bed, leaning down to cup her cheek and kiss her lightly on the lips. "Sleep well."

"I hope my sire doesn't bother you too much, Marcas."

He made his way to the door and said, "He'll be no bother."

How wrong he was.

CHAPTER TWENTY

——————◆——————

BRIGID WOKE WHEN Jennet and Tara entered, though she heard Tara whisper, "Hush. She's sound asleep."

She sat up, her eyes slowly adjusting to the darkness. "Nay, I'm awake now. How long have I been sleeping?"

"A couple of hours. We had to tease your sire for backing down to Marcas when he escorted you to your chamber." Tara giggled quietly. "It was perfect. Your father may have met his match. That is, if you're interested in him. Are you?"

Brigid hugged her knees to her chest before she rearranged the furs. "I am. It was a strange sensation. Part of me was actually sad to see my parents here. At first, I was so excited because I knew we'd have an escort back, but the oddest thing is…" She paused to gather her thoughts. "I'm not ready to leave yet. Are you two?"

Jennet answered while she disrobed and folded her clothing carefully before finding one of the night rails Nonie had left for each of them. "My instinct is to stay until we are certain our theory is correct. That would require us to remain here at least a fortnight."

Brigid teased, "And that has nothing to do with Ethan, does it? You two would make a nice couple." She shot a quick glance at Tara to see if she thought the same.

Tara clapped her hands and crooned, "Aye, you would. And I'm becoming quite fond of Shaw, but I have no idea if he feels the same."

They were interrupted by a light knock on the door. "Enter," Brigid said.

The door flew open and Sorcha rushed in, running over to her sister's side. She gave her a swift hug and whispered, "He's perfect for you. Pay no attention to Papa."

Brigid hoped she meant Marcas, but there were two other brothers. "Who?"

"Marcas, and you know it. I loved how he put Papa in his place. But I just need to be serious and ask you. Are you interested in him? Is there something there already?" Sorcha sat down on the bed, grasping Brigid's hand. Brigid adored Sorcha. She was closer to her than to Maggie or Molly, their adopted sisters. She'd always admired Sorcha for her soft heart and beautiful outlook, though she'd been teased about them many times. Uncle Quade often taunted her that she couldn't possibly be Logan's daughter because she was too nice.

Brigid sighed. "Aye, there is. But I don't know what to make of it. He just lost his wife to the heaves, so I thought 'twas too soon, but…"

"He did?" Sorcha asked, scrunching her face up in question. "I could be wrong. My instincts said he's as interested in you as you are in him, but mayhap not. But what? Please finish your thought."

"But he also told me he found out before she died that she was interested in someone else. She was still in love with the man she'd hoped to marry before their betrothal. Her father forced her to marry Marcas and she wasn't happy about it, but she did her duty. I should say no more, but he was never in love with her. It was a match between allies. Please don't repeat this."

"I hate how often that happens," Tara said. "But 'tis good for you. I didn't think he had warm feelings for his wife. Just something I sensed."

Sorcha kissed her sister's cheek. "Then go for him, Brigid. You know your choices of finding men are slim when Papa is around. There aren't many Ramsay men as bullheaded as Cailean who are willing to challenge our sire."

"I'll think on it. I'm tired. I need to go back to sleep." Brigid fell backwards, her head sinking into the pillow. Then she grabbed her sister's hand. "I'm glad you'll be here in the morn." Sorcha arranged Brigid's furs then turned to leave, waving before she stepped outside the door.

Brigid was too tired to think on any of it.

The next time she awakened, it was the middle of the night. She lay there considering everything, listening to the rhythmic breathing of her two cousins, but she couldn't fall back asleep. She sat up and rinsed her mouth, taking several gulps of the water she knew had been boiled. A short time later, she grabbed the largest fur, wrapped it around herself, and tiptoed out the door.

Padding down the passageway, she reveled in how quiet it was. Everyone had to be in bed. Reaching her destination, she tugged on the heavy door, enjoyed the rush of fresh air in her face, then climbed the staircase to the parapets.

She leaned over the wall to stare out over the beautiful landscape. Even in the dark, the area was breathtaking. Thick forests and the reflection of the moon on a firth that seemed to stretch forever was something she didn't see from the Ramsay parapets.

What was she to do? She knew why she'd awakened. Her entire being was in turmoil over a man with long dark hair, soft lips, and warm gray eyes. Watching him with his daughter only made her admire him more. He made her feel special, something that had been totally missing in her life—at least from a man she admired.

And that brought another thought, something she'd neglected to think on before. If she were to become involved with Marcas, she'd have two children who were young enough to consider her to be their mother. Tiernay would never remember Freda.

How did she feel about that?

Oddly enough, being mother to those two bairns gave her a warm feeling inside. There'd be no doubt she'd need help, but with Marcas, Nonie, and Gisela, she'd not be alone.

She jumped when the door opened behind her, and she took two steps farther down the walkway, waiting to see who it was.

Marcas moved out onto the stone floor and froze when he saw her, his eyebrows arching. "Had I known you were here, I would have come long ago, lass."

"I just arrived. I slept a few hours but now I can't."

"'Tis chilly out here. You must not take ill again." He came over and wrapped his arms around her from behind, his heat enveloping her. Then he took her by complete surprise, nuzzling her neck. "And why can you not sleep? You looked exhausted. Though I couldn't either."

"Because I'm confused."

"About what?" he asked gently.

"About how I feel now that my parents are here." She gazed out over the land. "'Tis more than beautiful here, Marcas. 'Tis breathtaking."

"I'm glad you can appreciate it. Some just consider it dark soil, and some give it evil connotations. There's said to be faerie lands within the isle, but others try to ignore that. I'll take you fishing before you take your leave. Our fish are the best. But I wish to hear more on what confuses you."

She turned around to face him. "I've traveled a bit, but only to other clans that are family. I've visited Cameron land and Grant land, and a few others. But this was an escapade. Once I got past my fear of you, I viewed the entire trip as a wonderful adventure, a place to act as myself without my father judging me or my mother looking at a man I had an interest in. And to be brutally honest, I don't know if I'm ready to leave yet."

He cupped her face and said, "I'm pleased to hear you say that. I'm confused, too, but in the most delicious way I've ever experienced. I like you and I'm drawn to you, more than I ever have been with any other lass, including my wife. I want to get to know you better—what makes you laugh, what makes you cry. I wish nothing more than to have the opportunity to explore each other, our minds and bodies. I mean that in a respectful way. I wouldn't do anything inappropriate until we were married, but lass, 'tis sheer torture being around you and being unable to touch you."

Brigid stared up at him, their gazes locked. She knew what she wanted more than anything. "Then please touch me as you wish to do. 'Tis what I want, too."

He gave a low growl and kissed her, only this kiss was different. It wasn't a tender kiss, or a soft exploration, but a kiss of need, of desire. A kiss telling her just how much he wanted her. Their tongues dueled and mated in a dance she loved, and all she wanted was more. She arched against him with a need she didn't understand, and his hand came up to cup her breast through the thin material of her night rail.

"Brigid, you are so beautiful, so soft." He kissed a trail down her neck, nuzzling her ear and down to the fine bones across her neck. His thumb teased her nipple through the night rail, and she jerked, surprised how much she enjoyed that simple touch.

His mouth found her lips again and he ravaged her, his breathing growing raspy, matching hers as they explored each other, his hands stroking her body in a soft caress she loved.

But then he ended it, and she wondered why. "Please don't stop, Marcas."

"Ah, lass, I must. You are an innocent, and you don't know how quickly this could become something it shouldn't be. I hope I didn't startle you with my desire for you. You are more than I ever dreamed of, beautiful and intelligent, compassionate and passionate. What more could I want in a woman?"

"I'm here." She didn't know how to tell him that she'd never shared this kind of intimacy with another and she wanted more.

"'Tis too soon. I'm happy that you wish to stay, and I'll not ask any more of you, lass."

Her heart nearly broke. "You don't want me?"

"Oh, I do, Brigid. I want every part of you, but you're not mine to have. At least, not yet. But Brigid Ramsay, I'm falling in love with you. Know that. Sometimes, it frightens the hell out of me, but it excites me more. I won't walk away from you unless you push me away."

She leaned her head against his chest, clinging to the last words he said. "I want you, too, Marcas. All of you. I've never loved anyone before, so I'm not sure what to expect, but I couldn't imagine it being stronger than how I feel about you."

She couldn't be more honest than that, but

she had an odd feeling she would get her heart broken. Now that her parents were here, would they ruin everything for her?

CHAPTER TWENTY-ONE

———◆———

T HE NEXT MORNING, Marcas came in
after checking the area outside their wall.
He had thoughts of sweet pink lips on his mind,
but he forced himself to think differently. He'd
checked the woods, the firth, and the main route
from Tarradale and found no signs of warriors in
hiding or in transit. He'd consulted with Alvery
and Mundi, who had told him they were warned
Clan Milton would be coming on the morrow.
MacHeth had sent a messenger who informed
them they'd heard the rumor and would come to
their aid if necessary.

It was time to talk with Logan Ramsay about
joining him to save his clan's heritage. It wouldn't
be an easy conversation, but he'd do it. And he
expected to get the full explanation of how they
found Kara. He'd hoped to learn the truth the
prior evening, but after their repast, Logan and
Gwyneth had gone to bed, promising to tell all
details the next morn.

Marcas stepped into the great hall, pleased
to hear multiple voices chatting over morning
porridge. He'd made certain that Nonie and

Jinny would only use boiled water everywhere. He'd also sent men out to bring barrels of water back from the well near the forest.

He hoped to never see such a tragedy fall upon his clan again.

Upon entering, his gaze settled on Brigid, finding her easily in the grouping because of her simple beauty. Tara was bubblier, while Jennet was quiet, like Ethan. But Brigid conversed and laughed as though she deserved the noble blood she carried. Clan Ramsay was one of the finest in all the land.

Marcas smiled and headed toward their group, but he was intercepted by a running toddler. "Papa!"

Kara launched herself into his arms, and he tossed her into the air. "How is my wee sweetling this morn?"

"I'm happy to be home, Papa. I miss Mama, but Nonie takes good care of me. And we have many visitors. I like them all."

Pleased to see her smile, he kissed her forehead before she wriggled down from him. "Go see Winnie." Her pet name for Gwyneth Ramsay had stuck, and he found it quite endearing. He noticed that Gwyneth didn't correct her either.

When he reached the table where Brigid sat, he asked, "All is well? The porridge suits everyone? I think we have plenty of honey to go around."

"'Tis delicious," Tara said.

He was about to speak to Brigid when Logan interrupted. "I'd like to meet in your solar, Matheson."

Marcas nodded. "Of course. I planned to meet with you soon, as promised last eve. Who else would you like to join us? I'll have Shaw, while Ethan is out at the gates."

"My son Gavin will join us."

"Have you eaten? I can have Nonie bring a tray of bread and cheese, if you please."

"Nay, we've eaten." Logan headed toward the door to the laird's solar.

Gavin said, "But I could eat a wee bit more."

"Never you mind, Gavin. You've eaten enough for three men already. We have business to discuss."

Gavin rolled his eyes, then laughed when Merewen said, "He's right. Just go along for now."

Marcas moved into the seat behind the writing table, his sire's chair. He guessed it did rightfully belong to him now. His sire hadn't had many meetings, as the clan had always functioned well on its own. It wasn't a large clan, usually around one hundred people. Most spent their time working the rich fields, planting oats, barley, and vegetables, or taking care of the orchards. Each family had their own goats for milk, and each tended their own part of the fields, took care of their own, and met in the great hall and the courtyard once a week for a big meal. The clan rarely battled, though they did keep a score of men training in the lists. Overseeing them had been Marcas's job.

Now, his job was to rebuild, but first, he needed Logan Ramsay's warriors to help him retain his land, land that had been in his family for decades.

"Please allow me to explain, and I will ask that

you save your questions until the end. Then I have a favor to ask of you."

Logan loudly snorted. Gavin snickered and took the seat next to his sire across from Marcas. Shaw joined them, settling in a chair next to his brother.

"My apologies for kidnapping your daughter and nieces. I should have asked. But to say we were saddened with grief is hardly right for how we felt. I'd lost both of my parents and wife. My sister and daughter were gravely ill. I'd watched many of my clan members pass, and I couldn't lose any more. I did what I thought was best. We planned to bring the healers named Brenna Ramsay and Jennie Cameron here, but we failed. Yet we made out better with the three than our anticipated two. I didn't realize the advanced ages of the two healers. I don't regret my decision, but I recognize that I owe you and the lasses our deepest apologies. If we can repay you with horseflesh or coin, I will do so."

"Why the hell didn't you just ask?" Logan said, his lips pursed.

"Time was of the essence. I did consider asking, but waiting until dawn to speak with the laird could have cost us more lives."

Gavin drawled, "Sounds like a story I heard once before, Papa."

Marcas was puzzled by this comment, but he didn't ask.

Logan said, "Keep your wise-arse comments to yourself. What I did was necessary and worked out for the best."

Marcas said, "I don't know of what you speak, but I'm hoping this entire situation will work out for the best, also. You're welcome to stay as long as you like. When you've decided how I can repay you for our oversight, please advise, and I'll do whatever I can to appease you and settle this."

Logan nodded.

Marcas couldn't wait any longer to find out the bastard who'd stolen his dear Kara away. He'd appeased the group last eve because he knew they were travel weary, but he needed answers to his questions. "Would you please tell me everything about the situation where you encountered my daughter? We'd searched everywhere for her on multiple occasions. She was taken from the keep after we left, from the arms of my sister, who slept with her near the hearth. Kara is not capable of opening the door herself, so someone assisted her."

Logan replied, "My daughter and her husband were seeing to their needs when I heard my daughter scream. When we found her, she was holding the lass and a man was set to run. We stopped and questioned him, but I'm afraid we can't give you the information you seek."

"Tell me what he looked like, what clan he belongs to, and I'll hunt the bastard down." Marcas couldn't stop his voice from growing agitated. "He tied my wee lassie with rope. He tore the tender skin on her ankles! Who was he?"

"I have no answers for you. The man who had her was clearly a traveling messenger. He claimed to be carrying a missive from someone in Inverness to Avoch. Said he was approached by a man to watch a child for two hours who paid him good coin. The man said he had no idea that the bairn would be in the condition she was."

"And you believed him?"

Logan nodded. "He untied the lass. That told me he had more consideration for her than her captor. He wore no plaid, no crest, no identifying information. I believe what he said. We questioned him about the other man, but he said he'd been all dressed in dark clothing and had no plaid either. Young man, light brown hair, I believe. Anything else, Gavin?"

"Nay, I agree with you on all that. He nearly pished his pants when Cailean grabbed him. He carried no sword, just a small dagger, and he never grabbed it. Didn't seem like the usual type of criminal to me. We let him go, and he left so quickly, I'm sure he was telling the truth."

Marcas's head fell into his hands. This was not what he wanted to hear. "Who would steal a child of three winters?"

"Did you ask your daughter?" Gavin asked. "We have a nephew around her age, and he would be able to tell us something."

"I did. She called him a bad man, that was it. She did say he hit her, made her cry. And gave her an oatcake. That was all she would say."

"Don't push her to remember any more. Let it go," Logan said. "She's dealt with enough."

"I agree. I'll not ask her again." His heart had nearly ripped in two when he watched the interplay of emotions cross her face when she told the story from her young memory. Pain was what she'd most remembered.

He'd kill the bastard with his bare hands.

Shaw said, "I'd hoped we would learn more about the fool. What do we do now?"

Logan said, "I'd do nothing. Whatever he wanted, whatever his purpose was, I don't think he got it. He'll be back. You have to be ready for him."

Marcas hadn't even considered it, but Logan was right. Perhaps he was as clever as his reputation foretold. But no matter how hard he mused, he couldn't come up with any reason why anyone would want a wee lass. Unless he'd been planning to sell her to a mother who'd lost her child, he had no other possible reasons.

"Your favor?" Logan asked.

Marcas cleared his throat, thinking about his words. "We have received information that a clan plans to attack us on the morrow. We have rich soil, many animals, and a fine keep. We've been advised that others were waiting for the curse to be resolved, that they knew we'd lost so many of our clan and guardsmen we would be easy to conquer. Would you be willing to stay and help us protect our clan? Do you have enough men to help us defend against two or three score warriors?"

"That's an insult," Logan scoffed. "We have five of the best archers in all the land who'll take half of them out before the enemy ever arrives. And we have some of the best swordsmen in all the land."

"I thought Alexander Grant and his son were the greatest swordsmen in the land."

"That may be. Gwynie and Molly are the greatest archers, and the Grants may be the best swordsmen, but Gavin is the only one best at both. With us here, you'll have plenty to help you beat off any local clan."

"I would be in your debt if you would assist us, Ramsay."

"Leave, Gavin," Logan said. "I wish to speak to the laird in private."

Gavin got up and left without question. Shaw looked at Marcas, who nodded, then followed Gavin out the door, closing it behind him.

Logan stood up, and Marcas did the same. Their statures brought them nearly eye-to-eye. "What are your intentions toward my daughter? Don't deny your interest. I see it in you and her."

Marcas again was impressed with Logan's directness. He felt he wouldn't be able to lie to this man who would know if he did. Honesty was best. "I'm not sure yet. Your daughter is an intelligent and talented young woman. I'm impressed with her compassion and her dedication to her task."

"And you find her beautiful."

"Aye, I'll not argue you there, but it wasn't the first thing I saw in her. She's an admirable lass, the way she carries herself, the way she speaks. I admire everything about her. Is she promised to anyone?"

"Nay, she's not. She'll make her own choice, with Gwynie's and my approval. Are you not grieving your wife, Matheson? Did you not just bury the woman? Seems pretty cold to me."

"Fair question, Ramsay. My wife and I were betrothed to gain an alliance between two clans. I'll be brutally honest with you, because I don't think anything else would be accepted. It was never a love match, but we got along well enough. That ended when I discovered she'd cuckolded me and was planning to return to her clan after the birth of our son."

Logan chuckled.

"You find that amusing? I did not."

"Nay, not that part. I just find it a good reason for someone to try to poison their wife. Don't you? Did you poison that well to kill your wife for her infidelity?"

Marcas had never considered such an accusation. He grabbed Logan by the collar and lifted him off the ground, a wee bit quicker than the older man. So incensed by Logan's accusation, he would put an end to that thought before the man stepped outside of his solar. "How dare you suggest I would kill my own parents and my wife and risk the well-being of everyone else in our clan over jealousy? You've overstayed your welcome, Ramsay. Please leave." Marcas set him down and turned away, his anger too powerful.

Logan opened the door and turned to speak to him. "I had to ask, Matheson. I believe you to be honorable. I have fifty guards arriving soon. We'll protect your castle for you. As for my daughter, 'tis yet to be determined."

Yet Marcas had a feeling Logan Ramsay would not be receptive to his asking for Brigid's hand in marriage. Not after accusing him of planning his wife's death.

How many others thought the same?

He couldn't stop himself from mentioning the possibility anyway. "I hope you may consider my offer for your daughter's hand. If not at this time, sometime in the future."

Logan didn't get the chance to respond. Shaw appeared in the doorway and said, "Clan Milton is on their way. Two score warriors."

Logan grinned. "Good. We have a battle to settle. I do love battles."

Marcas could only pray the Lord was on their side.

CHAPTER TWENTY-TWO

———————•◆•———————

BRIGID HAD NO idea what had been discussed in the solar other than what Gavin had said when he came out. He told her they'd be taking some horses home and that after they'd told Marcas about how they'd found Kara, he still hadn't come up with a possible name for the villain who had kidnapped the wee lass.

"Then Da kicked my arse out."

Brigid scowled and Sorcha smiled, squeezing Brigid's hand under the table, though Brigid didn't understand why.

The next thing she knew, they received word the clan was under attack, and her mother grabbed her along with Sorcha, Merewen, and Gavin, and said, "We're going into the trees. Let's take a few out before they know what hit them."

Brigid raced upstairs and donned her leggings and tunic, pleased she was feeling back to her usual self at last. Her mother had brought a bow and quiver for her, which she grabbed in the hall and followed them out.

Marcas was barking orders to their men while her father went after their guards near the stables.

How she wished to comfort Marcas, but he was far too busy. She followed her mother and vowed to see the Mathesons triumph over the enemy.

Ethan led the way. "If we go out this side door through the wall, you can hide in the trees in Gallow Hill Woods. Clan Milton will come from that direction, so it would work best if you could take several out as they pass by you. Then the rest of us will fight inside the wall and some outside. Once they pass, you can sneak back inside the door and shoot from the parapets.

Brigid asked, "Ethan, are you sure they are intent on attacking? Should we shoot no matter what or wait to see what they do once they pass?"

"Clan Milton loves to battle. If they come by at a full gallop with their weapons raised, and they will, then shoot them. You will hear their battle cry. 'Tis the surest sign to shoot."

Ethan left them, and her mother moved through the trees, studying each one along with the angle and view of the path near the firth. Then she started to point, assigning them the best spots. "Gavin, help Brigid into that tree. It's perfect seat for her, but a little tall for her to climb, and she's not in top shape."

Their mother moved with Sorcha and Merewen while Gavin gave Brigid a boost into the tree. "Gavin, did Marcas say anything to Papa about me?" she whispered, not wanting her mother to hear.

"Nay, but Papa kicked me out at the end. I'm quite sure you were about to be the topic. It's pretty obvious he's taken with you. The question is, how do you feel?"

She found her position in the tree and anchored herself, setting her arrows just right, then looked down at her brother. "I do like him verra much, but how did you know, Gavin?"

"Know what?" he asked, peering up through the branches.

"How did you know Merewen was the one? I've had verra little experience with men, as you know, thanks to Papa, you, and Cailean."

"Brigid, you're only seven and ten. No need to rush it, but if you have to ask me that question, then he's probably not the one. You'll know when you've found him."

"You weren't that sure with Merewen, from what I recall, or am I wrong? Don't speak lies."

"No lies, but for men, 'tis easier."

"Why? What made you fall in love with Merewen?"

He laughed. "Two things. Her skill with her bow."

"And?"

Then he laughed and left, glancing back over his shoulder. "Her arse in her leggings. You lasses aren't so simple."

"Gavin, I hate you sometimes." Her arse. What the hell kind of reason was that?

She waited an interminable amount of time, watching her mother and the others get into position. She could see the area in front of Eddirdale Castle and swore there was a new group of Ramsay warriors. Her sire had said more were coming. Perhaps they'd arrived. If so,

Clan Matheson would be successful.

A sudden loud screech echoed through the area followed by her mother yelling, "They're coming with weapons raised."

Brigid nocked her bow and readied herself, firing as soon as she saw her mother's arrows find their target. One fell off his horse, then another, and another. There were too many for the few archers to take out, but they did do some damage.

Her mother hopped down from her tree and ran toward the curtain wall, yelling, "Get inside! We'll shoot from the wall."

The others climbed down hurriedly. Brigid landed hard, but she didn't fall. She was last to the curtain wall and nearly inside when she heard something behind her. "Brigid, help me. Please."

She couldn't keep running afraid someone was injured, so she turned around to look. Sorcha was ahead of her, yelling, "Come on, Brigid."

"Just a minute. I'll be right there."

But she wouldn't.

Instead, she was struck in the head, and fell hard to the ground.

———— ◆ ————

Marcas felt as if he was about to heave in ten directions. Saving his castle was on his shoulders alone. It was up to him to see this done right. They must drive Clan Milton back.

He headed to the gates, barking orders, when Logan put a hand on his shoulder, making him walk through the gates and look at the number of Ramsay warriors coming their way. "If you have not much experience in battle, I would let Cailean and Kyle tell you what to do. They're experts, and our warriors have more experience than your men."

Marcas thought for just a second, saw Shaw give him a pleading nod, and said, "We'd be in your debt if you would lead the battle."

Logan moved over and spoke to Cailean and Kyle. Marcas went to their men of a dozen and said, "Ramsay warriors will take the lead. Alvery, I want you on the curtain wall. Torcall, take our men and join Kyle, he'll give instructions."

Logan came back and said, "'Tis your castle. You should be with Kyle and Cailean. You can follow their actions." Then he pointed to the wall. "I'll be up there watching for you. Don't move until my archers have had their chance to take the leads out. Wait for my word."

Marcas looked to both brothers and said, "Shaw and I will go. Ethan will be on the curtain wall with you." He took his mount from Timm, whose eyes were so wide he thought the poor lad might collapse. "'Twill be fine, Timm. You and your da will be fine."

"And you, too, my laird?" The lad teared up, gazing up at Marcas as he mounted.

Marcas often forgot the innocence of youth. "We have the Ramsays here to help us. You may not have noticed, but they have some of the best archers in all the land."

"Lady Brigid is a fine archer. I've seen her. Godspeed with you." Then he ran back to the stables to help the others to saddle and get the horses ready for battle. The strain in the air was palpable, more from his men than the Ramsay men. Some of them looked outright giddy over the promise of battle. The Ramsay clan had experience his men did not.

Once he mounted, Marcas made his way to the front of the curtain wall, heading toward Clan Milton, when he stopped, the sight of the beauty in the trees paralyzing him. Brigid's hair plaited, her form in tunic and leggings, and her bow at the ready, she looked like the most powerful warrior queen in all the land.

A voice called out to him, "Matheson, get her out of your head or you'll die."

He spun his head around, surprised to see Logan Ramsay on the curtain wall staring at him. Cailean drew up on one side of him and Kyle on the other. Kyle said, "He speaks the truth. Emotion doesn't belong in you right now. You need to protect all your clan, not just Brigid."

Hell, when had he become so obvious?

Cailean winked at him with a wide grin on his face, then turned in the direction of the approaching horses, patting his own horse's neck to ready him for battle, if Marcas were to guess. How did one ready a horse for battle?

They'd barely had five minutes to prepare before the Milton war whoop carried to them. Marcas set his horse in the right direction with Shaw next to him, ready to attack. At the last minute, he thought to look at Logan, standing tall and shaking his head not yet.

Then Marcas saw why. There in the trees were

the rest of the Ramsay archers, something he
hadn't noticed because he couldn't tear his gaze
from Brigid. It was a most unusual view because
most of them were female. But his gaze traveled
back to Brigid, moving with a fluidity he'd never
seen, firing her arrows one after the other as
though they were connected. Merewen was in
the next tree and did the same with so much
grace it astounded him. Their arrows took out a
dozen men before Clan Milton knew what hit
them.

And the one who fired fastest was Gwyneth
Ramsay. She missed one, but her other arrows all
found targets. Brigid's arrows had also all found
a target.

Logan bellowed to him, "Now! Attack!"

The brothers responded with the Matheson
war whoop and charged at the remainder of the
Miltons, clearly not skilled with their swords on
horseback. Marcas had made a point to train their
men many times on horseback, and it paid off.

The clash of blade against blade rang out over
Black Isle, men yelling as they were knocked from
their mounts, some trampled by horses, others
gaining their feet and retreating. Milton warriors
continued to fight on the ground, attempting to
slice the men on horseback, but they failed, some
taking a sword instead. Marcas was unaccustomed
to the sounds of screams and death, and he prayed
he'd never hear them again.

The Milton second-in-command was in
the back of his men, and his voice rang out,
"Retreat! Retreat!" The Ramsay warriors came

in, unwilling to let the Miltons disappear so easily, though their power with the sword had sent the Miltons running faster than they'd expected.

The battle was over in a matter of minutes.

Cailean had taken out two men with a ferocity Marcas had never seen, and the men behind his targets had turned their horses around and ran. Marcas had taken two men off their horses before he noticed the others retreating, so he'd turned around. It was clear why they'd retreated so quickly.

The Ramsay warriors combined with their paltry numbers made their cavalry look as if they numbered three or four score to Clan Milton's two score.

Clan Milton didn't stand a chance, and they knew it. Word would travel around Black Isle that they had help. They'd not be bothered again once it was known the Ramsay warriors supported the Mathesons.

Marcas searched the trees, looking for Brigid, but the archers had all dropped down and were making their way to the curtain wall. The crew on horseback began to celebrate, whooping and cheering their success, but Marcas couldn't join them until he saw Brigid.

Gwyneth was first, then Merewen, Sorcha, and Gavin, but—where the hell was Brigid? Seconds later, he knew something was wrong. The archers were looking for her, too.

"Brigid?"

That bellow caught Logan's attention and he barked up to his wife. "Gwynie, where's Brigid?"

"She was behind Sorcha. I don't know. I'll go look."

Marcas's heart raced as though it were to burst from his chest. He bolted off his horse and ran around the curtain wall, into the forest where the archers had been, searching for any sign of her. "Brigid!"

The worst thought he'd had in a long time took hold of him, and he couldn't shake it. Yet it came on so powerfully his hands started to tremble as he searched for footprints, horse tracks, anything.

Logan and Gwyneth searched with him. "What the hell, Gwynie? Did no one see anything?"

"Someone called out to her, it was someone she knew," Sorcha said. "She said she'd be right back."

In his heart, he knew what had happened. This was a ruse. A ruse to steal Brigid away since they'd gained Kara back.

Someone was out for him.

CHAPTER TWENTY-THREE

———————◆·———————

W HEN BRIGID AWAKENED, her belly threatened to heave again. It hadn't been that long since she'd been ill, and her appetite hadn't yet entirely returned. Then she understood why.

She was in a boat, with the smell of salty seawater carrying through the air to her. The rocking of the small vessel in the water did not help her nausea at all. The boat was barely large enough for the two of them, so where could they be heading in such a small vessel?

Setting her hands underneath her, she pushed herself to a sitting position, staring at the back of the man who'd taken her, his oars roaring furiously as they headed away from shore and toward the middle of the firth.

To the mudflats.

"Morris? What the hell are you doing with me? Where are you taking me?"

He stopped his rowing, turning the boat around so he could look at the shore they'd just left. Then he turned around to face her. "I'm getting what I rightly deserve."

"Morris, you've gone daft."

"Stop calling me that. The name is Hamon, Hamon Dingwall, and I've wasted so much time and energy to get what I want that I have nearly lost my mind, but I'm far from daft."

Hamon. She'd hadn't heard that name before. Her head pained her too much to have to think so hard. Her hand moved up to the bump in her scalp. Hellfire, what a headache she had now.

"What time and energy? And why did you lie to me about your name?" She rubbed her temple, turning her head away from the sun, though there were plenty of clouds to keep them shaded. The slight mist was definitely thicker near the shore, possibly hiding view of the boat from anyone who might be searching for her.

Like Marcas.

"You want the truth? Fine. I'll tell you because you cannot hurt me anymore. I loved Freda. I begged her not to marry Marcas, but her sire forced the match. Freda promised me two years. She'd give him a son and then leave him. We had plans to run away, to live in Inverness or in the woods somewhere no one could find us."

His anger seemed to abate as he stared over the water toward the mouth of the firth.

"'Twas two years, three years, then four. Finally, she gave him Tiernay, and she said she'd leave him. But then she didn't, said she'd wait another six moons before she'd leave. So I decided to rush the process a bit." He paused and turned to her, smiling. "You nearly caught me that day, but you were too dense to understand what I was doing."

"What are you talking about?"

"The well. I put soured goat's milk in it every time I passed by. I became a messenger for a few clans so no one would know me as Freda's lover. I had to see exactly how she was with Marcas. It was the only way, and when I saw them together, I just couldn't wait any longer." The sadness and regret on his face surprised her. He truly must have loved Freda. "I did what I had to do. She was mine, and I wanted her back. I tried to convince her to come away, but she had some reason she wanted to postpone leaving."

"I thought she told Marcas she was leaving him. That her sire was coming to smooth things over with Marcas's sire. Why couldn't you wait a wee bit longer?" She couldn't believe he'd made such a rash decision when Freda had planned to leave Marcas for good.

"It was the bairns. She wouldn't leave them both behind. Her hope was to convince him to allow Kara to go with her. She'd given him the son he needed, the heir she'd promised her sire to give him, but she wanted Kara. I was tired of waiting. I figured I'd get rid of the entire clan. I warned Freda. I told her what I was doing, but she didn't believe me. Then she got sick. I came to her; I begged her to stop drinking the water, but apparently, I'd put too much bad goat's milk in that time. Everyone began to die." He turned again to stare up across the firth. "Her husband's parents died, and I feared she'd be next. I tried to help her, but others got sick and died. I didn't know what else to do, so I left. And when she passed, I felt my heart was rent in two."

Then he swung his fist in the air. "It was all Matheson's fault. Then I kept throwing the bad milk in the well. I wanted him to die! He deserved it! Then I could take Kara and Tiernay and raise them as my own." His next words came out in an injured howl. "They're all I have left of my dearest Freda!"

He slapped the side of his head. "I could see my sorrow was my fault. I took Kara away and should have gone home. Why couldn't I be satisfied with just Freda's daughter? I could have watched her grow up to look just like my dear love, but nay. I wanted him dead.

"He deserved to die!" Hamon slapped his head again. "So I kept throwing sour, tainted milk into the well, expecting him to get sick, but he never did. And the Ramsays came along and ruined everything and stole Kara back. I was sickened." He closed his eyes and hung his head.

She leaned back, shocked at all she'd learned. Hamon had caused everything. This one man had murdered many over a simple jealousy. "How could you? How could you kill so many innocent people?"

His head shot up and his voice came out in a bellow. "Because I had to!"

Then he grabbed her by the hair, pulling her back to him. "But then, I learned of you. I see the way he looks at you. I've been hiding in the trees, watching his every move. I saw you in the woods with him, kissing him. He wants you, so I took you instead. It would have been easier if you would have agreed to meet me for an evening stroll, but you refused. Then I heard Clan Milton was going to attack. That was perfect. I took advantage of the situation."

"So what will you do with me?" The sinking feeling in her gut told her whatever he answered would not be good.

He chuckled. "You see, Freda told me how much Marcas hates swimming, especially where the firth is thick with weeds. I need not worry about him swimming out here to save you. He's too afraid. I'll make a trade with him. When I see them searching later this eve, I'll row closer and ask for an exchange."

"What exchange?"

"You for Kara. He'll pick you. And then I'll have a part of Freda forever."

Another sudden urge to heave overtook her. She didn't know how to tell Hamon that Marcas wouldn't pick her. Given the impossible choice, he'd choose the only one possible.

He'd keep Kara, because it was the right thing to do. If she knew anything of Marcas, it was that he was honorable and loved his bairns.

———— ♦ ————

The group assembled in the hall, everyone telling their version of the last time they saw Brigid. Gwyneth and Logan argued while their offspring and their spouses whispered a distance away from them.

In the keep's chaos, Ethan looked at Marcas desperately and said, "I'm going to the stables,

Chief. If you need me, send Shaw and I'll return." Then he scowled at the floor and muttered, "And I hope 'twill be quieter then."

Marcas's patience was wearing thin. They'd been caught up in the battle and not been careful enough. He should have insisted she stay inside the wall. Why the hell had they gone outside?

Shaw whispered to him, "There's no point in going back to determine where the mistake was made. You must figure out who would steal her. Who hates you enough to steal her away?"

"Why would anyone steal Brigid to get back at me? No one knew I was interested in her." He hadn't let anyone know how much she'd affected him. He'd made sure to keep his feelings a secret.

Shaw snorted. "Nay, no one saw the hungry eyes on you whenever the lass was around. If she'd have whistled, you'd have followed her like the last puppy in the litter."

Marcas scowled at Shaw but said nothing. Perhaps he hadn't been as successful at hiding his feelings as he'd thought.

After much rehashing and no solid ideas about who could have taken her, he got up to leave. Just then, the door opened, and Timm rushed in. "Chief, Ethan told me Brigid is missing. I was so busy with the horses I didn't know she was gone."

"Aye, someone stole her away, but we have no idea who would have done such a thing."

"But I have an idea."

"You do? Tell me, please." Logan and Gwyneth overheard him, and the entire hall quieted to listen to Timm, who quickly lost his courage to talk. "Go ahead, Timm," Marcas urged. "Tell me what you know."

"Well. Two times when Brigid was in the courtyard by herself, once when she was studying the well and the other time when she was practicing her archery—" He stopped and stared up at the ceiling. "—I think 'twas what she was doing. Or mayhap…"

"Timm. Get on with it."

Timm's eyes widened, but he continued, "She told me she met a man and wondered what clan he was from."

"What man?" Marcas had to keep himself calm because he knew Timm was about to give him the one clue he needed.

"She said his name was Morris, but I never saw him. She never said what he wanted either, but I chased to the top of the curtain wall the last time and saw this man leaving. He was alone."

"Who was it?"

"I'm not sure, but from the back, I think it was…" He paused, blushing and looking at everyone.

"Who?" Marcas was losing his patience.

Then Timm leaned over and whispered, "I think 'twas the man who would sneak in to see Freda. Hamon was his name."

Marcas was so stunned he couldn't speak. Had everyone known about Freda's indiscretion? Even the young lad? What would that fool want with Brigid? He didn't even know her.

Timm spun around and raced toward the door,

then stopped and ran back to Marcas. "Your pardon, Chief. May I take my leave?"

Marcas nodded. "Keep your eyes open, Timm. Good job."

Timm turned away, but then he stopped to face him again. "Oh, and I nearly forgot. I saw Hamon put a boat in the firth just after the battle when we were moving the dead."

Marcas ran over to Timm, lifted him, and tossed him up in the air with a loud whoop. "My thanks to you, Timm. Good work." He looked over at the Ramsay group and said, "I'm going to the firth."

CHAPTER TWENTY-FOUR

———— ♦ ————

BRIGID LOOKED OVER the water, just noticing the group gathering on the bank of the firth, not far from Clan Matheson. Fortunately, there was no wind. The voices carried quite clearly.

"I'm coming for you, Hamon!" Marcas bellowed, his voice carrying quite loudly across the water.

Brigid turned to see Hamon's reaction, and he smiled. "'Tis about time." Then he rowed a wee bit closer, she guessed to make sure they could converse easily enough. They were still at least ten boat lengths away when he stopped his forward progress. "The only way you'll get her back is if you bring Kara out to me. Fair exchange. A lass for a lass."

"My daughter? I'll not give you my daughter. I'll be in a boat and rowing your way to beat you daft, Dingwall."

"If you come out here without your daughter, I'll drown Brigid. You can watch her take her last breath."

The tide was starting to go out, but Brigid

had no idea how deep the water was here. True, she was a good swimmer, but she had no desire to swim in the cold water in her heavy wool clothing, and certainly not in the swampy area.

Creatures and eels and biting fish. Hellfire. She closed her eyes and said a quick prayer to be delivered safely into Marcas's arms.

She looked over the water, sparkling as the sun went down. Rays cast a sheen across the firth as if a last celebration before darkness descended. Then she caught action out of the corner of her eye. She squinted to get a better look, the sun playing tricks on her view. Marcas was getting in the boat without Kara. That was the best-case scenario in her mind. He could not put Kara in the boat because it was simply too risky. Hamon's reasoning had gone in the wrong direction. He was unpredictable and dangerous, especially with a toddler. How she prayed Marcas realized his best chance of saving her was using the archers. The distance was close enough to hit him, but once they moved back out, the distance could be too far.

Then something caught her. The man in the boat didn't look exactly like Marcas. She was unsure but continued to stare. Was it his brother? Or *was* it Marcas? Was it Ethan as a ruse? She said nothing, guessing Hamon didn't know the two well enough to notice the difference. But either way, since there was no lass in the boat, her doom would be upon her soon. She wouldn't drown. She knew how to fight and her sire would know how to get her away. He'd done it before, and he'd do it again.

She had absolute faith in her parents.

And Marcas. He wouldn't allow her to drown either. After all the tales she'd heard over the years—of Cailean saving Sorcha on the cliff, her uncle Quade saving her aunt by standing on his horse and using his bow, her father and mother saving Bethia with Donnan making the final move—now her heroic event was about to happen. Hamon was going to try to kill her, but Marcas wouldn't allow it.

Then her gut feeling changed as Brigid had a sudden inkling she would be going in the water soon.

Her luck had run out.

———— ◆ ————

Marcas turned to the other men—Shaw, Ethan, Logan, Gavin, and Cailean. "I have to go out there."

Ethan said, "He just said if you go out there alone, he'll drown her. You cannot go out alone."

Marcas looked at his brother and said, "I'm not going in the boat. You are. And you're going to row as slowly as you can to give me time to get ahead of you."

Shaw rubbed his jaw and looked at all the others. "What the hell are you planning, Marcas? We'll come up with something. We can find another boat and come at him from a different direction. Grab two boats and overpower him. The tide's going out. We'll have mud flats to walk on in another two hours, or mayhap sooner."

"I'm not waiting that long."

"What are you doing?"

"I'm swimming out to get her. Ethan can go in the boat—he looks enough like me to fool that man with the sun going down. I'll get in down the bank, swim through the swamp and get her out of his hands. Ramsay, I'm counting on you and your men to distract him with constant chatter. Your daughter tells me you're excellent at intimidating the enemy. Will you help me? I don't want Ethan to say a word. Shaw will go with me. Can you do that?"

Logan chuckled. "Chatter? Naught I love more than that. I'll have that bastard begging to go the other way. Cailean, go get the archers. We can take him out if he gets close enough. I want them hidden on shore or in the couple of trees near the bank."

"Wise choice," Marcas said, looking at the group. "I'll do my best to arrange him as a clear target." Cailean took off toward the keep. "Any questions?"

"Aye," Ethan said. "I have one. Marcas, you hate swimming in the swampy part of the firth."

Marcas sighed. Hell. His brother was absolutely right. "I know, Ethan. But have you a better idea? I'll do what I must."

Ethan looked at Marcas. "You love her. You wouldn't go otherwise."

Marcas looked at the Ramsay men, then back at Ethan before he spoke. No reason to lie at this point. "Aye. I love her. I hope she'll be my wife someday. But first, I need to get to her, and I'll not allow a bit of swamp to stop me." He wouldn't admit that his love was so strong he couldn't trust anyone else to go to her. It was more important he be there for her.

"Godspeed," Ethan said, climbing into the boat. "I promise to row slowly."

"Ethan, you must not look for me or he'll be on to us. You listen for sounds. And keep your back to him. We want him to think you are me."

"I promise, Marcas."

Marcas and Shaw strode back away from the bank toward the forest until they were well hidden in the dark. Then they made their way down the firth, making sure they were hidden by brush and tree cover, to a spot Marcas thought safest to enter the water. He said to Shaw. "Once I'm in, get another boat ready in case we fight."

"Will do, Chief."

Marcas looked at his brother oddly. "You never call me that. Why now?"

"Because you're acting like a chieftain, just like Da did. Godspeed with you. She's worth it. You deserve some happiness." He clasped his brother's shoulder, then walked away. "I'll get the boat, mayhap two. Torcall and Mundi are anxious to help you, also."

Marcas turned around and stared at the water, the weeds, the trees hanging over the bank, and the branches dipping low into the water. It was the only way. He knew it.

He tossed his plaid and tunic off to the side, removed his boots and wool hose, and stood there in just his trews. He could do this. He waded in.

Marcas had to will himself not to react to every brush of weed or a fish. He reminded himself the creatures were more afraid of him and would go the other way unless attacked. He vowed to let the weeds cling to his hair to help with his disguise. He couldn't have the bastard see him.

He loved Brigid with all his heart, and he would save her, no matter what.

A loud voice echoed over the water. "You dumb bastard, this is Brigid's father! Do you want to know what I plan to do when I finally get my hands on you? It won't be pretty to see, I can promise you that."

Marcas smiled and used the distraction to slip fully into the water, saying a quick prayer to be guided in the right direction. Then he heard a splash near the boat. When he was able to look, sure enough, the worst had happened.

Brigid was in the water. He watched long enough to make sure her head came back out and that Hamon wasn't attempting to drown her yet. His gut clenched until her head bobbed up and her hand firmly grasped the side of the boat. Brigid was strong and would fight Hamon. She had to know there were many trying to get to her.

He swam with his eyes above water, going at a slow easy stroke, turning his head to the side for air to keep his breathing as quiet as possible. Brigid grabbed the side of the boat and hung on.

Hang on tight, love, I'm coming for you.

Hamon said to her, "Who the hell is your sire, talking to me like that?"

"My sire was a spy for the Scottish Crown. So was my mother. My sister and her husband still are. And they're all trained archers." Her voice came out strong, challenging him, as if to dare him to think he could win. "They can kill with one arrow, right between your eyes, though that would kill you instantly, and I'd prefer to see you suffer more. An arrow in your arse would be better. Be careful." She snickered.

He couldn't have been more proud of her.

"She's telling the truth, you dumb piece of shite. My wife's favorite place to aim her arrow is at a man's bollocks. She pinned one to a tree for touching Brigid when she was young. Think you she'll let you go just because Brigid is older? You're a fool if you do. Brigid is her youngest, her wee bairn long ago, and she'll dig your eyes out to save her."

Marcas made a note to remember to thank the man for the entertainment that took his mind off the weeds he swam through, their waving tentacles teasing his feet. He thought he felt a tail of a fish or two, but they'd not hurt him.

"I don't see any archers around, old man. Say goodbye to your daughter. The water's cold and she'll not survive for long. If you want her back, you better get Kara and send her out in another boat. It looks to me that Marcas is alone. I'll hold your daughter's head underwater as soon as he's within a boat length of me and I can see for certain Kara isn't with him. He stole the love of my life from me. I want her daughter. Give her to me."

"You'll never live that long, you daft bastard."

Marcas swam and swam, listening to the banter between Ramsay and Dingwall. He'd have to tell Brigid how right she was about her sire. When he came closer to the boat, to his surprise he found the tide had gone out more than he'd thought, and he found a mudflat where he could set his feet down and still keep his head above water. He was about four boat lengths away, but he could see Brigid shivering and submerged to her neck. She held on to the boat with both hands.

Keeping his head low, he glanced around. After all, he'd fished in these waters his entire life, and he had an odd feeling that, even in the dark, he was near a group of boulders. He walked forward, praying he could find the boulders, because if nothing else, he could settle Brigid on one of the stronger ones and know she'd not go under. She wouldn't be able to swim far because she still wore all her clothes, including a mantle which would drag her under easily.

He had to find those boulders! A large, flat rock was usually the first to pop up as the tide went out, and since it spent more time out of the water than in, it held the least amount of slime on the top edge, making it less slippery than many of the rocks in the firth.

I'm coming, love.

The water was indeed chilly, the kind that went deep into the bones, but he ignored it. He saw movement in a tree on the bank, a body climbing up into it. He couldn't tell who, but the attack was imminent. If he could get a touch closer, he'd jump at Dingwall and knock him over the far side of the boat.

Weighing his options, he noticed that Ethan was getting closer. It was time to act.

He thought of the possibility of getting Brigid into the boat first. Then he decided that getting her to the rock and the mud flat was safer. It would give the archer a clearer shot of the fool, though the distance was a reach, especially in the dark, even with the sky nearly cloudless.

Marcas added a few weeds to his hair because he just noticed something he hadn't before. The mudflat was closer to the surface near the boat. He had one opportunity to catch the fool completely by surprise.

Out of the corner of his eye, he noticed Brigid finally saw him. He held his finger to his lips, then grabbed more seagrasses and hung them down over his face, finally making his decision.

He had to move fast. Dingwall reacted to something Ramsay said, and the fool made his biggest mistake. He stood up in the boat.

Marcas darted out of the water with a roar, his head covered with weeds, and climbed up on the mudflat, his arms out on both sides. Dingwall whirled around with a start, reaching for his dagger, but Marcas was faster. He threw himself across the water and knocked the bastard out of the boat, landing in the firth on the far side.

When Dingwall went under, Marcas reached for Brigid, grabbing her around the waist and swimming on his back, supporting her above him until his feet found purchase in the mud again.

He'd never been so happy to see anyone in his life. When he managed to stand, she threw her arms around his neck and whimpered, but he had to move her. Dingwall was coming toward him.

"Look, there's a boulder. Stand on it and it will keep you out of the water. It's flat." They scrambled to get her safe while others yelled at him. Ethan, Hamon, Ramsay—their voices bellowed across the water, but he understood nothing, so focused was he on getting Brigid to the rock. She was actually able to sit on it. "Can you hang on there?"

She nodded, her lips quivering from the cold, but she was a fighter. She'd make it. He gave her a quick kiss on the lips and spun around just in time to see Dingwall coming at him with a roar. Marcas stepped away from the boulder toward the mudflat so he could stand and get his bearings.

Ramsay yelled, "Where'd you go, you slimy bastard? I can't see you!"

Brigid whispered, "Square him. Papa's telling you to square him."

Marcas finally understood. He needed to make a target for the archers. He backed up until he found a rock he could stand on, and Dingwall rose out of the water, going for his neck. Marcas fought, giving all his strength to his legs, his arms wrapped around the man, trying to contain him, and then stood up, turning Dingwall's back to the bank. As if they planned it, Ethan lifted one of his oars in front of Dingwall's back, showing the archers where to shoot.

As soon as the arrows sluiced through the air,

their sound lighting up the night, Ethan dropped into his boat. Two arrows hit Hamon, one high and one low, but he froze, his gaze on Marcas. The man tried to grab onto him, and Marcas fought to push him into the water. Ethan came up on the mudflat and used his oar to shove Hamon off to the side, and he fell face first into the water.

"Well done, Ethan."

Marcas crawled over to Brigid, sitting next to her on the boulder and wrapping his arms around her. "You are hale?"

"I'm fine. Chilled to the bone, but I'll heal."

He kissed her forehead and said, "I love you, Brigid Ramsay. Marry me. Please say you'll be my wife. I don't want to ever lose you."

She giggled, the sound carrying across the water. When she could, she said, "Aye, I'll marry you, Marcas Matheson. Especially because you make a verra scary swamp monster."

Ethan pointed to the bank. "Your father has a fire going. Get in the boat and get her warm," he said. "Shaw is coming in another boat and we'll bring him in."

"Come, my sweet swamp maiden. Let's go to shore."

They rode back, Ethan and Shaw directly behind them with Dingwall face down in the boat being towed by Marcas's brothers.

Marcas had to laugh and be honest. "You're right, your sire is an expert at taunting men. I had to force myself to ignore him. I only pray he'll welcome my offer and not treat me the same."

Brigid laughed, sitting in front of him while he

rowed back to shore, cheers and applause carrying out to them. Cailean pulled them in, and Marcas lifted her out and set her on a log next to the fire. "You need to stop your shivering. I'm going to peel the weeds from myself and find something to warm you."

Torcall had brought his clothing, and Marcas found his plaid and wrapped it over Brigid's trembling shoulders. "We'll get you inside soon."

"I'm fine by the fire. 'Tis drying me a bit and it feels wonderful. Do what you must."

Marcas strode over to Logan, pulling weeds from his hair and tossing them to the ground as he approached the old warrior. "You did a fine job taunting the man. He was nearly daft because he wanted to beat you silly."

"Didn't touch me either." Then Logan clasped his shoulder and quietly said, "My thanks for saving Brigie. She'll always be my wee lassie."

Marcas swore he saw tears in the old man's eyes. "I love her. 'Tis all I'll say for now."

"Good, because I wish to see which one of my archers got the bastard." Ethan and Shaw jumped out of their boat, pulling it up on shore, while Cailean took the tow rope from Ethan's and pulled that boat up next.

"I believe he's dead," Cailean announced. Dingwall was turned on his side. Logan moved to close his eyes, then rolled him onto his belly, looking at the arrows in his hide. He burst into laughter.

"What, Papa?" Brigid yelled.

"Logan, what the hell?" Gwynie shouted. "Out

with it."

When he could finally control his laughter, he turned to Sorcha and said, "You are indeed your mother's daughter, lass. Nice job."

"I am? Did I hit him? Was it my arrow that stopped him? Where did I hit him?" She hurried to the boat, but her father's next comment stopped her in her tracks.

"Merewen got him in his flank, probably the one that killed him, but you caught him best, Sorcha. I'm proud of you."

"Where, Papa? Cailean won't let me near."

"Right in his arse, lass."

The group burst into laughter and applauded.

"Well done, daughter," Gwynie said, hugging Sorcha.

CHAPTER TWENTY-FIVE

———————◆———————

BRIGID SAT NEAR the hearth early the next
morning, still wrapped up in plaids and furs.
What little she recalled of last night made her
smile. The best part had been sitting by the fire
after she'd finally made it out of the firth. The
heat of the flames had warmed her almost as
much as the love of all those around her. Her
gaze had followed the sparks flying in the wind,
making the night seem magical.

It had been magical. Marcas had saved her, her
family was there to support her, yet moments
before in the cold of the firth, she had feared the
worst. A log dropped and shot off another slew of
sparks into the air as if agreeing with her.

She'd been fussed over by all her family and
Marcas's clan, too, the heat of the fire warming
her enough to stop her shivering outside. Once
by the hearth in the keep, she'd fallen asleep in
her chair and couldn't recall a thing afterward.

Her mother and Merewen joined her just as
Marcas came inside, her sire behind him. "You're
awake," her sire said. "We wish to hear all the
bastard told you."

Tara and Jennet hurried down the staircase just in time, grabbing a goblet of warm barley broth and pulling stools over to join the group. Gisela entered from the kitchens, a loaf of fresh bread in her hand.

Marcas came over, kissed Brigid's cheek, and asked, "You are better? You wouldn't stop shivering last eve."

"I am fine, though still a bit chilled," she admitted. "But I do have much to tell you. I hadn't had the energy to sort it out in my mind last eve, but I laid in bed this morn for nearly an hour thinking on all he'd confessed."

"Confessed?" Marcas asked, his brow arching as he pulled a chair next to hers. "Please do tell."

Once everyone settled, she addressed her comments to Marcas. "He did everything."

Shaw and Ethan came in the door just then. "Who did everything?"

The group quieted as they awaited her answer.

"Shall I tell everyone about your wife? 'Tis an important part of this. Hamon told me about Freda."

Marcas rubbed the stubble on his jaw. "Go ahead. There are not many of us left, and I consider you all family."

Brigid turned her comments to the group. "Marcas's wife Freda was in love with Hamon Dingwall. He was the man who told me he was Morris as he approached me in the courtyard. No one else ever saw him. When I first met him, he was leaning over the well, and I hadn't thought of the connection. He told me he'd stopped for refreshment."

She turned back to face Marcas. "She had promised to leave you after she gave you a son, so Hamon became excited once she had Tiernay, thinking she would leave you right away, but she wasn't fast enough for him. He had begged Freda to leave you and come home but she'd stalled. So he wished to do more damage by trying to kill you, Marcas. He apparently had warned Freda that he was going to throw soured goat's milk into the well, but she didn't believe him."

The admission brought gasps from both Jennet and Tara, something Brigid expected, and she turned back to the group. "This was a new concept to him. When he threw the soured milk into the well, he'd hoped to sicken a few, but he didn't expect to hear how many took ill. Then Freda was angry with him because your parents were ill. Then, of course, she also became ill."

Brigid allowed this to sink in for a few moments, taking a few sips of the warm barley broth again. The chill from the firth still sat deep in her bones.

Ethan spoke up, his arms out wide as if he couldn't quite absorb the issue. "This? All of our deaths, losing our parents, the misfortune of our numerous clan members was all because of Freda's relationship with another man? This was all because of jealousy?"

Brigid nodded, then reached for Marcas's hand, squeezing it. "None of this was your fault, Marcas. None. He stole Kara away from Gisela while she slept because Freda had given him a key to enter the door at the wall. He wanted something of

Freda's to keep forever."

"He wanted our daughter?" Marcas asked, letting go of Brigid's hand and standing to pace. After two passes, he stopped and said, "So why take you out in the boat?"

This would be difficult for him to hear, but he needed the truth. "He took me because he saw your interest in me. He climbed the trees often and watched from there. He saw us when we walked outside the gates and when you kissed me."

"He kissed you?" her father roared.

She was about to say something, but her mother was quicker. "Oh, Logan. Stop. Your wee bairn is a young woman and you have to let her go. Living on Ramsay land was not going to find her a husband. There's only one MacAdam."

Her father crossed his arms and grumbled just as Sorcha and Cailean joined them.

"But the boat?" Marcas persisted.

"He took me out into the firth because Freda told him how you hated the firth and swimming in the weeds. He thought you'd never try to swim out to the boat. And he never realized Ethan wasn't you until you jumped out of the water like a swamp monster. He nearly fell out of the boat then."

The group broke into separate conversations about all that had happened just as Nonie came with a platter of porridge servings. Edda came in behind her carrying Tiernay, her belly larger and larger.

Jennet asked, "When is your time, Edda?"

She shrugged her shoulders. "I do not know. I've not seen a healer but I am worrying a wee bit."

"Why?"

"Because I'm having pains in my belly. Mama says I could be going soon. Should that mean anything?" She rubbed her hands across the broad expanse of her belly, as if she could stop whatever was taking place inside.

Jennet stared at Brigid wide-eyed, a look that told Brigid her dearest cousin was frustrated at others' ignorance about what happened inside their bodies. Carrying a child was something that lasted for so many moons that women had a remarkable chance to become curious about the process, but apparently such knowledge didn't interest Edda.

Brigid said, "Come, sit down next to me, Edda. Tiernay can sit and chew on a piece of bread."

Edda sat down, then clutched her belly.

"A pain?" Tara asked, drawing closer.

"Aye," Edda said through clenched teeth. "I hope it does not get any worse or I don't wish to have this bairn."

Jennet spun around and headed to the kitchens while Brigid patted the lass's knee. "We'll help you get through it. Perhaps you should allow us to check you over now."

Jinny came barreling out of the kitchen, one word spewing from her lips. "Aye! Please check her. Do something."

Edda noticed her mother's expression of one who was about to burst into tears. Jinny was normally in control of her emotions. A big moment must be approaching.

Edda just nodded, grabbing her belly as she was consumed with another pain.

———————◆———————

Marcas sat on a large boulder, not far from the gravesite where his parents had been laid to rest. He shook his head as if someone were watching him. He'd come out here for a reason.

He had to speak to his father.

The freshly dug graves had been marked with the largest handmade crosses, meant to mark the grave of the Matheson lairds and their family. Marcas's father was laid not far from his father, who was laid near his father before him.

"Papa, I'm so sorry. I still am reeling from hearing the truth about Freda, about how she wished to leave me for another, and how because she didn't move quickly, her beloved poisoned you and most of our clan. It sickens me to know how much this is my fault."

Shaw's voice carried to him from a distance. "Hellfire, how can you say such a thing?" Gisela was directly behind him.

Marcus turned to his siblings. "If I'd been able to earn Freda's love, mayhap this would not have happened. But I did not meet her needs, so she sought love elsewhere."

Gisela said, "Marcas, please stop berating yourself for something that had nothing to do with you. If Papa were here, he'd tell you it was his fault for forcing you to marry Freda."

"I could have refused him," Marcas mumbled.

Shaw countered, "Nay, you never refused our sire. None of this was your fault."

"How can you say that? She was my wife." Marcas stood, his hands on his hips.

"Because she didn't suit you," Gisela said. "That kind of reasoning could be used to blame me, too. I should have said something to you. Freda was a phony. I hated her for you. She was a liar and spoiled and so many other things I don't need to say now but should have said before. The truth is you deserved someone better than Freda."

Shaw nodded his head in agreement. "You couldn't force someone to love you when she only loved herself. It was a poor match. Even Papa knew it."

"What?" Marcas turned to look at the gravesite as if his sire could answer. "Da? Is Shaw telling the truth?"

Gisela moved close to her brother and looped her arm through his. "Mama knew it, too." She stared up at the trees overhead, sighed, and said, "She told me that Freda had loved another, but Freda's mother had told her to forget about Hamon, though she never gave me his name. But she never did."

"You and Mama spoke of this without saying anything to me?" He couldn't believe all he'd heard in the last day. Everyone had known about Freda and her lover. They'd likely known it before he had. He felt like such a fool.

"Aye," Gisela replied haughtily. "I hated the way that bitch treated you. I went to Mama after Kara was born. I was afraid the wee lassie would act like her mother. Freda wanted everyone to wait on her and was rarely kind to you. She wouldn't even nurse her own bairns. She had the healer find someone to nurse them when you were not around."

Marcas was so stunned that he sat back down on the boulder. "She didn't put our bairns to her own breast?"

"Nay. Ellice found other new mothers to nurse the bairns. Well, she did for a bit. Then with Tiernay, when the other woman's milk dried up, she gave him goat's milk and water from the well. He might never have sickened if he'd only drank his mother's milk."

Shaw added, "Papa knew he'd made a mistake. He went to Freda's sire about the match and was reminded she'd promised to deliver you one son. So she did. But who knew all the rest that would follow? 'Twas a sad situation, but the guilty parties are all dead. I don't see what can be done about it."

Gisela smirked and said, "I do."

"What?" Marcas asked, lifting his head.

"Marry Brigid. You two make a wonderful couple. I hope you ask her to be your wife."

"And I hope she accepts," Shaw added.

Marcas chuckled. "I did, and she has. Now I just need to speak with her sire."

Shaw took two steps backward, holding his palms up to his brother. "I'll not help you with that."

CHAPTER TWENTY-SIX

———— ◆ ————

B RIGID SAT ON a stool at the head of the bed while Jennet and Tara checked Edda's progress. Nonie and Jinny had set the chamber up for them as soon as Tara had reported Edda would be having her bairn soon.

Brigid had to admit she was a wee bit excited. She loved delivering new life into the world. She'd gone so many times with Aunt Brenna that she could probably do a birth easily enough on her own. The joy that came to all when that wee bairn finally took its first breath was still something that brought tears to her eyes.

Would she ever have a child of her own?

Brigid and Jennet had assisted Jennet's mother ever since they were around five or six summers. Curiosity had been the original reason for Brigid, though she was also interested in following her cousin. She'd always trailed behind Jennet, her best friend, her elder by a year, but Brigid had learned a long time ago that her mind was not the same as Jennet's. Her mother often old her, "Brigid, you have your own talents. 'Tis up to you to find them. They're there. Do what *you* wish to do."

At first, she thought she'd be willing to stitch skin or stare into peoples' insides like Jennet, but she hadn't found it interesting for long. Brigid preferred to help deliver babies or take care of wee bairns.

Tara did her examination, then covered Edda with a plaid again before she made her announcement to everyone in the chamber. "Edda, you'll be delivering your wee bairn within a day, I believe. We must make sure we have all we'll need for this momentous occasion."

Brigid stood, but Jennet held her hand out to her. "Brigid, you must be exhausted still. I'll do the running. You stay here with her." Then she leaned over to whisper in her ear. "You've always been better at delivering bairns than me."

Brigid sat back to stare at her cousin. When had she ever been told she was better at anything than Jennet?

Jennet chuckled, a rare sound. "You don't believe me? Of course you are. You know I've never liked this part of healing. But I do what I must. You? You're so much better at calming women and motivating them to go through this ritual with the best outlook. You have the knack of guiding them through a difficult phase when most women wish to give up. 'Tis a rare and useful skill I don't have."

"I do?" Brigid whispered, never having considered what Jennet had just told her. She'd known she enjoyed being with women in this special stage, but she'd never once imagined herself as talented at it.

Then her dear cousin did something most uncharacteristic. She snorted.

What the hell did that mean?

"I just don't have the patience, and you do," Jennet said. "I'd prefer to shake them until the bairn popped out of them." Then, she laughed at her own jest again, and left.

Tara looked at Brigid and said, "I've not seen Jennet jest like that. She must be serious. Yet her confidence says much about you. Care to join me?" She glanced over at Edda who had fallen asleep, then pointed to another stool at the end of the bed.

"All right. I'll wash up and don a different gown. I do feel much better."

"Good," Tara said. "Because I don't think Jennet will be back, and I could use an extra set of hands."

Tara was right.

———————◆———————

Marcas had postponed the one thing he needed to do for long enough. When he saw Brigid's father exiting the stables, he headed straight for him. "My lord, may I have a word with you in my solar?"

Logan narrowed his gaze at the man, but then nodded slowly.

Marcas wouldn't be so easily intimidated. He could see the old warrior had practiced this "look" he gave anyone he wished to intimidate.

Not this day.

"Edda is nearing her time. I heard the three healers are with her, and I am most grateful," Marcas said, doing his best to find a topic that wouldn't inspire any harsh words from the man. He held the door open for him as they stepped inside the keep and moved into the great hall.

Jennet was busy giving orders to Nonie, Sorcha, and Merewen to help while Jinny stood by and persisted. "Nay, give me something to do, please. I'll not be able to wait with naught to do." Jennet also gave her a few tasks, then moved on.

Marcas called out, "The bairn is near, Jinny?"

"Aye, mayhap by the morrow, they say." Her face brightened, but she rubbed her hands together in front of her before running them down her gown. "I have chores, laird. The stew is simmering and the bread is made, but we must prepare for my first grandbairn. Please excuse me, but I must move on." She grinned and went on her way toward the kitchens.

New life was coming to Clan Matheson. Marcas had to admit he was overjoyed. He prayed the bairn arrived safely, or they'd be accused of still having a curse upon them. He led the way to his solar with Logan behind him, but as he stopped to open the door for the man, a loud voice interrupted and a body charged at them.

"Nay, you'll not. Not without me, Logan Ramsay." Gwyneth flew across the great hall as though she were no more than ten summers old.

Marcas held the door for her, instead, and she pushed ahead of both of them. Logan smirked. "My wife never misses anything." Then he winked at Marcas.

He wasn't quite sure what to make of the whole spectacle, of the woman insisting she be involved in a discussion between men, or the fact that her husband allowed it, or the wink. But he took the seat on the far side of the table and held his hand to indicate they were to take the two seats across from him.

Gwyneth was already seated. "So why are we here, Marcas?" The woman got right to the point.

Marcas figured this was a good thing. They had to suspect why he called Logan inside his solar and no one else, not even his brothers. That told him they'd be agreeable, for sure.

Or so he hoped. If he were lucky, one of them would be on his side.

"I'm sure you've both seen that I've become fond of your daughter," Marcas started. "I hope you've had the chance to ask her about her feelings for me. I find I am willing to offer to make her my wife. I'm asking you for her hand in marriage and…"

"Nay." Logan gave his answer and got up out of his seat, heading toward the door.

Gwyneth said, "Aye, I give you my permission. Forget him."

Logan whirled around so quickly his plaid lofted into the air. "Gwynie, do not cross me on this. She's not ready."

Gwyneth bolted out of her chair and crossed her arms to face her husband. Marcas had to admit he'd never seen another woman challenge her husband as this woman was about to do.

"Logan, there isn't enough time in the world for *you* to be ready, and that is who is truly not ready. I'd prefer to still be alive to see our daughter married. Fuss over Beatris and help find Simone a husband from your own list, but Brigid has found hers. Give your approval so we can stay for the wedding."

"Gwynie, have you lost your mind? Why would you want Brigid to marry someone who lives so far away? We'll never see her. I'll find someone for her to marry on Ramsay land. I know you've told me before it is time for her to find someone, and I'll admit my fault in this. I was loathe to admit she is of age. Now I see my mistake. We'll go home and find someone for her."

"Nay," Gwyneth insisted. Her pursed lips told Marcas it was time for him to speak up.

"With all due respect, my lord…" Marcas said.

"Stop calling me that. I'm not your lord." Logan shook his head. "See, Gwynie. He's daft."

"He's being polite, showing you respect. I wouldn't. I'd tell you to kiss my arse." The glare was a mighty powerful one, and Marcas had to wonder if Brigid could do the same.

He hoped not.

Logan grinned and said, "Wife, you know 'tis one of my favorite things to do. Why would you tell me that? Bend over and I'll kiss it right this moment. That won't make me change my mind."

Marcas's jaw nearly dropped to the floor, but he kept himself under control. "I'm not here to cause an argument," he said to the two of them. "Please sit down."

They both sat after glaring at each other. Then he continued, once he finally had their attention. "I love your daughter. I think you should ask her what she wants."

"Doesn't matter," Logan said. "Still too soon."

"The hell it doesn't matter, Logan. I thought you'd be better about this daughter marrying." Gwyneth tugged on her plait, swirling the end of it in circles, something Marcas had noticed her do before in a moment of tension.

"I never had problems with the other marriages."

Gwyneth let out a low growl. "You didn't want our other daughters married either."

Logan refused to look her in the eye. "There have been a few problems. But not with Maggie."

"You made Will promise to marry her before you'd allow him to steal her out of prison." The woman slapped her hands down on her thighs with such vigor, he wondered if she would hit anything else soon.

Marcas did his best not to arch his brow at this revelation, a story he hadn't heard yet, but about which he'd be sure to ask.

Gwyneth continued, explaining to Marcas, "Will was going to spend the night with her. He had to take her away from Edinburgh, and we couldn't be the ones to do so because the king would come after us."

Logan crossed his arms, getting defensive over her words, but he said nothing, allowing his wife to give the explanation.

Gwyneth's attention reverted to her husband, the look on her face telling everyone she wasn't happy. "Clearly it was the only way you'd get anyone to save her, Logan. No one else could have done so but Will. If he hadn't stolen her away and spent the night with her in a cave, they both would have had their heads in a noose before dawn. It was the only way to keep her alive."

"So I paid the ultimate price."

"And do you regret it?" Her tone softened a wee bit.

"Nay, he's a good man." His voice came out in a low grumble, but he still wouldn't look her in the eye.

"And we had to tie you up before Cailean could take Sorcha away from the wedding. I'll not go through that again, Logan Ramsay. Agree to this marriage, or you'll be single again."

Logan snorted. "Gwynie, you don't mean that."

Her voice rose again. "Well, if you ever wish to kiss my arse again, you'll agree to this wedding."

Marcas fought the urge to run from this extremely private conversation. He didn't know if he'd ever be able to repeat it to anyone.

Logan finally turned to look at his wife, and Marcas saw a raw vulnerability there he hadn't seen before. This man adored Brigid as he did all his bairns.

"He's a good man, Logan," she said, her voice quieting.

Marcas thought it a perfect time to speak up. "I promise to protect her with my life. Do you doubt that?"

"Nay, I know you will. You already proved that point out in the firth."

"I promise we'll visit Ramsay land twice a year," Marcas offered. He noticed Gwyneth smile at that. "And you're welcome on Black Isle anytime."

Logan gave the loudest sigh he'd ever heard, but then said, "I'll give my approval. But you must visit twice a year, and we will be here to visit often."

"You're welcome to move here, if you like."

Gwyneth bolted out of her seat and said, "Nay! Do not tell him that!"

Logan grinned, pushed back his chair, and exited the room.

What the hell did that mean?

CHAPTER TWENTY-SEVEN

———— • ————

B RIGID AND TARA stared at each other, the sweat visible on Tara's forehead as Brigid's own trickled between her breasts. She wiped both their brows, then turned to Nonie. "Please find Jennet and tell her she's needed right away." The birth was proving to be more difficult than they'd expected, and difficult births often had disastrous outcomes.

Edda wailed, leaning forward with another push that would undoubtedly leave her with no resolution. She pushed and pushed with all her might, her arms laced around her own knees as leverage, but the bairn was not coming out. Jinny sat next to her daughter, mopping her brow and giving her encouraging words as she tried to complete the nearly impossible feat of allowing a baby to descend from her private parts.

When the urge stopped, Edda fell back onto the bed and whimpered, "What's wrong? Why won't this bairn leave me? I cannot do this much longer."

Brigid leaned forward and reached for Edda's hand. "The bairn isn't turned in the right position."

"What does that mean?" the poor woman asked, huffing and puffing from the hard work she'd been doing.

The door opened, and Jennet entered, quickly finding another stool at the end of the bed. Nearby were clean linens to catch the bairn once it was born and took its first breath.

"What's wrong?" Jennet whispered.

"'Tis what we just asked," Jinny explained, gripping her daughter's hands tightly. "There must be something you can do."

Brigid continued in her most soothing tone. "There is. With Jennet here, she and Tara are going to push on Edda's belly at every spasm, or when she feels the need to push. Bairns are supposed to have their heads come out first. This wee one has her bottom down first, and 'tis a difficult position."

"So you'll push it out of me? Won't that hurt more?" Edda looked from one face to the next, hoping for good news, or any news to end this arduous process.

Brigid patted the top of her foot. "Nay, I don't think you'll feel the difference. What we have to do is shift the bairn, turn it so the head or the feet come out first. We hope it will be the head, but if it's the feet, we can attend to that, too."

"Have you done this before?"

Tara said, "I haven't but they have. Aunt Brenna has repositioned bairns many times."

Jennet and Tara moved to lean over Edda's belly. Brigid glanced at Jennet to give her encouragement. The one time her dearest cousin struggled was when a patient was awake and screaming. She couldn't handle the extra pressure of it. Jennet preferred her patients asleep or at least with a bit of ale in their bellies.

Aunt Jennie had had some special powder the monks had brought back for her to use to help ease a patient's pain, but the girls knew to never use it during delivery of a bairn. They needed the mother's assistance, or the birth wouldn't work.

"Tell us right before you feel the gripping in your belly, and you can push from the inside while Jennet and Tara push outside."

Brigid palpated Edda's belly. "I'm sorry if this hurts, but I'm trying to determine the bairn's exact position.

"It does not hurt," Edda said with a sniffle.

"I think this is the head," she said, showing Tara with her hands. "So we must try to ease it down. Or if it doesn't move all the way, we'll have to try feet first. I'll reach inside when she has the contraction and try to locate an appendage."

Foot would be better than hands, she thought.

They had done this before on three occasions, but always with Aunt Brenna's expert guidance. On one occasion, the baby came out head-first after a great amount of manipulation; on the second, the bairn was born feet first. But on the third occasion, both mother and bairn died.

Aunt Brenna had cried that she'd wished to just cut the woman's belly and pull the bairn out, but she knew it was too risky.

Brigid knew what else was at stake here. If the

bairn wasn't born safely, the curse on Black Isle would seem to continue.

"I feel one coming!" Edda leaned forward to push while Jennet pushed in one direction and Tara pushed the other way, the two movements together meant to rotate the bairn in the womb. They were trying to turn the baby as if it were a wheel. Edda grunted and groaned with all her might, but nothing happened.

Jennet asked, "Could you see anything, Brigid? Any feet? Hair?"

She'd looked as close as she dared holding the candle to light the area, but Brigid had seen neither. Nor had she seen any movement at all. She set the candle down in the best position to light the area she needed to examine.

"Another is coming already!" Edda said.

The two women pushed on her belly, as Tara asked, "Anything, Brigid?"

"Nay."

Edda let out a loud breath when the spasm ended and yelled, "Why me? Why is this not working. Lord, please help me. I cannot take much more!"

Jennet looked at Edda, then Brigid, wide-eyed.

Brigid had to do something. "Edda, you're doing a great job. If you could give me two more big pushes, I think I can do it."

"You're just saying that. I'm not. I can't even deliver my own bairn into the world. I'm such a failure. I'm so sorry, Mama."

Jinny began to cry, mumbling incoherent words to her daughter.

Brigid wouldn't let Edda descend into a place they couldn't pull her back from. They needed her assistance. "Tell me again when you feel the pressure about to come on, Edda."

"Another one is coming!" she gasped, almost immediately.

Tara looked at Brigid. "What are you doing?"

"I'm going inside in search of a foot. Fortunately, I have verra small hands." Brigid inserted one hand as far into Edda as she could, knowing the contraction would push hard on her own wrist, but guessing if the pressure wouldn't hurt a bairn's skull, it couldn't hurt her. Then she felt it. Something. An arm or a leg, all she had to do was figure out which one. Pulling on an arm would be worse. A bairn would never come out sideways, so she prayed it was a foot.

The contraction strengthened, surrounding her hand, and at Edda's firm push, or Tara's or Jennet's, there was a sudden shift in the bairn, and she was immediately able to feel a second appendage next to the first, convincing her what she'd felt was a foot, not an arm. She gripped the two together and said, "I have the feet. Push!"

Edda pushed with all her might. Once the contraction eased a touch, Brigid was able to pull her hand out and slip the two feet out Edda's opening. She looked up at Jennet and Tara and nodded.

"I have two feet, Edda. One more good push and I think the bairn will come out." She used her sleeve to wipe the sweat from her brow while they waited.

Jinny began to pray over and over again.

Edda lifted up with a shout, "'Tis coming again!" She pushed and pushed with Jennet's help, and Brigid grabbed a blanket just in time as she pulled the bairn out with a whoosh, swinging her upside down to give the cord room to come out, then dropping her into her blanket-covered arm and wrapping her up quickly.

Everyone cheered with awe.

"What is it?" Edda squealed.

Brigid and Tara both looked and announced, "'Tis a beautiful lassie." Brigid cleared the liquid from the bairn's mouth and held it up as her auntie often did, opening the babe's mouth until she let out a loud squeal to announce herself, her face red as the brightest apple, breaking into a hardy cry of fury over having been so abruptly disturbed and taken from the comforting womb of her mother.

Tara and Jennet jumped into action, helping Brigid with all the tasks necessary after the birth. Cleaning up the bairn and setting her to her mother's breast in her arms, taking care of the birth that comes after the bairn, cutting the cord, cleaning up what they could—there was much to do. It was a finely orchestrated dance Brigid and Jennet had done many times together.

Tara said, "Brigid, you were wonderful. I was getting worried."

Jennet said, "I'd call your work brilliant, cousin. You are so much better at this than I am."

Brigid nearly stopped what she was doing, wishing to offer a different opinion from what

Jennet had said. "Jennet, I've never been better at healing than you."

Jennet spoke matter-of-factly, as if everyone knew the same truth she did. "Not being a healer, but you've always been a better midwife than me, Brigid. You have the touch and the patience I don't have."

Brigid's mind churned with all Jennet had said and the tension of the birth. Edda was beaming with her lassie in her arms, who calmly settled at her mother's breast.

But Brigid didn't feel right. Nonie took one look at her and said, "My lady, you've overdone it. You've finished with the hard part. Jinny and I will clean her up and get her in a fresh gown."

Jennet nodded and pushed at Brigid. "I think you need to get something to eat. "We'll finish. You did the hard part."

Brigid washed her hands and took off the bloodied overgown she'd donned, then ran out the door. She couldn't leave fast enough with the sudden urge to sob coming over her. Racing down the passageway, she opened the door to the parapets and sighed at the fresh breeze that lifted her hair off her face. Then she climbed the staircase blindly.

Once on the parapets, she ran straight into a rock-hard chest, its heat flowing to her in the night's cold air. She recognized Marcas by his scent alone. Brigid fell into his chest, her pent-up tears exploding.

Marcas wrapped his arms around her and cuddled her, his chin resting on the top of her head as she sobbed, thankful at his allowing her this time to let go.

"One question for you, lass, and I'll leave you to your tears."

She nodded against his chest.

"Is the bairn here and well?"

She nodded again, blubbering out the words, "A wee lassie." Then she sobbed again into his chest and wrapped her arms around his waist, clinging to him as if he was the only boat in the water.

Just as he'd been in the firth.

"Then you did a fine job, aye?"

She nodded again, still crying.

"My thanks to you and your cousins. I didn't know we'd need your talents for this, but I'm grateful you were here to help Edda and Jinny. I cannot wait to meet the new lassie."

"I didn't think I had any special talent, but Jennet just said I'm the better midwife." Then she blubbered a wee bit more.

"That makes you sad?"

"Nay, it makes me feel special. I never knew. She was always better than me at everything."

He kissed Brigid's forehead. "Not to me," he said. He didn't speak again for a long time, but then whispered, "You are hale, are you not? You just need the release?"

She sighed and turned her head so she could speak, still unable to let go of him. "I do this often after a difficult situation when we're trying to help someone. While I'm in the middle of it,

I just keep going, but once all is done, I cry like a bairn. Forgive me for my tears all over you, Marcas. I can stop now."

"Cry your heart out if it helps, Brigid. I'm here for you." He sat on a ledge near the wall so they were face-to-face. "And I always will be, if you'll have me."

Somehow, she knew the truth of that statement. No matter what happened, Marcas would always be there to save her from the evils of the world, whether they were evils in her own mind or real. He'd comfort her, soothe her, and love her forever. He had the heart of a loyal man. He'd known tragedy unlike most, and he'd come through it strong.

She whispered against his chest. "I love everything about you, Marcas Matheson. I don't wish to ever leave Black Isle." Then she leaned back to stare into his eyes. "I remember what you asked me before. If in doubt, know that I will happily marry you. Unfortunately, you have to ask for my sire's approval. 'Twill not be an easy task for you."

He cupped her face and planted a soft kiss on her lips. "I already have and he agreed."

"He did?" she asked, shocked, her lip protruding in a definite pout. "Aww, he does not love me as much as my sisters then."

"He loves you the same. He completely refused me at first. 'Twas your mother who threatened him. After a bit of tussle back and forth, she got his consent."

"Oh, I cannot wait to hear all about it."

Marcas stared at her, his eyes widening. "I'll never tell. Nay, you do not wish to know."

CHAPTER TWENTY-EIGHT

————◆————

MARCAS STEPPED OUTSIDE of the wall two days later. Life finally held hope and the promise of much happiness for him, with the wedding planned to take place two days later. He'd eaten the evening meal with his clan and the Ramsays, then ducked outside to check on the area. Once the lasses got into a discussion of the wedding and what they wished to do to decorate the hall, he knew it was time for him to leave. Logan had gone off with Gwyneth to Inverness to meet up with others of their clan after they shopped the market in the burgh.

Apparently, Brigid's mother loved to shop as much as Brigid did and she was off to find the softest fabric for her next set of tunic and leggings. Logan had promised his daughter he'd help her mother find a gown for the wedding.

Gwyneth had made no such promise, instead glaring at her husband.

He'd not gone far from their gates when Cailean and Kyle met up with him, stopping him to speak with them. Cailean had a grin on his face and said, "We're taking you away from here."

Marcas didn't know what to make of that statement, or the man's odd grin, but he looked to Kyle for more of an explanation.

Kyle said, "I know how this sounds, but you must trust us. Brigid is awaiting you in a cottage hidden in the forest."

Marcas arched a brow in question at Kyle, the thought of Brigid alone in a cottage both enticing and frightening at the same time. "Why?"

Cailean said, "Look. We're trying to make it easier on you. 'Twas Brigid and Sorcha's idea because they know their sire. He's away, so Brigid wishes to…ummm…" Cailean rubbed his jaw, clearly uncomfortable with the subject. Marcas had no idea where the conversation was headed.

"Just go," Kyle said. "You have to make her yours before Logan returns. 'Tis the only argument that will work on him. You need to handfast with her, and he won't try to put a stop to the wedding. 'Tis in your best interest. We'll keep everyone away from the cottage. You have until the morrow."

"You're serious? He would stop it?"

"If you don't," Cailean said, "You'll be fortunate to still have your bollocks after the wedding. I had to nearly die before he let me be."

"Go to the cottage, at least speak with Brigid," Kyle said. "What you do after that is up to you."

Marcas thought this last suggestion made the most sense, as long as they weren't jesting to get him away from his own warriors. He mounted his horse and followed along, mulling over their words along the way.

After they arrived, Kyle said, "You've been

married before, so I know you need no advice.
Just remember that you're around a large number
of Ramsay warriors. In other words, no tears
from Brigid."

Then the two left.

Marcas made his way over to the door of the
cottage, knocking lightly and opening it when
he heard Brigid's voice invite him in. He stepped
inside and closed the door behind him, still
curious about this entire event.

What he saw upon entering pulled every
thought from his mind. Brigid stood in front of
the hearth in a transparent gown, a nervous smile
on her face, so beautiful he couldn't speak. He
moved closer until he stood in front of her, letting
out the breath he didn't know he'd been holding.
He took in everything about her—the smile on
her face, the chestnut waves floating down to her
hips, the curve of her breast visible in the light of
the flames behind her.

He gazed into her forest green eyes and settled
his hand on the curve of her hip. "You are
stunning. You're sure 'tis what you wish, lass? You
know it cannot be undone."

"Aye," she said, standing on her tiptoes to plant
a soft kiss on his lips. "I want this more than you
could know. I love you, Marcas. I wish for you to
love me."

"Not until we handfast. We must pledge our
troth to each other." He used his plaid, a shade
greener than the Ramsay plaid, and wrapped it
over their twined hands. "I pledge my troth to
you, Brigid Ramsay. I pledge to love and protect

you forever. Do you pledge your troth to me?"

"Aye, I do. Love me, Marcas Matheson."

He groaned, his lips descending on hers with a growl he didn't mean to be so loud, but he hoped it let her know how much he wanted this, too. He lifted her in his arms and set her on the bed, the coverlet already pulled back. Reaching for his plaid, he said, "You're sure? Would you like me to undress from under the covers?" He didn't wish to upset her, not knowing how much she knew of what was about to take place.

She gave him a saucy look, shook her head, and lifted her own gown over her head, tossing it onto the floor. "Nay, I want all of you, Marcas Matheson."

He rid himself of his clothes and his boots, then slid under the covers next to her. Kissing her everywhere he dared, he caressed her and made love to her with all of his being, taking his time to make sure she was ready for him.

Taking her maidenhead bothered him for a bit, but since it didn't appear to bother her, he buried himself deep inside her, calling her by name as he brought her to her own climax, and lost himself in all that was Brigid Ramsay.

She was his new wife, the woman who'd brought him to a place he'd expected to be, a place of happiness, serenity, and hope.

———◆———

The day of her wedding, Brigid stood in the chamber, Sorcha fussing over her gown while Merewen and Molly fiddled with her hair. Her mother sat in a chair in the corner, fighting with her own gown, ignoring everyone else.

"Mama, I know you hate it, but you must only wear it for a few more hours. If you leave it be, it will stay unwrinkled longer." Sorcha cast a glance back at their mother. She'd always preferred leggings and only wore gowns to please her beloved brother Rab.

"Only for my brother would I do this." Gwyneth's scowl told them all how she felt about parting with her leggings, if only for a short time.

Brigid's Uncle Rab was a priest, and he'd come all the way from West Lothian to marry the couple, along with the rest of her brothers and sister, nieces and nephews, and many of her cousins.

Her mother jumped to her feet and left, slamming the door behind her.

Sorcha grabbed Brigid's arm and whispered, "So was it not as wonderful as you thought?" They hadn't had the chance to speak in private after Brigid's night in the cottage.

Brigid peered at Merewen and Molly and giggled. "Oh, 'twas the most wonderful night ever. Many thanks to you for helping make it take place."

"We all know how Papa can get. You deserved that happiness and now he'll not stop you." Sorcha continued to fuss with Brigid's hair, making sure every strand was in place.

Pledging their troth to one another privately had made it all the more special. She'd known plenty in her clan and Clan Grant who had handfasted, but she'd never given the process much thought until Marcas had wrapped his plaid around their intertwined hands and pledged his troth to her. She'd nearly sobbed with happiness, but she'd controlled herself, pledging the same to him. They'd spent one entirely blissful night together, many of their siblings acting as watchdogs against her father, in case he returned early.

She'd calmed down after that wonderful night, so pleased to know how strong their love was and that her father couldn't drag her away as he'd threatened to do. Brigid belonged with Marcas now, and even her sire wouldn't argue that.

Merewen stood back once she finished tying the last ribbon on the back of Brigid's gown. "Brigid, you are absolutely stunning."

A quick rap sounded at the door, and it opened, her mother returning with Simone and Beatris behind her. Beatris giggled and hugged Brigid while Simone looked at her in awe.

Brigid said, "Merewen, have I told you how pleased I am that you and Gavin are staying on Black Isle for at least a moon along with Tara and Jennet? It truly means much to me."

Gwyneth said, "At least four times, Brigid. I'll have no chance of bringing anyone home with me if you keep telling them.'

Brigid moved over to give her mother a short squeeze. "Oh, Mama. 'Tis only for a short time."

"I know. And it all makes perfect sense, but I need to go back with the bairns. 'Tis where I belong now. With my grandbairns. I must allow all of you to set your own paths. They do need archers in Clan Matheson, so 'twas a wise thing Marcas did when he asked Gavin and Merewen to stay and train some. 'Tis necessary."

Molly said, "You'll still have Sorcha and me at home. Maggie will be around enough."

"I'm surprised you didn't choose to stay, Sorcha," Merewen said. "You're a fine archer, too."

"I'm doing my sister a favor. Taking Cailean along will give my father a target. It takes the attention away from Marcas."

"Poor Cailean," Molly said.

Sorcha gave an indelicate snort. "He loves it. Don't let him convince you otherwise. Enough talking. Are you ready to get married, sister?"

Brigid nodded, giving Beatris a squeeze.

While Sorcha arranged everyone, Simone looked up at Brigid. "The shade of green makes your eyes stand out, and the way Sorcha did your hair is stunning. The weaving of the flowers in the back is perfect. I wish you could see it."

A knock sounded at the door, and Bethia strode in, then she stopped and gasped. "Oh, Brigie, you are so beautiful. Papa will be crying for sure. Sorcha, you are still gifted with a needle. She looks like an angel in the middle of the forest in that green. The shades of pink in the ribbons are perfect."

Everyone headed out, following Brigid, but when she reached the end of the passageway, she waited for her mother, looping her arm through hers. "Mama, are you happy?"

Gwyneth kissed her forehead. "Verra. You were your father's wee lassie for so long I didn't think he'd ever let you go. I'm proud of him for agreeing."

"No trickery today, I hope," Brigid said. "Meaning no rope."

"Don't worry," she said, patting her hand. "I have it hidden in case I need it."

Brigid made her way down the stairs and stopped halfway down. Everyone in the hall held a special place in her heart, but it was her father's gaze that stopped her. She could see the tears from this far away.

"Papa, I'm not leaving you."

Her mother moved over and kissed her father, then said to the others. "Off to the chapel with you. Give Brigid and her father a moment alone."

Once the door closed, Brigid finished heading down the staircase. "Papa, I'll be fine. I love him with all my heart. I tried to find someone on Ramsay land but it just didn't happen."

The tears slid down his cheeks unabashedly, and once she stood in front of him, she stood on her tiptoes and kissed his cheek. "I love you, Papa."

He whispered, "You are so beautiful, Brigie. I suppose I should call you Brigid now."

"'Tis all right. You still call Mama Gwynie. It tells her you love her. I don't like it when you call her Gwyneth."

"Verra astute of you, Brigie," Logan smirked, which stopped his tears as he gave emphasis to her name. "I'll miss you, but you're not too far away from me. 'Tis a fine man you chose, so I cannot argue. I'll count on him to hold his promise to visit twice a year."

The door opened, and Torrian stuck his head in. "They're waiting for you. Better get ahead of the dark clouds coming."

Her father held his arm out to her and she took it, just noticing Beatris sneaking under Torrian's arm to hand her a beautiful bouquet of white and yellow flowers. "My thanks to you, sweetling. They're perfect."

Once outside, they took a slow stroll over to the chapel, her uncle Rab in his flowing robes waiting out front for them. The courtyard was half full of clan members, the ones she knew and several who were new, returning at word that the curse was over.

Clan Matheson had come back to life. A pig roasted off to the side, awaiting the festivities, but she only had eyes for her handsome husband. Ethan stood on one side of Marcas and Shaw on the other. Gisela held Tiernay. Once Logan and Brigid drew up next to Marcas, wee Kara stood between Brigid and Marcas and held one hand up to each, getting ready to escort them into the church, Logan following.

Brigid's gaze locked on her husband. She thought her heart would burst with happiness. She'd never dreamed to find someone who would love her so unconditionally, someone who could make her heart sing with one look.

Then they did what the two of them did best together.

They laughed.

Marcas had never been happier. The wedding had been lovely, and they'd managed to beat the storm. Everyone had gathered inside the hall for festivities before the skies opened up. But the rain had been short-lived, and then the sun had come out.

The hall was full of tables covered with various dishes, and a few minstrels sang and played their lutes for dancing.

At one point, Tara called to the new couple and waved her hand at the door. They joined her on the steps outside, leaving everyone inside enjoying the revelry. Tara pointed to an area off in the trees over the firth. "Look, 'tis most special. I think 'tis meant for you both."

A rainbow.

Tara said, "Mama believes you've just had your union blessed, so I wanted you to see it."

Marcas was in awe at the colors spanning the sky, not that he'd never seen a rainbow before. He'd seen many over the course of his life, but the colors in this one were so brilliant they had to mean something.

He glanced at Brigid, whose eyes were still locked on the stunning display of nature's beauty, the brightness casting a sheen across the firth as it flickered in the light. They moved to a place that allowed them both to see it better.

Tara stood behind them and said, "Before I leave you two to enjoy it alone, I'll tell you this. My sister, who is a seer, would tell you it's someone telling you they're happy for you. I would guess it to be your parents, Marcas. 'Tis their way of being here."

Then she disappeared.

"Oh, Marcas," Brigid said, squeezing his hand. "Do you believe it could be true?"

He looked at the scene again and whispered, "Aye, because I hope 'tis true. I miss them terribly, but somehow in my heart, I know they approve of you and our marriage."

A wee voice came from behind them, and they both turned to see Kara standing at the top of the steps, Gisela holding her hand tightly. Marcas's sister had tears in her eyes and nodded to him, telling him she'd overheard and agreed with them.

But it was Kara's voice who caught him. "Look, Papa," she said, pointing to the bank of the firth. "'Tis Mama. Greetings, Mama."

She giggled as she stared at the rainbow, then back to the area on the bank she'd pointed to before. Marcas had no idea why she had said that about Freda because he saw nothing. He glanced at Brigid, who shrugged her shoulders, then back to his daughter, her face still lit up and her wee finger pointing.

Gisela, her voice choking with tears, asked, "What else does she say, Kara?"

"She says I cannot come see her. But she loves me and she'll see me again someday. And she says she wishes to tell Papa something."

"What?" Marcas asked, almost afraid to ask.

"She says she's happy for you." Then Kara's hand came up and waved. "Bye, Mama."

CHAPTER TWENTY-NINE

———— ◆ ————

S EVERAL HOURS LATER, after enjoying the company, food, and dancing, Marcas looked at his wife, and she gave him a small nod. He took Brigid by the hand and led her to his horse, anxious to get away from the crowd and be alone with his dear wife. But apparently, it wasn't to be yet.

Logan's voice carried over the crowd, stopping Marcas in his tracks. "Hold it, Matheson. You'll not take my daughter anywhere when you only intend to ravage her. She's staying here."

Marcas spun around, not surprised to see Gwyneth with rope in her hands, ready to do the same thing they'd done to Logan at Sorcha's wedding. But Marcas wouldn't allow it.

He held his hand up to Gwyneth, Gavin, and Torrian, all with wide grins on their faces.

"That'll not be needed."

They all froze, staring at him wide-eyed, waiting to see what would happen next.

Logan's chest puffed out a bit more, if that were possible. He could be an arrogant bastard. "Good, glad to see we understand each other, laddie. Let my daughter go. Brigie, come over here." He waved to his daughter and pointed to a spot next to him.

Marcas maneuvered himself in front of Brigid, lightly pushing her behind him. "She's my wife, Ramsay, and she's going with me."

"The hell she is," Logan spit out with a growl. "Brigid, now!"

Marcas removed his sword from its sheath and tossed it to the ground. "She's my wife, and I'll take care of her. I don't need you in the middle of our affairs."

"That's exactly what I was afraid of. You'll not be ravaging her."

Marcas took a step closer to Logan and said, "I'm not afraid of you, Ramsay, and I'll ravage her if she wishes. Now you need to stand down, now and forever. If she has any complaints, I'm sure she'll let you know."

"Stand down? Have you been sleeping with faeries and inhaling their dust? I don't stand down." Logan's hands went to his hips and he tossed his sword to the ground as well. "'Tis my daughter, and you'll always have to answer to me."

"We need to end this now. I'll not be looking over my shoulder for you all the while we're married." He took two steps closer and matched Ramsay's stance, his gaze locked on Brigid's father's. "Take your best swing, old man."

Marcas heard the slew of gasps across the crowd. He'd heard enough of all Cailean had endured at the hands of this brute, and he wouldn't take it. One more step forward. "Hit me. I'm not afraid of you."

A bevy of emotions crossed the old warrior's face, but the one that caught Marcas most was the slight misting in the man's eyes. Having a daughter of his own, Marcas couldn't blame Logan for worrying about his youngest, so he dropped the tone of his voice and said, "I swear to you I'll always protect her. I adore her. She's my life. I'll never let anything happen to her, so you need not worry."

Logan dropped his eyes to the ground, and the crowd silently waited for his reaction. Marcas waited because he had to. He couldn't tolerate this man constantly meddling in their lives.

A long pause later and Logan lifted his gaze to Marcas's, a wide smile crossing his features before he dropped his stance and moved forward to clasp Marcas's shoulder. "'Twas just a test, Chief. Wanted to see if you're man enough to protect her." He looked past him and said, "Brigie, you chose well. If you change your mind, you know where to find me."

The crowd erupted in cheers while Marcas lifted Brigid onto his horse, then mounted behind her, both of them waving to the crowd. They'd only gone a short distance when he heard Cailean say, "I'm not afraid of you anymore, Logan."

Logan said, "Well, you better be. That only worked on me once."

"Oh, Papa…" Sorcha drawled.

Brigid turned around to watch the antics, looking over Marcas's shoulder. Then, she chuckled.

Without turning around, he said, "Your sire is watching us, isn't he?"

"Aye, and he probably always will."

EPILOGUE

———— ◆ ————

LOGAN DIDN'T WISH to do what Brenna wanted him to. He had no desire to travel back to Black Isle.

True, he hadn't seen his dearest Brigid for a short time, but it hadn't been that long, and the toughest part was the reason he was making this visit.

His beloved eldest brother, Quade, previous laird of Clan Ramsay, had taken a turn for the worse. He'd been getting sicker each day, for no reason his wife could figure out.. Brenna had sent for Logan immediately.

"You need to go for Jennet."

"Brenna, he's my brother, too. Mayhap I'd like to stay with him."

"There's naught you can do, Logan, and Micheil will be here soon. I've already sent Kyle with a message to him, but you must go to the Black Isle. Bring her back." Brenna swiped a tear away.

"I'd like to see him first." Gwyneth came up behind him and whispered in his ear. He turned. "I know, Gwynie, but he's my brother. I don't wish to come home and have him gone."

"Come, you may see him." Brenna led the two of them into the healer's chamber off the great hall, which she'd had installed right after she'd married Quade.

His brother had struggled with hip pain for so long he preferred to ride his horse over anything else, but this, this was too much. Watching him slowly deteriorate with no explanation was unacceptable. He'd always trusted Brenna to keep their clan on the mend, but she had no idea what Quade's illness was or how it had started.

She feared the worst, that he could be dead soon. Brenna set a stool next to the bed, then moved to the other side, pointing for Logan to sit. Brenna sat on the other side of the bed, her smile appearing magically, looking not much different than the lass he'd stolen from Grant land so long ago to save Quade.

She was a beautiful lass with a big heart and the wisest woman he knew. He almost said it aloud.

Then, he changed his mind with a smirk. Quade would love to hear him mouth the words, but he wouldn't in her presence. She wasn't just the wisest woman he knew; she was the wisest *person* he knew. Where she'd gained all her talent and wisdom, he'd never know, but she'd not only shared it with his clan, she had also given them three beautiful bairns with Quade—Bethia, Gregor, and Jennet.

She may even have given the world someone wiser than she—Jennet.

Logan sighed, looking at his brother, Quade's mind still as sharp as ever. That much he could tell. He reached for Quade's hand, and he barely moved at all.

"He's too weak to do much, Logan."

Logan had no idea what his problem was, but if anyone could heal him, it was Brenna. He nodded and gave his brother's hand a little squeeze, surprised to have him squeeze back so hard, it hurt.

"What the hell, Quade? What do you want me to do?"

His brother's eyes burned with a need, and he finally spoke, his breath raspy, "Go get her."

Logan was surprised at what an effort it cost Quade to speak. Hellfire, he wished to yell at Brenna. How did she remain so calm in all events? How did she not scream at her husband to get off the blasted bed?

"All right," he conceded. "I'll do my best. You want me to bring Jennet home?"

Quade nodded, his green eyes larger than Logan had ever seen. Then he squeezed Logan's hand again.

"All right, I'll go for her, but I'd prefer not." Logan ran his hand down his face. "I'd prefer to stay here with you." He belonged next to his brother. What if Quade died while he was away? He'd never forgive himself. It was his duty to be at his brother's side, just as it would be his duty to be at Gwynie's side when her time came.

His brother squeezed his hand harder, then managed to roll himself over onto his side giving him the leverage to move his hand up to Logan's throat.

Nearly.

Logan wasn't that foolish. "You choked me enough times when we were laddies, Quade. Even now I'm wise to your ways. Fine. I'll go. Just as soon as..."

"Bring my daughter back now, Logan." Quade grabbed the top of his brother's tunic, wadding it up enough to move him off the stool.

"All right!" He grabbed his brother's hand and shoved it away. "You want me to go get Jennet and I'll oblige you, you miserable old goat."

Quade nodded furiously, dropping his hand and falling back onto the bed. Logan got up from the stool and strode to the window, pulling the fur back and glancing across the courtyard edge, the only part he could see. "But I should stay with you, Quade. I don't wish to leave you."

True, he'd love to go to Black Isle to see how Brigid fared and visit his new son, Marcas. He wondered how Clan Matheson had grown. Even Gavin and Merewen had stayed back.

But not now. This was his older brother, his mentor, his best friend.

This was Quade.

Brenna came over and stood behind him. "Remember a verra long time ago when you made a promise to me? I'm calling you on it. You said you owed me."

Logan chuckled. "I remember it well. I stole your dear mother's healing book, but I returned it. And because I stole it, I gave you one request. I said I'd do whatever you asked of me without question. My memory serves me well, Brenna, and you already used it up when I protected you the night of the bedding ceremony."

Gwynie just uttered one word. "Logan…"

Then his brother kicked the bed, threw the linens off, and moved to come after him. Instead, he fell to the floor.

Gwynie arched a brow at Logan while Brenna raced to the bed. "He's too weak to walk. Come, we have to get him back in."

The three hoisted the tall man back onto the bed, his green eyes following Logan. Hellfire, he hated when his brother did that. Quade knew exactly how to make him feel guilty. "I still think I was born first, you craggy old man."

He smirked at his brother, and for the first time, Quade's eyes lit up with laughter.

Torrian came in. "If he doesn't go, I will, Da."

Quade managed to say, "Nay, Logan goes."

"I know," Logan retorted. "Torrian belongs here with Lily and Brenna and his own family. I'm going. Gwynie, you need to stay here. Please. You know I'll be going too fast for you."

Logan made his way toward the door, turning around when he got to the opening. "You better have your arse out of that bed when I return, old man."

Then he closed the door, just before something thrown crashed against it.

At least he knew his brother's mind was still all there.

THE END

D EAR READER,
Thanks for reading! As you can see, this is a new series, and I have no idea how many books will be in this series yet! See what my muse says as I go along.

Jennet is next.

Happy reading,

Keira Montclair

keiramontclair@gmail.com
www.keiramontclair.com
http://facebook.com/KeiraMontclair/
http://www.pinterest.com/KeiraMontclair/

OTHER NOVELS BY KEIRA MONTCLAIR

#2 TRUSTING A SCOT

STAND-ALONE BOOKS
THE BANISHED HIGHLANDER
REFORMING THE DUKE-REGENCY
WOLF AND THE WILD SCOTS
FALLING FOR THE CHIEFTAIN-3RD in a
collaborative trilogy

**THE SUMMERHILL SERIES-
CONTEMPORARY ROMANCE**
#1-ONE SUMMERHILL DAY
#2-A FRESH START FOR TWO
#3-THREE REASONS TO LOVE

ABOUT THE AUTHOR

Keira Montclair is the pen name of an author who lives in South Carolina with her husband. She loves to write fast-paced, emotional romance, especially with children as secondary characters.

When she's not writing, she loves to spend time with her grandchildren. She's worked as a high school math teacher, a registered nurse, and an office manager. She loves ballet, mathematics, puzzles, learning anything new, and creating new characters for her readers to fall in love with.

She writes historical romantic suspense. Her bestselling series is a family saga that follows two medieval Scottish clans through four generations and now numbers over thirty books.

Contact her through her website:
www.keiramontclair.com

Made in the USA
Las Vegas, NV
26 May 2021

23686372R00166